Sister Caravaggio

A Novel

First published in 2014 by
Liberties Press
140 Terenure Road North | Terenure | Dublin 6W
T: +353 (1) 405 5701| www.libertiespress.com | E: info@libertiespress.com

Trade enquiries to Gill & Macmillan Distribution
Hume Avenue | Park West | Dublin 12
T: +353 (1) 500 9534 | F: +353 (1) 500 9595 | E: sales@gillmacmillan.ie

ISBN: 978-1-909718-41-8
2 4 6 8 10 9 7 5 3 1

A CIP record for this title is available from the British Library.

Cover design by Liberties Press
Internal design by Liberties Press

All the characters in this book are fictitious, and any resemblance to actual persons, living or dead, is purely coincidental.

Sister Caravaggio

A Novel

Maeve Binchy
Peter Cunningham
Neil Donnelly
Cormac Millar
Éilís Ní Dhuibhne
Mary O'Donnell
Peter Sheridan

Devised and edited by
Peter Cunningham

About the Authors

Maeve Binchy's best-selling novels have been translated into thirty-seven languages and have sold over forty million copies worldwide. Her first novel, *Light a Penny Candle*, was published in 1982. Several of her books have been adapted for cinema and television, most notably *Circle of Friends* and *Tara Road*. She was married to the writer and broadcaster Gordon Snell for thirty-five years, and died in 2012. www.maevebinchy.com

Peter Cunningham is best known for his novels set in Monument, his fictional version of Waterford, where he grew up. *The Sea and the Silence* was awarded the Prix de l'Europe in 2013. *Consequences of the Heart* was short-listed for the Kerry Listowel Writer's Prize. His novel, *The Taoiseach*, was a controversial bestseller. He has written the Joe Grace series of thrillers under the name Peter Wilben. (www.peterwilben.com) He is a member of Aosdána, the Irish association of writers, musicians and artists. www.petercunninghambooks.com

Neil Donnelly is best known for the plays, *The Station Master*, *Upstarts*, *The Silver Dollar Boys*, *Chalk Farm Blues*, *Flying Home*, *The Duty Master* and *Butterfly*.

Cormac Millar is the author of two crime novels, *An Irish Solution* (Penguin, 2004) and *The Grounds* (Penguin, 2006). As Cormac Ó Cuilleanáin, he is a professor at Trinity College Dublin, and an academic author and translator. This was perhaps inevitable, given his family background. www.cormacmillar.com

Éilís Ní Dhuibhne has published many novels, collections of short stories, books for children. She has won several literary awards, including the Stewart Parker Award for Drama, three Bisto Awards for children's books, and the American Association of Irish Studies Butler Award for Prose. Her novel *The Dancers Dancing* was shortlisted for the Orange Prize for Fiction. She is a member of Aosdána. www.eilisnidhuibhne.com

Mary O'Donnell is the award-winning author of fourteen books, including poetry and fiction. Her latest novel, *Where They Lie,* was described by the *Irish Independent* as 'a timeless story of loss, grief and tribal loyalties'. Her fiction has appeared in *The Fiddlehead* literary journal (Canada), and many anthologies, including *Phoenix Irish Short Stories*, and *The Hennessy Book of Irish Fiction*. She lectures in Creative Writing at NUI Maynooth and with Carlow University Pittsburgh. She is a member of Aosdána. www.maryodonnell.com

Peter Sheridan is a leading figure in the Irish theatre. Among his plays are *No Entry, Down All The Days* (from the book by Christy Brown), *The Liberty Suit* (in collaboration with Gerard Mannix Flynn), *Diary of a Hunger Strike* and *Finders Keepers*. He has written two memoirs on his family, *44: A Dublin Memoir* (nominated for an Irish Times Non-Fiction Literature award) and *47 Roses*. His latest book, *Break a Leg*, was published in 2013 and is now also a stage play. He is a member of Aosdána.

Chapter One

Doon Abbey, County Kildare, Ireland
Present Day, 10 June, 1 AM

During the long passage of those sultry summer nights, Sister Alice often wondered if she had really shot the man. Squeezed the trigger with soft and knowing stealth and then watched his head explode. Sometimes she could see the passage of the bullet in its flight. Could that have been her? Dismay seized Sister Alice as the old images returned. At such moments, God seemed very far away.

In the flickering glow of the night-light, she looked down at her right hand with its long, unadorned fingers that lately had clasped a rosary instead of a Glock G17 9mm. Sister Alice – Sister Mercy Superior had allowed her to keep her own name until the end of her novitiate – closed her eyes as a squeaking bat manoeuvred the airspace beneath the listing walls of Doon Abbey. The centuries sighed from the turrets and walls and from the elaborate finials that surmounted the castle's Gothic windows. Moonbeams bathed the moss-covered buttresses and conjured intricate shapes from the ancient escarpments. Sister Alice knew that later she would hear the passage of mice in the corridor going about their nocturnal business, as they had done for generations, safe from the attention of Panda, the convent's muscular black-and-white tomcat, who slept with Sister Mary Magdalene two cells away.

Now and then she heard a jet plane in the distant sky and thought: *I'm going to die here and no one will ever know.* But wasn't that the whole point? she asked herself. Had she not chosen to renounce the world and enter an enclosed order? To cut herself off from all mortal friendships and her former life? *Especially* her former life. Sister Alice tugged a lock of her cropped raven hair until it hurt. Ah! the bliss of self-mortification. *Ouch!*

It was after one in the morning when Sister Alice suddenly sat up in bed. What had she just heard? There it was again; the sound of an engine on the breeze. She immediately tried to categorise it. Two litres, petrol engine, small rupture in the exhaust . . . Stop! She would have to try to forget all that. Meditate on a psalm. Think of the warm love of Our Lord. A brook of goodness. But why had the engine suddenly cut out? Here I go again, she thought, with a sigh of longing for the peace that the other sisters had found but she had not.

Sister Alice became aware that the corridor outside her cell was in darkness – the two wall lights, with their long-life bulbs, had gone out. She frowned. Then she heard the distant engine again, but only for a few seconds before it drained into the night.

The nearest public road was half a mile away, and so the engine sounds heard during the day came mainly from the convent's farmyard, where broad-shouldered Sister Diana fed silage to cattle using a front loader fitted to the Massey Ferguson. A local young man, Joe Foley, was employed part-time to help with the milking, but Alice was almost sure that Joe's car ran on petrol.

She prayed for sleep. Where was the wind from tonight, she wondered? From the east, she decided – which meant that the engine she had heard might well have come from the public road. Her restless ear picked up the soft sound of cows masticating in the front meadow, a comforting repetition that spoke of healthy udders and lapping cream. Occasionally she heard an owl calling to its mate, and then Sister Alice was overwhelmed by another longing.

Doon Abbey
10 June, 2 AM

'Gabrielle?'

'What is it, Eleanor?'

'What's that noise?'

'I heard nothing. Go back to sleep.'

The Misses Hogan, twins in their eighty-fifth year, had lived all their lives in Doon Abbey's single-storey gate lodge. Their father had been a greyhound trainer whose great-grandfather, legend had it, had won the gate lodge in a poker game from the then owner of Doon. Gabrielle and Eleanor had both been primary school teachers in County Kildare, albeit in different schools. Since their retirement in the early 1980s, they had been the backbone of the Doonlish branch of the Irish Countrywomen's Association.

'I definitely heard something,' Eleanor whispered.

'Well, then, go and have a look,' Gabrielle replied.

Eleanor climbed from the double bed that had belonged to their parents and made her way to the bedroom window that looked out on the final stretch of Doon Abbey's long avenue. It was chilly out of bed, even though it was summer, and as she drew back the curtain an inch, Eleanor shivered. The half-moon filtered through light cloud, creating ever-moving shadows. Eleanor pressed her nose against the window glass.

'Goodness!' she exclaimed.

'What is it?'

'I'm not sure. Come and see.'

Gabrielle joined her sister by the window. A shadow slid away like a theatrical drape. There, on the far side of the avenue, a large woman was loading an object into a car.

All at once the car's engine burst into life. Its lights came on. The big woman turned and stared directly in at the gate lodge. As one, Eleanor and Gabrielle sank out of sight. They could hear the car driving away. They stayed down for five minutes, terrified. Although they had not been able to see her features clearly, there had been an aura of menace about that big woman that had sent icy tremors into the twins' elderly bones.

At last they raised their heads. The moon danced through the shadows but the large woman had gone.

'Maybe it was just a bad dream,' Gabrielle said as they returned to bed.

'Maybe it was,' Eleanor agreed.

Within two minutes, they were snoring in unison.

Doon Abbey
10 June, 4 AM

Summer darkness lay warmly on the one hundred acres of the estate at whose centre Doon Abbey proudly, if shakily, stood. Doon Castle had originally been built as a fortified square, but now only two and a half sides of the square remained. The base of the square was the east face of the abbey, the elevation that greeted visitors as they emerged from the wooded half-mile-long avenue that connected the convent with the outside world.

The nuns' cells and bathrooms were located on the first floor of the east wing, as was Sister Mercy Superior's room, above the arch. Halfway along the south wing was the small convent chapel constructed in the late nineteenth century and finished in Baroque design. The choir stalls for the chapel were carved from local oak, and numbered thirty-six: two tiers of nine stalls on each side, facing one another behind the altar.

At the mid-point of the twentieth century, all these stalls had been filled by the pious women who lived the silent and enclosed life in Doon Abbey, manufacturing altar breads that were sold all over Ireland. But that business, like so many others, was in decline. The surviving five nuns of Doon Abbey now relied almost entirely for their income on the tourists who came to Doon Abbey and formed patient queues to enter the tiny chapel, six at a time, to gaze and wonder at Caravaggio's *The Agony of Judas Iscariot*.

★

Sister Alice tried to settle on a single image from scripture and bring it with her into sleep. The trouble was that every time she visualised Our Lord on the Sea of Galilee, she saw Galway Bay and the little pub in which she and Ned had so often eaten oysters. Our Lord entering Jerusalem on a donkey gave way almost immediately to the donkey rides she and Ned had once hilariously taken on the beach in Bundoran. Ned, with his big tummy sticking out as he bounced along. How could she ever forget it? Even the Last Supper shamefully morphed into the Michelin-starred restaurant in central Dublin where Ned had brought her on that final night, to try and persuade her one last time.

A blurred image of her own face looked back from the burnished copper stand in which the night-light sat. The strong nose, the large eyes, the sensuous lips. Could she hack this for the rest of her life, she wondered? With no human verbal exchanges, except during instruction from Sister Columba, the low-sized novice mistress, and cut off from the outside world?

Sister Alice had come to look forward to the sight of the few outsiders who turned up each morning for Mass and to receive Holy Communion. The Misses Hogan were always first in, and if not, it was Jeremy Meadowfield, a tall, handsome man in his mid-thirties, with a large mop of blond hair and startling blue eyes. Meadowfield was a convert to Catholicism, Sister Alice had learned from Sister Columba, who recounted with pride how Sister Winifred, a nun no longer in Doon Abbey, had instructed Mr Meadowfield in his Catholic doctrine. He was an English accountant, Alice had heard, and he now prepared Doon Abbey's books for the banks and the taxman.

The only other regular was Davy Rainbow, a local journalist with the *Doonlish Enquirer*, whose article a few years before on Doon Abbey's 'hidden Caravaggio' had attracted national attention. In its gilt frame, the canvas measured less than ninety centimetres square. It was technically described as a 'fragment' and was most likely a sketch for a larger work, yet there was no denying the power of the painting, and its allure for visitors.

★

Sister Alice prayed for sleep to take her painlessly to the bell for lauds at half past four. The reassuringly cold bite of an Irish summer dawn. The deep comfort of Gregorian chant in the chapel, the cool calmness of the carved wooden choir stalls, and the incomparable sight of light rising slowly to illuminate the stained-glass window, setting it alight until the window's colours drenched the floor of the chapel in a holy flood.

She sat up, suddenly awake, and choked back a scream. 'Ned!' she cried soundlessly.

The first light of dawn flickered in through the window of her cell.

Something has happened, Sister Alice thought as she dressed hurriedly, the images from her dream still foremost in her mind. The bell for lauds pealed. Something had changed, she was sure, as she made her way out to the chapel, but she could not yet say what it was.

Doonlish
10 June, 4.30 AM

Davy Rainbow counted out the cash carefully on his bed. He liked order, so he sorted the fifties, twenties and tens into neat piles. Still not enough. He shivered as he heard a thump outside, and went still. Going to the window, he peered out. Christ, his nerves were in fritters. He had covered enough court cases in his day to know exactly how severe the penalty would be for the crime he had just committed.

Davy was lightly built and low in stature. On the Curragh, where he had grown up, his father had wanted him to become a jockey. When the old man heard that Davy was going to work for a newspaper, he had nearly had a fit.

Davy took a long swallow from the glass. The neat alcohol charged into his bloodstream and fizzed up his spine. This was the last day – or night – he was going to drink, he told himself. He had made the same vow before, but this time he was adamant. If only he could pay off what he owed.

He lay on the bed and took out her photograph. She had been so – so *serene*, was the only word he could think of. So *kind*. A woman had never treated him like that before. He began to weep. When they had gone for their long walks together, occasionally he would look up at her lovely profile and inhale her calm beauty. Memories of those intimate moments now pierced Davy. He took up the bottle and slugged from it directly. Her picture was hazy – a face picked out from a crowd – but, even so, her strength and her femininity made his head swirl.

Where was she now? What was she doing? If he could have her, Davy thought as he slipped into sleep, if she could be his only for an hour, he would promise before God never to drink or gamble again.

Doon Abbey
10 June, 4.45 AM

Daylight was filling the horizon as Sister Alice crossed the cloister and neared the chapel door. The first chorus of birds could be heard as Panda, the convent tomcat, strolled languidly towards the kitchens, his scarlet neck collar bright in the early morning. Alice was so grateful for the dawn. She would pray well this morning and put her earlier misgivings behind her. She saw the imposing figure of Sister Mercy Superior emerging from another door of the east wing, the burly nun's hands wrapped around her opposing arms to fend off the cold.

At that moment, in the portal of the chapel, the figure of Sister Mary Magdalene appeared. Alice smiled, for she liked the pleasant-faced and kind librarian, who was nearer to her in age than any of the others. But now Sister Alice frowned. Sister Mary Magdalene's normally serene features were distorted. Her mouth open, as if in a mute cry of grief, she was pointing back into the chapel, where she had just come from.

And in one awful moment Sister Alice understood.

★

Detective Sergeant Alice Dunwoody had made the momentous decision to become a nun only three months beforehand, entering Doon Abbey as a novice. Sister Alice, as she now was, knew that she had enemies. There were the usual grudges from the petty thieves, drug-pushers and wife-beaters whom she had seen put away. And there was Bruno Scanlon Senior, known throughout Dublin's inner city as a particularly vicious criminal who had spent more than half his adult life in prison. He had, a decade before, handed over the running of part of his crime empire to his son, Bruno Scanlon Junior, who had inherited his father's cruel streak but not his intelligence. Bruno Junior ran his drugs operation from a disused treacle factory in the docklands, where his opponents, members of other gangs, were routinely executed and their bodies chained to the floating concrete-pile foundations of the building. When the media eventually found out what was going on, they dubbed the internecine gangland violence 'The Toffee Wars'.

Alice had spent two years building up a file on Bruno Junior. Working closely with young Detective Sebastian Hayes, who became a close friend during that difficult time, Alice had painstakingly tracked down two drug-pushers, who, in exchange for immunity from prosecution, had agreed to testify against Bruno Junior.

It was meant to be a straightforward arrest. Alice, along with Sebastian and ten uniformed gardaí, surrounded the treacle factory. She wanted to make the arrest herself. She entered the building by way of the rusty fire escape which led directly to Bruno Junior's office. Her lithe figure swung upwards for three floors. As she drew back to kick in the door, its glass panel sprayed outwards, shattered by a bullet.

Glass shards ripped into Alice's face. Too late, she realised there must have been a tip-off. She came into the office rolling, her gun held two-handed. She could taste blood on her mouth. The next couple of seconds expanded into a timeframe particular to intense action and sudden death. Bruno Junior was behind his desk, his eyes wild. He was holding a firearm. He brought his shooting hand down towards Alice. She rolled once and heard the silencer-muffled bullet thud into the patch of linoleum on which she had just been stretched. Another thud sent a glass ashtray flying. She could clearly see the irises of Bruno Junior's small, cabbage-coloured eyes.

'Drop it, Bruno!' she screamed.

He was, however, programmed for Death – hers or his own – with a capital 'D'. He made the mistake of aiming too carefully. Alice, with the certainty of hundreds of hours spent on the firing range, squeezed with the utmost softness to keep the Glock steady. Bruno Junior's mouth seemed to enlarge. The wall behind him went Technicolor. The Toffee Wars were over.

Doon Abbey
13 June, 2 PM

Sister Alice sprinted down the old cart track between rows of overgrown laurels. Attired, by permission of Sister Columba, in a tracksuit and a pair of sturdy boots, she relished the release of energy as her body settled into its old balance and rhythms and her blood moved smoothly, as it had for all those years on the athletics field.

It was exceedingly frustrating to be at the centre of a theft that must have been on the lips of the nation, but equally to be unaware of what was really going on. For, as garda patrol cars, with their revolving blue strobe lights, came and went interminably, soon followed by throngs of media, Sister Mercy Superior led her nuns in the strict regime of the convent as if Doon Abbey's Caravaggio was still hanging on the chapel wall.

Sister Alice yearned to participate, yet she was unable to speak to anyone, or to read a newspaper, listen to the radio, make a phone call or watch television. At the very least, she thought, each nun in the tiny community should have been interviewed by the gardaí investigating the crime. But Sister Mercy Superior's iron insistence that God came first meant that no exception to Doon Abbey's daily regimen and vow of silence would be tolerated.

Sister Alice wanted to at least tell someone about the high-powered engine with the ruptured exhaust pipe that she had heard on the night of the theft, but she was forbidden to do so.

When the forensics people in their white suits had completed their tasks, the crime-scene tapes were removed and the community moved back into the chapel for vespers, just a light patch on the wall over the side altar indicated where the Caravaggio fragment had once hung.

Sister Alice realised that the religious community's reaction to the theft of the Caravaggio perfectly illustrated the value of the life she had chosen. And yet . . . and yet Sister Alice's deeply founded and ever-present sense of justice twitched ever more strongly as the days went by. Communing with God was fine, most of the time, but even He had lost His rag once or twice when He had been outraged by events. He had whipped the money-lenders from the Temple, for example. He was no pushover, Our Lord, and if He was here now, Sister Alice was convinced, He would want the Caravaggio found and returned.

Sprinting flat out, pushing herself to the limit of endurance and praying for inner peace, Sister Alice rounded a bend and came face to face with a large man.

A number of things happened very fast. The big man drew back his fist. Reflexively, Sister Alice pivoted, sprang in the air and swung at him with her extended right leg, the heel of her boot whistling in a deadly parabola. In the fraction of a second in which she was airborne, Alice realised that this attack might not be necessary, and adjusted the plane of her body so that she simply landed on two feet, cat-like and crouched opposite the man, her flattened hands out before her.

The man stared and slowly lowered his fist. He was overweight and middle-aged, with close-together small eyes and hair that grew on his head in ginger tufts.

'Just out for a little jog, Sister?' he blustered, recovering.

Alice looked at him coolly before turning her back and returning to the convent. The next day, during her instruction with Sister Columba, she recounted that she had found someone trespassing on convent ground and learned, after she described him, that the trespasser was Cyril O'Meara, the man who owned the adjoining farm and who claimed that the Fitz-Johns, the former owners of Doon Abbey, had robbed his family of its land.

13 June, 10 PM

She leaned forward to her vanity mirror, angled the tweezers and snipped the silky but wayward eyelash. She stepped back and appraised herself. She smiled at what she saw. Her eyes flashed. She looked not just good – she looked great. *You look great!* she whispered to her image. *You are one sexy and amazing-looking woman!*

Sitting on the bed, she eased on her tights: long, right leg first, sculpted toe, pointed like a ballerina's; left leg with its lovely smooth and rounded calf. For the last thirty minutes she had applied her battery-powered

Epilady to both legs. The tights glided languidly up her succulent thighs. She loved this moment, this sensual and timeless affirmation of womanhood.

'You're so *big!*' Mama had always said, with a mixture of guilt and despair, as if she, a small woman, was unaccountably to blame for having had such a large child.

She had always felt miserable when Mama commented on her size. She had hated herself. Her height, her big shoulders, her square hips. She had felt trapped in someone else's body. And the thing Mama had said! The word she had used . . . So cruel to say it even once to a little girl, let alone every day. So *brutal!* In bed, dreaming of the person she wanted to be, she had cried herself to sleep.

She applied the mascara that matched the green hills and valleys of her childhood. She had been sixteen years old, staying with her cousins who lived down the country over the fashion boutique her aunt ran. One evening, when they had all gone to the cinema, she found herself downstairs in the boutique. In the back office stood a steel wardrobe and a mirror. She opened the wardrobe and stood back, hands to her mouth. A rack of the most stunning dresses she had ever seen was hanging there.

First their scent: the beautiful world of the feminine enveloped her in its mystifying fragrance. And then their colours: no prism could have captured the variety and register of what that riotously joyful wardrobe contained.

Over the next two hours, she discovered how size was no barrier to beauty. She stripped to her underwear, then tried on one dress after another. The gorgeous fabrics, mainly silks, made her almost swoon. She collected them in her fists and buried her face in them. In a daring three-quarter-length orange dress with a plunging neckline, she no longer looked big and awkward; she looked positively *feline!* A dark green dress with a halter neck made her look ten years older and gave her an air of mystery.

Upstairs, in her aunt's bedroom, she found nail polish. With great care she painted each fingernail and toenail. A little foundation for her face and neck, a little powder. Green mascara: she had never known such a thing existed! She felt attractive; she felt astonishing.

Now, decades later, she zipped up her black voile dress, chose a pair of shoes with platform heels for the work ahead – the bigger the better, she thought – and made last-minute adjustments to the hair that fell in rich Titian tresses to her shoulders. She took a moment to review her image in the restored, gilt-framed looking glass that she had surrounded with a gay arrangement of fresh-cut roses, irises, sunflowers and hollyhocks. She smiled. From her wardrobe, she took a dark green gabardine coat, picked up her handbag, slipped on her dark glasses and made for the door.

Outside it was dark. She loved the dark, like the name she had given herself: Dark Heart. It was after eleven when she parked in an anonymous twenty-four-hour multi-storey in central Dublin. The streets were empty. She left the carpark, walked for half a mile, then got on a late-night feeder bus going to the north side. Sometimes men looked at her and she gave them a little smile. Alighting from the bus, she walked for another ten minutes. Her streets. She hailed a taxi.

'Not a bad evening, ma'am,' the taxi driver said as she sat in.

'Liffey Valley,' Dark Heart said.

Doon Abbey
14 June, 11 AM

Despite the avalanche of prayer in which she was immersed, Alice could not help her mind leaping ever more feverishly to the theft of the Caravaggio. The silence, other than prayer spoken out loud, or psalms, or hymns, was driving her to distraction. That morning in the kitchen, when only herself and Sister Mary Magdalene stood side by side, beating flour and water, Alice whispered, 'Do you know what's going on here?'

Sister Mary Magdalene, uniquely and by special permission of Sister

Mercy Superior, roved the ether in search of holy texts and sacred music on the laptop computer her family had donated to the convent. But now her kind and giving eyes blinked in shock at Alice's unexpected intrusion into her silent world. In consternation, she returned to her task at the mixing bowl.

Alice began to see Bruno Scanlon Senior in the evening shadows and even beyond the grille of the chapel, into which a trickle of Mass-goers had begun to return every morning. She also, worryingly, was having vivid dreams about Ned, in which her former boyfriend was attempting to flog the Caravaggio in Amsterdam.

She tried to restrain her mind by memorising the regulation of the Psalms; she could not concentrate. The numbers of the Psalms reminded her of the numbers of Dublin buses, and with the numbers of the buses came their origins and destinations – all of which served only to remind her of cases against criminals that she had pursued in those areas of Dublin. She was going to burst.

Then at half past six that evening, as she was leaving the refectory, she felt her sleeve tugged. She looked around and saw Sister Mary Magdalene standing there, eyes bulging. Motioning with her head from right to left in the universal gesture which said 'Follow me', Sister Mary Magdalene set out at a brisk pace across the cloister towards the old banqueting hall in the disused south wing.

It was a misty evening, with the sun still up there somewhere, doing its best to come through, just like Our Lord. Sister Alice felt sure that Sister Mary Magdalene was going to remonstrate with her for her sinful attempt at conversation the day before. But Sister Mary Magdalene, whose voice Alice in three months had only ever heard in choir, closed the door, turned to Sister Alice and said, 'I know this is not right, but, no more than you, can I keep it bottled up, because I have eyes in my head, and what I'm seeing fills me with dread that my chosen life here in Doon Abbey is in real danger of coming to an end. Yesterday, I was confronted with a sudden revelation that without the income from the Caravaggio, we are doomed. Like other communities I'm sure you've read about, we will most likely end up in a housing estate in Castledermot or the like, which is not why I became a nun. I have also seen things recently that have filled me with terror, but about which I am reluctant to speak, even to you. Although I am obedient and have given my life to God, as you have too, dearest Alice, I cannot stand by and watch everything I love be sold off. Since I think that too is your position, I am taking this huge risk this evening of asking you: what should we do?'

Sister Alice looked at Sister Mary Magdalene's honest but fearful expression and felt a surge of vindication.

'Tomorrow morning,' Alice said, 'we must go and talk to Sister Mercy Superior.'

Doon Abbey
15 June, 4 AM

Sister Alice lay awake, her thoughts of Sister Mercy Superior in free-flow.

Doon Abbey's head nun was a bulky woman, standing well over six feet tall, with powerful hands, iron-grey hair and thick black eyebrows above deep brown, almost black, eyes. That Sister Mercy Superior was pious and even serene in prayer, Sister Alice did not doubt. But if a sister in the kitchen baking altar breads scalded her hand and cried out in pain, a dark look from Sister Superior was enough to ensure that there would not be a second yelp. Doon Abbey's commanding head nun ran a tight ship, in which the ministry of the Aurelians – eternal prayerfulness in the name of Our Lord – was ever maintained.

And yet, Sister Alice had come to realise, Sister Mercy Superior had been elected to her current position only the month before Alice's arrival, replacing Sister Winifred Superior. Sister Winifred was no longer in the convent and, as Sister Alice had observed, none of the tidy headstones in the convent's cemetery bore her name.

But there was something else. Alice tried to blame her observation on her police training, which was striving to assert itself – but to no use. She lay in her cell and she was certain. Guilt had taken over Sister Mercy Superior's features; there was no other name for it. Sister Mercy Superior was hiding something.

Doon Abbey
15 June, 11 AM

A procedure was laid down for requesting a meeting with Sister Mercy Superior which involved Sister Alice and Sister Mary Magdalene applying through Sister Columba. At first the novice mistress, whose eyes became enlarged with curiosity, wanted to know the agenda, and became resentful when Alice insisted that she would reveal what she had to say only to Sister Mercy Superior.

'She is very busy,' Sister Columba said, puffing herself up like a tiny lizard.

'Listen, Sister,' Alice said gently, 'this is important.'

'I'll see how her diary looks for the next couple of weeks, but I cannot promise anything,' said Sister Columba stiffly.

Sister Mary Magdalene sighed deeply and turned away, defeated. But Sister Alice then said, 'I'm sorry, Sister. I don't think you understand. Either you set it up now, today, or we're just going up there.'

Sister Columba became even more short of breath and her face grew red with fury. But ten minutes later she was hauling her way up the marble staircase with some agility as Alice and Mary Magdalene trailed a respectful distance behind. On the landing, Sister Columba paused to regain her composure, then continued on down the oak-panelled corridor, past occasional crucifixes, pictures of assorted saints and, mounted in recesses, various adaptations of the indefatigable Infant of Prague. She reached the oak door and rapped on it.

'*Benedicamus Domino*,' she intoned.

'*Benedicamus Domino*,' came the muffled reply. The three women went in.

The room was brightly illuminated by morning light. Sister Mercy Superior sat at a square, plastic-topped table on an upright chair. Even seated, it was obvious how big she was. She glared at her visitors. Sister Columba spread her arms and hunched her shoulders in the gesture traditional to asserting innocence.

As Alice approached the table, she could see that Sister Mary Magdalene was shaking with fear. Alice wondered if she had now crossed a line that would result in her ejection from the convent. One part of her, the part that still thought of Ned every day, wished this would indeed be the case; but, simultaneously, the side of her which had decided to become a nun sank at the prospect of such a failure.

She took a deep breath and said, 'Sister Mary Magdalene and myself have been talking.'

As the head nun and the novice mistress exchanged scandalised glances, Alice realised that she had not opened with the most judicious remark. Nonetheless, she continued, 'Mary Magdalene and I love this place and we are giving our lives to it in the service of Our Lord, but that doesn't mean we should stand by and see our dreams destroyed. Please tell us what is going on.'

Sister Mercy Superior stared fiercely at her young novice.

'I *beg* your pardon, Sister Alice.'

Alice took a deep breath and continued: 'Look, there's a problem, isn't there? We're all intelligent women, and we're all in this together. Mary Magdalene and I want to help. We're young, smart and energetic. Include us, please. We can help you.'

'How dare you!' Sister Mercy Superior cried, quivering at the indignity. 'You imply that I am somehow responsible for seeing, as you put it, your "dreams destroyed"? We take you in here and allow you to share our home, and this is what we get in return? And as for you, Mary

Magdalene, I am *so* disappointed in you. Your treachery will not go unpunished, believe me.'

Sister Mary Magdalene let out a high-pitched cry, then slowly sank down into her brown habit as if her unseen legs had turned to jelly.

'And weak too,' Sister Mercy Superior rasped. 'Take her out of my sight.'

Sister Columba moved to gather up Sister Mary Magdalene – a difficult task, given their respective sizes.

'No! Wait!'

Sister Alice was standing between Sister Columba and the convent's prostrate librarian.

'I know this may be the last opportunity I have to say something, but I'll say it anyway,' Alice began. 'You two know what my job was before I joined the Aurelians, but Sister Mary Magdalene doesn't. I was a garda detective sergeant, Mary Magdalene, and a very good one at that.'

Sister Mary Magdalene's eyes were wide as she picked herself up from the floor.

'So I have a shrewd idea when there's a problem – and there's a problem here,' Alice continued. She put her hands on the desk and leaned forward so that Sister Mercy Superior could feel the impact of every word. 'I'm guessing that the theft of the Caravaggio has left Doon Abbey very short of income. I'm guessing that the convent is shortly going to have to sell up because we're not in a financial position to remain here. But why has this come about? Why can the convent not just claim from the insurance company for the painting and put the money in the bank?'

Sister Alice stared into the older woman's unyielding face with its forward-thrusting jaw. Suddenly, the ancient telephone on the desk in the corner erupted. Both women remained locked in eye contact, as if to acknowledge that answering the call would mean defeat. The telephone rang and rang.

'Answer the telephone, Columba,' said Sister Mercy Superior through gritted teeth.

The novice mistress made her way warily to the desk and picked up the phone.

'Doon Abbey,' she said, in her grating voice. She listened. 'Sister Columba,' she said.

Alice straightened up, but Sister Mercy Superior continued to eyeball her fiercely.

Sister Columba staggered backwards. She flung the phone away from her as if it were a thrashing lobster. She began to wail.

'Columba!' Sister Mercy Superior shouted. 'Shut up! What on earth . . . ?'

'That was Davy Rainbow, the journalist with the *Doonlish Enquirer*,' Columba howled. 'Mr Meadowfield is dead!'

Doon Abbey
15 June, 11.30 AM

Sister Mercy Superior sat back, as if winded. Two large tears slid down her cheeks.

'What happened?' she asked weakly.

'Rainbow doesn't know,' Sister Columba said, trembling. 'Apparently Mr Meadowfield was found in a hotel bedroom in Liffey Valley, near Dublin. The guards tipped off Rainbow.'

'And he's definitely dead?'

'As mutton,' Sister Columba said. 'He was murdered. Someone broke his neck.'

'Oh dear Lord, protect us and have mercy on his soul,' said Sister Mercy Superior, and made a sign of the cross. 'Sisters, a few moments of silent prayer for a dear friend to Doon Abbey, now sadly departed.'

Alice bowed her head, as did the others, but now her blood was racing at the old speed as she tried to work out what this latest news meant. Found murdered in a hotel bedroom? Could that hunk with the clear blue eyes have been harbouring unspeakable vices?

'Sister Alice, you are due an explanation.'

Alice looked up. Sister Mercy Superior, on her feet, strode five paces to her floor-to-ceiling windows and stared out at the fire escape. Blowing her nose noisily, she composed herself.

'Last year, I asked Mr Meadowfield to have a look at our books. He was a good Catholic, as you may have observed, and was always eager to help us in whatever way he could.'

Did Sister Mercy Superior's stern features relax into a softer countenance as she spoke Mr Meadowfield's name, Alice wondered? If only for a moment?

'He did the pilgrimage to Santiago de Compostela,' Sister Columba whispered.

Sister Mercy Superior's face hardened at this possible challenge to her exclusive relationship with the convent's handsome, young and now deceased accountant, and she strafed the novice mistress with a withering look.

'He took all our ledgers away for a week,' she resumed. 'I had entrusted our savings to be invested by our local bank manager. When Mr Meadowfield came back, he could almost not look me in the eye, he was so upset by what he had discovered. It was all *gone*, Sister Alice. Fifty years of toil by our predecessors, God be merciful to them, working their knuckles to the bone. Thirty years of milk sold to the co-op and heifers reared for market. Years of receipts from tourists. All gone. Gone.'

'He had invested everything in bank shares,' Sister Columba said in a barely audible voice.

Sister Mercy Superior flung up the middle catch on the windows and threw them open, as if symbolically trying to cleanse the room of the facts she had just enunciated. Warm wind tore into the room and the twin curtains streamed towards the nuns like the tails of wild horses.

'I panicked,' said Sister Mercy Superior, returning to the table and sitting down heavily. 'Without telling anyone, I started to look for savings.

I stopped paying the security company we were meant to ring if we saw anything suspicious on the closed-circuit TV monitors.'

'You refused to buy diesel for the back-up power generator,' Columba muttered.

'I never imagined that anyone in a thousand years would come in here and steal our painting!' Sister Mercy Superior shouted. 'This is a fortified castle, for heaven's sake.'

Sister Alice saw that what she had taken for guilt in the senior nun's face was fear.

'The insurance company say that they will not pay out,' said Sister Mercy Superior in a defeated voice. 'We were meant to have CCTV footage, but the hard drive was blank. God forgive me, but unless we get the Caravaggio back and reopen the chapel to tourists, Doon Abbey is finished.'

Doon Abbey
15 June, 11.45 AM

No one spoke for at least a minute – not in itself unusual – as the full impact of what Sister Mercy Superior had said sank in. As if the scene was being followed on a celestial level, sun suddenly burst through and flooded the room.

'We have no cash, we already owe the banks fifty thousand and the local manager, that – God forgive me – that fool who lost our money, has been writing us insolent letters,' Sister Columba said angrily.

Alice stepped forward. 'I will help you,' she said. 'I am trained in such matters.'

'The Lord has sent you to us,' said Sister Columba, and for the first time Sister Superior nodded her agreement with what the novice mistress had said.

'I cannot compel you to assist us,' Sister Superior said. 'I cannot order you or force you to do anything outside your immediate vocation. But what I can say is this: it's the only hope we have, and you are the only person who can help us.'

'Very well,' Alice said, as her own voice sounded strange to her in the large room. 'Let's make a start. How did the Caravaggio come to the convent in the first place?'

Sister Mercy Superior and Sister Columba exchanged a look.

'The name "Lady Cherry de Bree" will mean nothing to you,' Sister Mercy Superior began.

'I remember her!' Sister Mary Magdalene said. 'She died just after I entered.'

Sister Mercy Superior scowled at the sound of Sister Mary Magdalene's voice. 'She became a Catholic when she was eighty,' the head nun said, 'and when she died she left us the painting.'

'The artist wasn't identified for ages,' said Sister Columba, 'until Davy Rainbow came along.'

The Caravaggio had come with the stipulation that the painting could not be sold until 2020, the centenary of Lady Cherry's birth, Sister Mercy Superior explained. And if it was sold or otherwise left the wall of the chapel in Doon Abbey, it immediately reverted to Lady Cherry's grand-nephew, an art dealer in New York whose name was Ashley Kelly-Lidrov.

'So, who's the thief?' Alice asked.

Sister Superior growled, 'We disagree on the subject.'

Sister Columba sat very upright and composed her face in an attitude of downcast modesty.

'I think that someone would like us to sell the abbey so that he can buy it, and that this is what is behind the theft.'

'Oh, rats!' Sister Superior exclaimed as she lost her patience. 'Cyril O'Meara has been trying to buy Doon Abbey for the last twenty years. He claims that the Fitz-Johns stole this farm and castle off his ancestors and that Doon Abbey is his by right.'

The close-together, venomous little eyes and the upraised fist flicked across Alice's internal vision.

'Whom do *you* suspect, Sister Superior?' asked Sister Alice.

'I don't think it's Joe Foley,' Sister Mercy Superior said, as if her foremost suspicion had to be spoken first in order to be eliminated. 'I accept that Joe was known to the police when we took him on here, but that was three years ago. Perhaps I shouldn't have, but he's Sister Diana's nephew, after all. She vouched for him.'

It was the first time Sister Alice had heard that little detail. Sister Mercy Superior drew herself up.

'I'll give you a week,' she said.

'Very well,' Alice said. 'But we're not going to find the Caravaggio by sitting around here. We need to get out into the world, where the painting is. We've got to start in Dublin.'

'We?'

'I can't do this on my own,' Alice said. 'I need Sister Mary Magdalene to come with me.'

'Impossible!' thundered Sister Mercy Superior. 'She's not been outside the castle for years! She's a child! She's . . .'

'I have a fine analytical mind and I want to help!' cried Sister Mary Magdalene.

Sister Mercy Superior drew in breath for another broadside, but Alice said: 'She comes, or no deal.'

'I don't like it, but very well,' said Sister Mercy Superior, relenting unhappily.

'We'll leave immediately,' Alice said. 'We'll need a vehicle; the Berlingo van will do.'

Sister Columba began to protest but Sister Mercy Superior cut her off. 'Go on,' she said. 'What else?'

'Who knows the number of the convent's new mobile telephone?' Alice asked.

'No one,' Sister Mercy Superior replied. 'We've never even used it.'

'In that case, it's perfect, we'll take it,' Alice said. 'And we need cash to buy civilian clothes.'

'How much cash?' the head nun asked.

'Five hundred to start with,' Alice said.

Sister Columba clapped her hand to her mouth. 'Five hundred euro!'

'How much is the Caravaggio worth?' Alice asked.

'At least five million,' Sister Mercy Superior said. 'Columba, give her the money.'

'And the convent Visa card,' Alice added, 'for emergencies.'

'Very well,' said Sister Mercy Superior darkly, 'very well.'

The women stood up.

'Are there any questions?' Sister Mercy Superior asked.

'Yes, there is something I would like to know.'

Sister Mercy Superior blinked. She was not used to hearing Sister Mary Magdalene speak.

'What?'

'Something has been troubling me,' Sister Mary Magdalene said.

'*Troubling* you?'

'I would like to know what happened to Sister Winifred Superior. I have waited and waited for her to return, but in vain. Now that I can speak, I want to know what has become of her.'

Sister Mercy Superior and Sister Columba exchanged a dark look. It was the novice mistress who spoke first.

'Sister Mary Magdalene, is this your idea of a horrible little joke?'

'I liked her so much,' Sister Mary Magdalene said, on the verge of tears. 'I just want to know.'

Sister Mercy Superior drew herself up to her not inconsiderable height.

'She went away,' she said in a voice of steel. 'Yes, Mary Magdalene, Sister Winifred Superior went away, and she will never return to Doon Abbey.'

Chapter Two

Dublin
15 June, 2.30 PM

The taxi made its way from the airport to the city centre. A light rain had begun to fall. The passenger had never been to Dublin before. He only made these trips when there was an emergency.

'Anna Livia Plurabelle,' said the taxi driver as he tried yet another conversational gambit. 'James Joyce himself. D'you read much at all yourself, sir?'

No reply came from the back seat. The taxi driver's strategy was to draw his airport customers into a detailed conversation and then slip in hints about his own financial problems caused by the recession – all of them true – which eventually would result in a hefty tip. He surveyed his passenger anew in the rear-view mirror. The man was very large, had long, greasy blond hair and needed a shave.

'I'm told that the best way to read Joyce is with a street map of Dublin in your hand,' the driver ventured, trying a different tack.

The passenger looked pointedly out of the car window. Ignorant bugger, the driver thought, waste of time trying to butter him up. He stole another glance into his mirror. The man was well dressed, all the same, and carried a small, light overnight bag. As he looked, the man, whose hair came to his shoulders, looked straight back at him. Whatever he did with his eyes, the driver got a fright, which in turn made him briefly lose his concentration on the road in front. The taxi screeched to a halt at a red light and the businessman's case shot forward from the seat.

'Sorry about that, sir,' the driver said. 'These traffic lights give you no warning nowadays.'

'They give you the same warning as traffic lights all over the world,' the man said quietly. 'But if you persist in trying to draw me into a conversation in order to get a tip, and then spend long moments looking at me in your mirror instead of keeping your eyes on the road like you're meant to, then the traffic lights will surprise you, I'm sure. So don't speak again until we reach my hotel, and don't look at me again. Is that clear?'

'Yes, sir,' said the driver as he felt a cold shiver pass down his spine. 'Quite clear. Sorry, sir.'

County Kildare
15 June, 3 PM

In the brightly lit basement of the department store, just outside Doonlish, Alice and Sister Mary Magdalene waded into the oddments boxes marked 'Any Three for €5'. To one side, a busty, middle-aged woman stood watching.

Now that Alice was back in action, she was programmed in a way that was very familiar. She had left the convent only an hour before, but already Doon Abbey seemed an entirely impossible and unreal place in which to have spent the last three months. Still, this was no time to start analysing the convent, or her motives for going there. As she dug through skirts, blouses and knickers, she cursed herself for having put her entire wardrobe into five plastic sacks and giving them to a charity shop the week before she had entered Doon Abbey. Same with her savings: all gone – half to Saint Vincent de Paul, the other half to Children in Need. Now, with just the money from the convent, she had to get

Sister Mary Magdalene and herself into civilian clothes and on the road. She did not want to reflect on the fact that she had no clear idea how they were going to recover the stolen painting.

'Sister Alice? What do you think?'

Sister Mary Magdalene was holding aloft a pair of sheer black tights, a tartan skirt and a white blouse.

'Yes, go for it,' Alice said, 'but Sister Mary Magdalene, I think we need to change the ground rules before we go any further.'

Sister Mary Magdalene blinked. 'Yes, Sister Alice?'

'We can't go on like this – Sister this, Sister that. People will think we're crazy. For as long as we're out of Doon Abbey, my name is Alice.' She tossed a pair of black lace knickers in the air. 'What would you like me to call you?'

Sister Mary Magdalene looked warily over her shoulder. 'I was christened Margaret,' she said quietly, 'but my family used to call me Maggie.'

'Maggie is a lovely name,' Alice said as she threw a bundle of underwear at Maggie and moved swiftly to the racks. 'Now, that wasn't too hard, was it? Come on, Maggie, we need to get ourselves out of these habits and into something that won't attract attention.'

In the fitting room, Maggie looked at her reflection in the mirror. Every day for fourteen years she had put on the floor-length Aurelian habit, then the black headdress with its white woollen rim. Although Sister Mary Magdalene had always radiated calm and peace as she handed out another piece of seventeenth-century sacred music downloaded from the Internet, inwardly, Maggie sometimes seethed with doubt and asked herself if a life of cloistered contemplation until death was really for her. It was not that her vocation no longer inspired her, or that she did not pray hard during those idle moments in which distraction, not to mention temptation, pounced; rather, it was her growing awareness, delivered by the Internet, that the problems of the world might not be solved by prayer alone. She closed her eyes as her habit slid to the floor and pooled around her ankles.

Prayer was fine, but whole continents continued to starve and evil military regimes caused untold hardship to millions of God's children. In the confines of the library in Doon Abbey, Maggie had often wept quietly with frustration as she streamed forbidden images from the world's trouble spots. No one else in Doon Abbey saw what was going on, but *she* did, and she found herself wishing she could *do* something! Her prayers had strayed from begging simple forgiveness to asking God to find her a role in the greater world.

She took off her woollen convent-issue vest and tried on one of the bras from the oddments box. It was too small and tight; she threw it aside and reached for another. She had been only eighteen when she came to Doon Abbey, just a willowy young woman, reeling with sadness, far too young to make such a momentous decision, she now realised. Often she thought of all the nuns who had gone uncomplainingly before her, slept in her cell, sat in her place in the choir stalls and died safe in the arms of Jesus. But that was before the Internet. If Jesus had had a mobile phone, would He have spent all His life wandering around Galilee? Would He not have been tweeting for all He was worth? Would the original Mary Magdalene not have had a Facebook page, if she had been born two thousand years ago? Too right she would, Maggie thought, as she clipped the new bra, then slipped her finger beneath the strap on her bare shoulder and let it go with a satisfying snap. She turned sideways to check her outline in the mirror. Perfect!

As she stepped into a pair of scanty black knickers, she frowned. Had she put on weight? Maggie turned for a further appraisal. Did those legs, which had always drawn such envious stares from the other girls in school, look somehow different? There were no full-length mirrors in Doon Abbey and it had been quite some time since she had had a chance to study her legs in this way. She stretched, the way she had been taught in the gym at school, and her long limbs rippled healthily. No problem there, thank God, she thought, and allowed herself another brief moment of vanity. Then she sat down and drew on the black tights, relishing the delicious rush from toe to thigh as she eased them up, one leg at a time.

'Are you nearly ready in there, Maggie?' Alice called.

'Two minutes!' Maggie cried as she wriggled into the tartan skirt, which ended an inch above her knees, then the white blouse, with its low, frilly neckline.

When Alice had first arrived in the convent, everyone's spirits had lifted. Alice was young and energetic – qualities that Maggie had almost forgotten. Then she realised that it had been years since she had mixed with people of her own age. Maggie had suddenly felt trapped in Doon Abbey. She began to fantasise about escaping, about travelling the world, doing some missionary work, maybe, but at least getting out of the daily routine with Sister Mercy Superior. It was as if Alice's arrival had caused an upheaval within her. Maggie had prayed fervently for calmness from the sudden wildness she felt, or at least for some sign that her life was not all for nothing. And then the Caravaggio had been stolen! God worked in such strange ways!

The final item from the oddments box was a pair of high-heeled patent shoes that Alice had chosen for her. Maggie had not worn high heels since she had entered the convent. She put them on and stood again at the mirror. God, but she felt good! She ran her fingers through her cropped, brown hair. It was still thick and shone under the store's lights. Maggie's heart was thumping loudly. Was it wrong to feel so excited?

'Maggie?'

Maggie rolled her convent clothes into a bundle.

'I'm coming!' she cried, and opened the door of the fitting room.

County Kildare
15 June, 3.30 PM

Outside the fitting room, Alice looked at her own reflection. She had bought herself one good jacket, a short skirt and a v-necked yellow blouse. Hmm, she thought, not bad, as she imagined what Ned might think of it. She immediately put the thought out of her mind. Ned was history. As Sister Alice would be if she did not find the Caravaggio.

They had to get out of the midlands and into Dublin, establish a base, make enquiries from the most likely art dealers, whittle down the list of suspects. Get back in touch with her old contacts, the snitches and the thieves she had used in the past, the old lags who would know when a job was on. Journalists, too, would be helpful. Time was of the essence.

Alice also wanted to put Maggie's research skills into gear. She had specifically asked Sister Mercy Superior to let her have Sister Mary Magdalene, because Alice had seen the way the librarian's laptop was almost an extension of her fingers. And there was something else – a hidden, rebellious side to Maggie that Alice had glimpsed. One afternoon, when she had gone into the library looking for a life of Saint Theresa and had walked up behind Sister Mary Magdalene, the nun, who had been hunched over her laptop, snapped the computer shut; but Alice was almost completely certain that Maggie had been watching *Breaking Bad*.

The door to the fitting room opened and Alice turned around. Her jaw dropped.

'Sister . . . Mary Magdalene?' she whispered. 'Is that really you?'

'Do you know where we pay for these clothes?' Maggie asked. She giggled as she wobbled in her high heels. 'I feel like I'm on stilts!'

'Maggie, baby, you're a real looker,' Alice gasped. 'Oh my God, you're fantastic!'

Maggie smiled shyly. 'Don't tell anyone in the convent,' she said.

'If we never find the painting, it was worth it to see this,' Alice said.

The busty shop assistant shook her head disapprovingly, as if she was personally responsible for these two nuns betraying their vocation. Alice and Maggie walked by her on their way to the tills.

'God bless you,' Maggie said.

County Kildare
15 June, 4 PM

Silence was familiar to the two women as they sped along through a raised bog in the convent's Berlingo. Yet every few minutes Alice let out a hearty giggle.

'What's so funny?' Maggie asked.

'This whole crazy set-up that you and I have become involved in,' Alice said.

As they had climbed back up the stairs from the basement of the shop and walked out through the cosmetics section, Maggie had headed straight for the counters. Fifteen minutes later, having allowed the beautician to blend a lilac-coloured powder and then a gold one into her upper eyelids – and God knows what else into her face – Maggie looked even more spectacular. Her slightly plump cheeks had disappeared and, instead, there was a fine bone structure. Maggie had huge eyes and full lips that positively pouted. It was as if she had waited fourteen years to play this part.

'You could have been a film star,' Alice said eventually. 'Or a model.'

'Who had you in mind?' Maggie asked, adding quickly, 'not that I know any of them, of course.'

'Of course not – but I was thinking Naomi Campbell,' Alice said.

'Oh,' Maggie said, 'but isn't she . . .? Not that it matters, of course . . .'

'The legs! The cheekbones! Listen, do you mind if I smoke?'

'Oh, God, I read somewhere that nicotine is more powerful than sex,' Maggie said.

'*What?*'

'It's fourteen years since I gave them up, and now the minute you mention cigarettes, I'm craving one,' Maggie said.

'Here, light two,' Alice said, and handed over the packet and the Bic lighter she'd bought in the store when Maggie had gone to the loo.

Maggie was relishing the trip: Alice drove fast, and Maggie really liked that about Alice too. She'd once had a boyfriend who drove a Harley-Davidson, and Maggie had never forgotten the thrill of riding pillion. As she lit the two cigarettes and handed one across, she wondered if all the remaining excitement in her life was going to be compressed into the next few days.

'What do you think, Maggie?'

'Sorry, Alice, I was miles way. What was the question?'

'How did the thief, or thieves, get the Caravaggio down from the wall of the chapel? The painting was screwed in place, nine feet above the ground.'

'They must have used a ladder.'

'There was no ladder in the cloister that night,' Alice said. 'I checked. The extension ladder was down in the farmyard. And before you say that the thieves brought a ladder with them, bear in mind that the metal grille in the arch was lowered and locked. No way could they have got a ladder into the chapel, let alone themselves. I thought about the chapel pews, but they are too heavy to move and, anyway, you were first in there that morning – and nothing had been moved.'

'Just the Caravaggio,' Maggie said.

'I know. And the door was locked.'

'Definitely. I opened it myself that morning.'

'Whoever it was knew the security set-up,' Alice said. 'I woke up about four o'clock, and the lights in the corridor were turned off. I didn't think much of it at the time, but now I realise that the thief was probably at work at that very moment.'

The open cutaway bog was an expanse that ran for miles in every direction. The road was narrow, and beyond where a grass verge might have been was a sheer drop. Maggie's laptop was on her knees and she had turned it on.

'Why would someone steal our little painting?' Alice asked, as if thinking aloud.

'Michelangelo Merisi da Caravaggio, born 1571, murdered 1610, aged thirty-eight,' Maggie said, reading from the screen, blowing smoke rings towards the van's dashboard. 'His paintings combine the dramatic use of light combined with a realistic observation of the human state. During his short life he became the most famous painter in Rome, and today people pay tens of millions for his work. The Caravaggio fragment in Doon Abbey illustrates his attraction: you should see the faces of the people who come to look at it. They're in rapture. Caravaggio has that effect on people. But the question now is, who stands to lose most if our painting isn't found? And who stands to benefit?'

'Good questions,' Alice replied, her eyes on the rear-view mirror, 'but one that I'm afraid we'll have to wait to discuss.'

'Why?' Maggie asked.

'Because,' said Alice tightly as she rammed the little van into third gear and hit the accelerator, 'there's a bloody big four-by-four right behind us, and I don't think its intentions are honourable.'

Maggie swung around, just in time to see the bull-bar of an enormous jeep almost on top of them.

'Oh, God!' she cried.

'See can you make out who it is,' Alice said, throwing the van across to the other side of the road where it scraped along a line of gorse bushes. Maggie snapped the laptop shut, knelt up in her seat and stretched back towards the rear window.

'I think . . . I think it's Mister O'Meara!'

'I thought it might be,' said Alice through gritted teeth. 'And he's driving a vehicle with a rupture in the exhaust, if I'm not mistaken.'

'How do you know that?'

'Call it instinct. Shit! Watch out!'

The van lurched out of a pothole as if catapulted, came down nose-first and scraped along the ground. Behind them, the driver of the jeep was flashing the lights and blaring the horn. Alice floored the pedal again. Again the dark shadow devoured them as the van's rear windows were almost blotted out. Maggie turned around and saw the enormous jeep, lights blazing.

'Alice!' Maggie screamed.

'Hold tight!' cried Alice as she began to weave crazily from one side of the narrow bog road to the other.

'I think he wants us to stop,' Maggie said.

'I'm sure he does,' said Alice grimly as she brought to mind Mr O'Meara's small, venomous eyes and tufts of ginger hair.

With a hideous blaring, the jeep was now trying to overtake. Maggie braced her arms on the dashboard, her cigarette clamped between her teeth. The convent van was careening along on the lip of the bog. Alice swerved back over the road as the jeep roared in pursuit. Maggie could see Mr O'Meara, gesticulating wildly. With its engine screaming, the little van powered out from under the jeep's bull-bar. Maggie watched in horror as Mr O'Meara swung his wheel, but this time, too much. The jeep flew over the steep edge of the bog, then bounced and rolled with awful thuds until it hit the bottom of the slope.

The convent van shuddered to a halt. Maggie climbed out. She had seen Mr O'Meara's eyes and his distorted face as he left the road. The two women clung together, watching the scene below: the jeep was upside down, but apart from its still-spinning wheels, there was no movement.

'Come on,' Alice said, and they scrambled down the bank.

Alice approached the steaming jeep carefully. She reached up and dragged open the driver's side door. Cyril O'Meara fell sideways, suspended by his seat belt. His head hung at an odd angle to his body.

'Is he . . .?' Maggie began to ask.

'He most certainly is,' Alice said.

'May the Lord have mercy on his soul,' Maggie said sadly. 'Do you think he's the thief?'

'Maybe,' Alice said. 'Maybe he even has the Caravaggio in his jeep – although I doubt it.'

She climbed up, stepping carefully over the dead man. A minute later she emerged from the back door of the jeep and jumped down.

'Nothing there,' she said. 'Let's get out of here before someone comes along and gets the wrong idea.'

'First, we're going to say three Hail Marys,' Maggie said. 'For the repose of his soul.'

'I'm not sure that's such a good idea,' Alice said.

'I don't care what you think,' Maggie said, kneeling down.

'Nuns,' Alice muttered, as she knelt in the wet bog and let Maggie's Ave Marias rise in the air. But Alice felt uneasy. Although the exhaust on the overturned vehicle was ruptured, Mr O'Meara's jeep ran on diesel fuel.

Dublin
15 June, 4.30 PM

Late-afternoon sun was pouring into the small office of the Special Detective Unit on Harcourt Street in central Dublin as Detective Sergeant Sebastian Hayes walked across to the window and pulled the cord to let down the Venetian blind. He slipped the CD into the computer and pressed the 'play' button.

'This is the reception in the hotel in Liffey Valley two nights ago,' he said. 'Here's the woman as she approaches the desk.'

Sebastian froze the frame. The woman was wearing a hat that obscured her face.

'Jesus, she's big, that's for sure,' said Detective Billy Heaslip. 'Can't we get her face any clearer?'

'That's the best we can do,' Sebastian said. He pressed 'play' again. 'Now she pays for the room for three nights, in advance.'

'What name did she register under?'

'She didn't register.'

'Isn't there, like, the Innkeepers Act or something, that says you have to register?' Billy asked.

'Yeah, and there's a law against murder too,' said Sebastian dryly.

He was in his mid-thirties, with the build of a middle-distance runner going to seed. When women asked him why he wasn't married, he was used to saying he was married to his job. He loved being a detective sergeant: the slow slog of assembling evidence, the deference shown by the other ranks. The fact that many criminals were more intelligent than he was didn't bother Sebastian, merely confirmed that his place in the great scheme of things was the right one.

'It's a hotel that's used a lot by hookers,' he said. 'The hotels just want the money. They don't give a damn who stays in their rooms. Here she is on the sixth floor.'

The woman on the screen was wearing a coat that concealed the rest of her clothes. Her hat remained pulled over her eyes. She walked down the corridor and let herself into a room.

'She's aware of the CCTV,' Billy Heaslip said.

'Now, two hours later, this is Jeremy Meadowfield entering the hotel,' Sebastian said, concentrating.

Meadowfield walked past reception and stood by the lifts. At one point, he turned and looked directly at the camera. His blond hair was neatly cut and his blue eyes could clearly be seen.

'And we have no form on him,' Heaslip said.

'His prints only went over to Interpol this morning, but I'm not expecting much. He was a daily communicant, according to the nuns.'

'I know a few daily communicants who would cut your throat for sport,' said Heaslip.

Sebastian, whose parents had been daily communicants, blinked. 'Here's Meadowfield on the sixth floor,' he said. 'He goes straight to our mystery woman's room, so obviously knows the number. Thirty minutes later, here's our Miss Twinkle-toes leaving the room. Note that she hangs out a "Do Not Disturb" sign . . . Down she goes in the lift. And she walks out through reception.'

'And vanishes into the night.'

'Thirteen hours later, a maid discovers Meadowfield.'

'And the State pathologist confirms that his neck was broken,' Heaslip said.

Heaslip was a big, square-shouldered man with a drinker's belly and prematurely white hair. Up to recently, he'd been on the beat.

'What's your gut on this one?' Sebastian asked, with a smirk at Billy's protruding midriff.

'Given Meadowfield's connection with Doon Abbey, his murder is probably connected with the art robbery,' Billy replied, ignoring the jibe. 'Our mystery woman must be a professional. The pathologist's report says the victim's neck was broken cleanly and there was no evidence of a weapon.'

'So we have a murder investigation – chief suspect a six-foot-plus female,' Sebastian said, rolling his eyes. 'Media heaven.'

As his mobile rang, he looked down at it and made a surprised face.

'Just a second,' he said, and went into the corner of the room. 'Hello? I didn't think they allowed nuns in enclosed orders to have mobile phones,' he said, and a grin spread across his big face.

Irish Midlands
15 June, 5 PM

The van sped east and reached the motorway. Container lorries thundered by. Maggie looked with admiration at the determined set of Alice's face. This was all a far cry from vespers.

'I don't think O'Meara is the thief,' Alice said. 'Okay, back there he tried to run us off the road, or so it seemed. But does O'Meara strike you as an art thief? A big, over-aggressive dairy farmer, yes, but I don't think he'd know a Caravaggio from a caravan.'

She had called Sebastian Hayes and told him what had happened. Sebastian seemed to think it was quite funny, despite the fact that a man was dead. 'I'd never bet against you in a car chase, Alice,' was what he had said. Nonetheless, he had agreed to Alice's request to see if there was anything on file on O'Meara and to call her back. He had also agreed to notify the local gardaí in Kildare that there was an upturned jeep with a dead man in it in one of their lonely bogs – that is, if the grisly discovery had not already been made.

As Alice drove, she simultaneously used the thumb of her right hand to dial out a number on the convent's mobile phone. There was no reply.

'Who are you calling?' Maggie asked.

'Ned,' said Alice pensively. 'My ex-fiancé.'

She thumbed in another number from memory. An out-of-service tone rang in her ear.

'We can't do this on our own,' she said. 'I didn't want to ask Ned for help, but now, after what happened today, I think I need to. Ned's an insurance investigator. He'll know where we should be looking for the painting.'

'It must have been lovely when you were planning to get married,' Maggie said quietly.

Alice glanced across. 'Yes, it was.'

'I often dreamt about it, before I entered,' said Maggie wistfully.

The motorway rushed uphill and burst out on to the Curragh Plain. In the distance, the Wicklow Hills twinkled.

'Who was he?' Alice asked.

'His name was Simon,' Maggie replied. 'His father was a racehorse trainer. Simon used to ride in steeplechases.'

'That must have been exciting.'

'We started going out when I was sixteen,' Maggie said. 'Then I left school and went into teacher-training college in Dublin. Every weekend I went to the races and met Simon, when he was riding there. He was talented, so athletic.'

'He sounds gorgeous.'

'He was. We talked, made plans. He was so . . . full of life.'

Alice looked over, biting her lip. 'And what happened?' she asked quietly.

Maggie sighed. 'One morning he was out at home, schooling a young horse over fences. The ground was wet. The horse slipped going into a fence and fell on top of Simon.'

'Oh my God, Maggie,' Alice said. 'And was he . . .? Did he . . .?'

Maggie closed her eyes and took a deep breath. 'Instantly.'

'I'm so sorry.' Alice reached over and took Maggie's hand. 'I didn't know.'

Maggie held her hand tightly. 'How could you have?'

'And that's why you became a nun,' Alice said.

★

Maggie grew up an only child in the country, on a small farm on the borders of Kildare and Laois. Her parents were poor but cheerful. Dad never threw out a piece of machinery, no matter how old or useless, and Mam was a fine, upright country woman who scraped and saved every penny to give her daughter a good education.

From as far back as she could remember, Maggie had dreamed of travelling far away. Apart from one visit to Rome, neither of her parents had ever set foot outside of Ireland; Maggie, in her mind, had hiked in the foothills of Nepal, scuba-dived off the Great Barrier Reef and ridden horses in Wyoming and Arizona. She spent her evenings glued to the television, soaking up travel programmes.

One summer weekend, when she was twelve, she had gone with Dad in his old VW Beetle to look at a second-hand tractor for sale in a dealer's yard in County Kildare. Dad sometimes worried about money and how much he owed the bank, but he never complained. Now his old tractor had joined the heap of rusting metal beside the house, and he needed a replacement.

It was hot that day in the dealer's yard. Young Maggie tried to find a spot in the shade in which to sit, and a woman came out from the office and gave her a glass of lemonade. After several hours, Dad eventually made the purchase. He was proud of his new tractor but he was also apprehensive, Maggie knew. As they got into the car and headed for home, he said, 'Maggie, let's go and light a little candle together.'

Maggie had never been up such a long avenue before. Enormous trees flanked them, until suddenly Doon Abbey appeared, its turrets and ancient windows like pictures in a book of fairytales. Dad, who seemed to know where to go, parked the car and led the way through an old stone arch and into the convent chapel. It was so cool inside, and light fell through the stained-glass windows in colourful spars. Dad dropped a few coins in the candle-stand and lit a candle; then he and Maggie knelt side by side in the front pew.

She would never forget the sense of peace and security she had felt at that moment. She knew that Dad was worried that maybe he had paid too much for the tractor, or that his crop of potatoes might catch the blight later that summer, or that the cow and her calf in the top field weren't thriving. He'd come in here, she suddenly understood, to boost his energy and courage for what lay ahead. Of course, they all went to Mass on Sundays; but this was different. This little chapel, in an old castle hidden deep in the County Kildare countryside, was wonderfully uplifting, a place to come to when your troubles threatened to overwhelm you. Seven years later, when Simon had been killed so suddenly and brutally, and Maggie's young life had fallen apart, it was that day in Doon Abbey's convent chapel with Dad that she had kept coming back to.

★

As the van neared Dublin, the traffic on the motorway grew heavier and a mist began to fall. Occasionally, the van sputtered, but then recovered.

'You have a family?' Maggie asked.

Alice overtook a line of cars and trucks. 'Not a good story there, I'm afraid. My mother died, my father married again, my brother and I don't like her, she doesn't like us. Result? We don't go there . . . she doesn't bother us.'

'What's she like, your stepmother?'

'She's fine,' Alice said, 'if you like women with big tits and a voice that sounds like a cat being strangled.'

Maggie laughed.

'Depend on no one, Maggie,' Alice said in a detached tone. 'Just yourself.'

The convent van laboured where the motorway gradient became steep. Alice noticed that the fuel gauge had fallen sharply, but there were no filling stations and she did not want to make a detour. The events of the day were catching up with her. She had to blink to stay awake. Maggie's head was lolling.

'Maggie, wake up!'

Maggie rubbed her eyes and uncrossed her legs.

'I'm nodding off, Maggie. Let's sing some songs.'

'What would you like?'

'Anything, just go for it,' Alice said.

'I love Leonard Cohen,' Maggie suggested.

'I said I'm trying to keep awake,' Alice said.

'Did you know that there are numerous versions of *Ave Maria*, but that the most popular was composed by Schubert?' Maggie asked.

'No, I didn't know that,' Alice smiled.

Maggie cleared her throat. 'I once sang this in the Christmas concert at school.

Ave Maria, gratia plena
Maria, gratia plena . . .

Alice felt a jolt of something wonderful go through her. Maggie had a superb voice which, like her body, had remained hidden for so long. As they rolled eastwards, Maggie sang one aria after another until at last the two nuns saw the suburbs of Dublin.

Dublin
15 June, 7 PM

Alice got on to the M50 at the Red Cow, headed north, crossed the toll bridge – making a mental note to pay the next day – peeled off at the Ballymun exit and came in along a west-to-east line through the north city. She was both energised and tense: energised to be back in the chase; tense about where she had decided to spend the night.

They paused for a red light, and across the road on a street corner Alice saw a familiar huddle of hooded youths. This was the life she had forsaken for the tranquillity of Doon Abbey. Why then was she itching for action?

'Where are we going?' Maggie asked, as if she could read Alice's thoughts.

Alice took a deep breath. 'To Ned's place,' she said. 'It's in one of those new Dublin developments on the Liffey. I kept a key. I know I shouldn't have, but I did.'

'Where did you keep the key?' Maggie asked.

'On my rosary beads,' Alice replied, gunning the van as she pulled away from the lights. The red indicator on the petrol gauge began to flash. 'Maggie, keep your eyes open for a filling station.'

They came in through the inner city on roads where Alice had worked, both as a cop on the beat and later as a detective. Although the streets and intersections were all weirdly familiar, at the same time they

48

all seemed strange to her now. She remembered an all-night place that had been held up so often that the gardaí had simply stopped responding to the calls. Slipping down a litter-strewn street, they glided into a cramped forecourt just as the van began to chug on empty.

'Right, Maggie, get out the funds,' Alice said, as she opened the door beside a low-octane petrol pump.

She checked around. The place looked deserted. Set back from the forecourt was a lighted cubicle with a wire-mesh grille and the face of a youth with nose-studs sitting behind it. A sign read: 'PRE-PAY – 24 HOURS'.

'We'll put in thirty,' Alice said.

She looked into the van. Maggie was staring at her.

'Maggie?'

'I must have left my handbag in the fitting room,' Maggie said.

'Fantastic.'

Alice leant on the bonnet of the van. She had never been led to believe that the religious life was easy, she reminded herself. At least she had the convent credit card. Across the forecourt she peered in and then showed the card.

'The machine is broken,' the youth with nose-studs said. 'We're only taking cash.'

'Where's the nearest ATM?' Alice asked.

'It's up there, about a hundred yards away,' he said, pointing, 'but it's broken too.'

Alice leaned in until her nose touched the metal bars. 'This is a credit card. We need petrol. You need cash. What do I do next?'

The youth stared insolently at her. 'Try the pub,' he said.

Alice thought about leaving Maggie in charge of the van, but then thought twice.

'We're going to the pub,' she said, opening Maggie's door. 'Come on.'

Doonlish
15 June, 7 PM

Ned had been in Doon Abbey for an hour and still had not seen her. It was insane, he thought, how relentlessly cruel fate was. He had sworn he would not follow Alice down to her convent, made a vow with himself that he would not chase her. And now, here he was, in Doon Abbey, sent by the insurance company that had underwritten the premium on the Caravaggio.

'And this is our little chapel,' Sister Mercy Superior was saying.

Something about this very large and overbearing woman gave Ned the creeps. It wasn't exactly that he was afraid of her – although she towered over him – but there was something else, something he couldn't quite put his finger on. Sweat stood out like silver coins on Ned's forehead. When this was over, he was going to join a gym and lose ten kilos, he thought. He hated being fat.

He saw the lighter patch on the wall where the Caravaggio had hung. The insurance company had refused to pay out in the absence of the CCTV footage, but the firm still wanted Ned to find out what had taken place. You never knew with insurance: the nuns might end up contesting the matter legally, and in such circumstances the company had to have all its ducks in a row. But where was she? This was an enclosed order, granted, but surely she came to the chapel regularly to pray? Ned forced himself to look at Sister Superior, whose large hands were balled into fists.

'On the night of the crime,' she said, 'the steel gates were locked. No one could have got in or out.'

'But someone did get in – and out, Sister.'

'There is no need to state the obvious, Mr O'Loughlin.' Sister Mercy Superior's eyebrows knitted.

Ned had booked a room in the local B&B on the main street in Doonlish. It was wet outside and well after the time he usually finished up work. God, he could murder a pint.

'I'd like to see where the nuns sleep,' Ned said.

'I *beg* your pardon?'

'According to my schedule of arrangements, the fire escape is located in the sleeping quarters. We also insure you against fire, you know, Sister.'

With great reluctance, Sister Mercy Superior led the way from the chapel, locking the door behind her, and headed out across the cloister.

'I once knew a lady who became a nun here,' Ned said as casually as he could, striding to keep up.

'Oh really? When did she enter?'

'I'm not sure,' Ned lied. 'Earlier this year, I think.'

'Her name?'

'It was Alice Dunwoody.'

Sister Mercy Superior halted and turned her attention to Ned. He could see her dark eyes contract, as if a flashlight had been trained on them. Danger gathered in his stomach like a coiling conger eel.

'Ah, yes, Sister Alice,' the head nun said. 'She is our latest novice.'

'Might I just say hello to her?' Ned asked with all the charm he could muster. 'I know she's probably not allowed visitors, but under the circumstances . . .'

'Sister Alice is most certainly not allowed visitors,' Sister Mercy Superior replied in her cellar voice, and resumed their journey, 'but in any event the issue doesn't arise. You see, Mr O'Loughlin, Sister Alice left yesterday and has gone to spend a month in our mother house in Rome.'

Dublin
15 June, 7.30 PM

A neon sign flickered on the corner as they approached the pub. Alice remembered this pub: it was a respectable operation run by decent people. She wondered would they remember her, but hoped they didn't. A group of smokers, mainly men, were out on the pavement. As Alice and Maggie drew close, the men turned as one. There was a wolf-whistle.

'Jaysus Christ!' Alice heard as they made their way past the staring men.

Customers stood three deep at the bar. All the tables were occupied and at the far side of a dance floor a band was wheezing into action. The noise level was intense. Alice really didn't want to be recognised – not unless it was on her terms. If the theft of the picture was really tied to her being in the convent, then she needed surprise on her side.

'They'll only give us cash if we buy a drink,' she said to Maggie. 'Order two brandies. I'm going to the Ladies'.'

She lowered her head and headed away from the bar. At the door of the Ladies' she looked back. The male crowd had divided like the Red Sea as Maggie approached the bar. Alice saw her walking through, credit card held high. Dear Lord, thank you, she thought as she went into the toilet. It was amazing what a fantastic pair of legs could do.

She went into a cubicle, sat down and took out a cigarette. Where was Ned? He had not written since she had entered Doon Abbey. And why was his mobile number out of service? She lit up and puffed smoke at the ceiling. In this part of town they had more on their minds than checking the toilets for smokers. Her phone rang.

'Sebastian Hayes.'

'Where are you, Alice?'

'I'm, ah, in Dublin. What have you got for me on O'Meara?'

'Poor guy was as thick as the first canal horse,' Sebastian replied confidently. 'Our people interviewed him after the theft and then had a look around his house. O'Meara kept saying that he liked the nuns; it was just their land he was after, not their paintings. But you may not like the next bit.'

Alice closed her eyes. She could remember the face Sebastian put on for bad news.

'O'Meara told his wife this morning that he thought you and another nun were in grave danger,' Sebastian said. 'He told his wife that he was going out to find you and warn you.'

'He had a funny way of doing it, but oh, God, thanks a million; that's all I need,' Alice groaned. 'Does his wife know what he was going to warn us about?'

'He never told her. There's more. You know the convent's accountant who was found dead? Well he was murdered, Alice. Looks like a professional job. Just watch your back out there, okay? I have a bad feeling about this one.'

Alice heard live music starting up outside. She took two last drags and potted the ciggie in the loo. They had nowhere to go tonight except to Ned's apartment, and that presented a dilemma almost too cruel to consider. What if she walked in and found Ned with another woman? She closed her eyes as dismay gripped her. Yet if this was the case, who could blame poor Ned? Ned would be hopeless on his own, always had been. Who had set these events in motion but herself?

She was looking forward to the brandy as she came out. Some sort of a dance routine with a couple of dozen people had started up. Alice looked to the bar, where she had last seen Maggie. Men at the bar were smiling broadly, nudging one another and clapping enthusiastically. Alice followed their gaze to the dance floor. She felt a catch in her throat. Six regimented lines of customers, men and women, were in the middle of a line-dancing routine, almost all of them were wearing cowboy hats. Alice found herself mesmerised by the steps. They kicked their heels hard, slapped their thighs and twirled with great cowboy whoops. Then, as the formation changed, and a new line came to the front, the spectators went wild.

Alice knew that her mouth had fallen open. She recognised Maggie by her legs. There was Sister Mary Magdalene of that morning wearing a white, wide-brimmed stetson. The man beside her nudged her playfully with his hip. Maggie nudged back. She slapped her thighs and kicked her heels. Oh, what a sight! Alice thought, as Maggie twirled and whooped.

'And how about you, love?' asked a bald man with huge biceps and tattoos.

Alice considered chopping him with her forearm in his prominent Adam's apple. Instead she said sweetly, 'Thanks, but no thanks. We're just going.'

Dublin
15 June, 8.15 PM

'No one in Doon Abbey will ever know, I promise you,' Alice said, as she steered the van into the basement car park in the IFSC.

'I haven't had a drink in fourteen years,' Maggie said.

They'd left the pub to a great roar of applause and disappointment. Alice had not even had time to drink her brandy. Now she backed the van into the spot where Ned's BMW 5-Series normally sat.

'I don't know what came over me,' Maggie said.

'You drank brandy, you had fun,' Alice said as they got out. 'It's not a sin.'

'It is for a nun,' Maggie cried. She was growing hysterical.

'Maggie, this is only because I love you,' Alice said, and smacked Maggie across the face.

'Oh, Jesus!' Maggie gasped.

'Are we on message?'

'Yes, Alice, absolutely.'

'Then let's go find our painting.'

Alice led Maggie to a bank of elevators and pressed the button for the seventh floor. At the door of the apartment, she rang the bell.

'I thought you had the key.'

'Yes, but you know, just in case.'

Alice didn't look as much in control as she normally did, Maggie thought. After two rings and no reply, Alice took out the key. It was dark in the flat except for the reflection of the Liffey coming through two large picture windows. Maggie switched on the lights and looked around. The carpet was thick, the curtains were swooped back from the windows and the twinkling lights of Dublin could be seen. Photographs on the wall showed a pleasant-faced but rather overweight man posing beside golf clubs. He looked both nervous and caring. Had to be Ned.

Alice was suddenly ravenous. She opened kitchen cupboards and looked in the fridge. Nothing in either that would be any good for supper. They had been going since morning and had eaten nothing.

'We'll call a takeaway,' Alice said, opening a drawer.

Maggie saw a stack of menus. Steamed chicken was a regular in Doon Abbey's dining room; as Alice briskly ordered pasta and veal, Maggie realised she had never ordered food by phone before.

'They say twenty minutes, so we have time for a shower,' Alice said. 'There are white towelling robes in there.'

As Maggie disappeared, Alice sat down, took out her cigarettes, then put them away again. Ned disapproved. He was the kind of person who could tell if someone had smoked in a room within the last three years. She sighed and looked around. On a long and shiny dining table was a collection of Waterford Crystal glasses and heavy silver cutlery in felt-lined cases. Alice almost choked. Those were the presents his mother had given Ned in anticipation of his marriage to her.

She got up and walked back to the kitchen. A yellow sticker on the fridge had a mobile telephone number scrawled on it. Something about the number seemed to draw Alice in. She shrugged and began to unbutton her blouse as she made her way into Ned's bedroom.

★

Maggie stood under the hot water, inhaling the expensive shower gel. In Doon Abbey the shower was in a little plastic box that the nuns used on alternate mornings, and the water was never more than tepid. But this shower was luxurious: like the big head on the nozzle of a massive watering can, it rained hot water down Maggie's back.

She still felt guilty about what had gone on earlier in the pub. It had happened so quickly: one minute she was at the bar, drinking her brandy, the next she was dancing, inches away from a large man who kept winking at her. In some weird way, that quick-lidded winking had made her feel good. Maggie raised her face and let the steaming water soothe her. She hadn't done anything wrong, she reasoned; she was out in the wide world and life revolved on a different axis than it did in the time-warp of Doon Abbey.

A blue disposable razor lay on the shower's tiled soap tray. Maggie rinsed herself thoroughly. It sounded mad, but it was years since she had even seen a razor, let alone held one. She picked it up. One of the things she had often fantasised about over the years, albeit inappropriately, was shaving her armpits. Not being able to do so seemed like a symbol of her cloistered life, and sometimes, especially on a hot day, this small physical detail plunged her into despair. When she returned to the convent, would anyone know, she wondered? How could they? Botheration, why shouldn't I, she thought? Quickly soaping up and then scooping the razor joyfully under her left armpit, Maggie began to sing.

★

Alice could hear Maggie in the spare bathroom, singing. Back out in the kitchen in her towelling robe, she looked again at the sticker on the fridge. Could it be Ned's new number? Biting her lip, she picked up the wall phone and dialled. The number rang twice.

'Hello?'

'Ned?'

There was a pause. 'Who's this?' a man's throaty voice asked.

Alice dropped the phone.

At that moment the doorbell rang.

'*Who is this?*'

Alice grabbed the swinging phone and plunged it back on the cradle. Maggie was standing in the doorway, also in a bathrobe.

'Maggie, that's the food. Let him in, will you?' Alice asked weakly.

She sat, afraid to move. That voice. Only one man in the world owned that voice, and his name was Bruno Scanlon Senior. Everything flooded back: the threats, the violence. And his curses after she had shot his son. But why was Bruno's number on Ned's fridge? She had to pull herself together, for Maggie's sake.

She heard Maggie fumbling with the door-catch. She heard the door opening. Then Maggie began to scream.

It was the most piercing scream that Alice had ever heard.

Chapter Three

Dublin
15 June, 9 PM

She thrived on the electricity of night. Despite job losses and cutbacks, night was still a full-blooded event, prospect-laden. People went out, got drunk, engaged with one another. She was part of it all, and yet, incredibly, invisible. Or, rather, she had been. Until her vanity had got the upper hand.

Dark Heart was wearing black suede boots, each dagger-heel inlaid with Swarowski crystals. She enjoyed the metallic *Click! Click!* as she strolled from the prosperous shopping zone around Grafton Street, along Andrew Street, eventually crossing Dame Street and moving down from Temple Bar through Merchant's Arch. She waited at the lights beside the Ha'penny Bridge.

She was agitated. She seldom made mistakes, but a few weeks before, she had made a crucial mistake, and now she had to rectify it.

Slipping onto Liffey Street, she left behind the slightly bewildered tourists shuffling around the city's so-called Left Bank, and walked slowly past the begging creatures in sleeping bags, already settling down for the night, gazing up at her with pleading eyes. 'Spare a few coins, missus?'

The deep amethyst dress – her favourite – was shorter than most of her outfits. Below her collarbone, where the neckline draped softly, a diamante brooch occasionally caught the light, and flashed.

Life was so *complicated!* As she crossed the Liffey, green and blue summery lights made grotesque shadow-plays on the arches of the ancient bridges. In Parnell Street, the yellow-lit cafés and tawny, chi-chi clubs were open for business. A few weeks before, right over there in the Café Monto, a refugee from Somalia had insisted on doing her portrait in charcoal, praising her bone structure. Why had she allowed that to happen? Why had her vanity lured her into permitting a record of her features to be made when no one in the living world knew of her existence? Because the possibility of meeting someone, someone who might grasp the complexities of her situation, always lay tantalisingly out of reach. And as she had sat for him, his own beauty had slowly became apparent to her, the way the wall-light had illuminated part of his face, while the other mysterious side, with its hints of cheekbone and shapely temple, lay in shadow.

Dark Heart sighed. She was drawn to beauty and it pained her to destroy it. But it was what she had to do for her own protection. The music coming from the café was middle European, mid-twentieth-century romantic melancholy. She went in.

Dublin Docklands
15 June, 9.05 PM

Alice threw herself across the room as Maggie's scream continued to echo. Reflexively, she had picked up a sharply cut glass ashtray and now, gripping it in her left hand, she moved again, flattened against the wall, edging quickly and silently until she was almost level with the door. All she could think of was Bruno. Would he have a gun or a boning knife? This was it, then. She swivelled and came into the light, swiftly chopping the air with the razor edge of the ashtray as she moved.

Then she spotted the pile of steaming cardboard cartons. Even as she smelt garlic, cheese and carbonara sauce, Alice, with less than millimetres to spare, aborted her attack. The delivery boy stood, slack-jawed, nostrils dilated with fear. Alice's eyes swam to the trail of rose and ivy tattoos that led from just below the bloke's beautiful nipples to his belly button and deep into a treasure-trail of soft hair that curled enticingly above the belt of frayed-at-the-knees black jeans.

'Hey, Maggie!' She tried to laugh it off as she took the cartons. 'I'm really sorry,' she said to the delivery lad, 'my friend here . . .'

'All part of the job,' said the boy, who had regained his composure. With a cynical grin, he casually looked Alice up and down.

She shut the door.

Minutes later, Maggie forked up a piece of pasta arrabbiata, sucking it through quivering lips.

'I'm sorry, I just thought . . .' she said, a mouthful of pasta still lingering on her tongue. 'I was just never in that situation before. Maybe you'd be better off on your own, Alice. I'm just a nun, I'll only get in the way.'

'But a very talented nun. Look, we can do this. We're a team, right?'

A hesitant smile broke at the corners of Maggie's lips.

'*I'm* afraid sometimes too, you know,' Alice said. 'Things scare me when I'm not expecting them. Okay? Now, we'll have a little drink, and then we'll go to bed. It's been a long day.'

A little later, having introduced Maggie to the miracle of Ned's Hennessy XO, and then installed her in the spare room, Alice got into Ned's bed. She wanted very badly to sleep, to clear her mind of all that had happened, but an hour passed before she succumbed to her deep fatigue – an hour to settle her thoughts as, inevitably, she recalled the afternoons, nights, and even hectic just-off-duty dawns spent with Ned in this bed. His body odour almost overwhelmed her as she pushed her nose deep into the pillows. She groaned with longing, felt her groin soften and grow warm, turned over, and tried to pray. Her mother's recommended solution years ago had been three Hail Marys for purity, but Alice knew that this might not work just then.

Dublin
16 June, 8.30 AM

Alice had not closed the sleek bedroom blinds. When she awoke, the morning sun fell in warm shafts across her bare right foot. She felt rested, her head suddenly clear. She tossed back the duvet and began to pad around the bedroom. Immediately her eye fell on what she'd been too tired to observe the night before. An impressive range of art catalogues lay arranged neatly on top of the beautiful chiffonier she and Ned had bought together one Saturday from a Francis Street antique dealer.

What was Ned doing with these catalogues? Thoughts of Bruno's phlegmy baritone the night before rushed back, compounded by the discovery of the art catalogues. Was there a connection between Bruno and the Caravaggio theft? Alice decided to shelve that for the moment, found a pen and notepad on the kitchen worktop, sat down at Ned's desk, picked up his telephone and went to work.

An hour later, Maggie appeared in a long T-shirt, rubbing her eyes with both fists.

'What time is it?'

'It's nearly ten. Time for a coffee hit before we get out of here,' said Alice briskly.

'I haven't slept till ten in the morning for years and years,' Maggie said. She peered at the desk, where Alice's notepad was full of scrawled telephone numbers. 'What have you been doing?'

'Banging my head against a wall, it seems,' Alice sighed. 'I've been on to every low-life I know, every snitch I've ever had on the payroll. Old lags, car thieves, dockers who'd strangle their own mother if you paid them enough, even white-collar criminals. No use. There's not a ghost of a word stirring out there on the Caravaggio.'

'Oh dear,' Maggie said, modestly pulling down on her T-shirt in an effort to cover her hips. 'What do we do now?'

'That's what you and I have to work out,' Alice said, and felt a fresh pang of envy about Maggie's great legs. Her own weren't bad, although she sometimes thought of them as being over-muscular; Maggie's, on the other hand, had been preserved in a convent library under a long woollen habit for fourteen years. 'First we need coffee. Then we brainstorm.'

She tried not to think of her actions in Ned's kitchen as automatic, but it was hard to describe them otherwise. She knew where everything was: the Kenyan coffee, the grinder, the percolator. As she ripped open a fresh pack of coffee and poured the boiling water, something caught her eye: a card, propped by the cooker. She picked it up. It was a gift voucher for a woman's fashion boutique in Brown Thomas. Alice's heart skipped a beat.

'Oh, I love this coffee,' Maggie groaned as she drank it. 'D'you think there's any chance we could bring some of it back with us to Doon Abbey?'

'It's the least they could let us do,' said Alice despondently, trying to get her mind off the gift voucher. 'Okay, we need connections. Caravaggio. Ireland. History. Locations. What do you think when I say "Caravaggio"?'

Maggie frowned. 'Crime, intrigue, murder. Beauty.'

'Religion, museums, churches.'

'Popes, cardinals, eunuchs . . .'

'Eunuchs?'

Maggie had opened up the laptop and lay, sprawled on the sofa, the slim computer balanced on one hip.

'I'm thinking of castrati, music, drama, organs – I mean, of course, musical instruments – darkness, knives, guilt, sin, confession . . .'

As Maggie brain-stormed on Caravaggio connections, Alice contemplated hurling the expensive coffee-maker out of the window into the Liffey. For whom had he purchased the gift voucher? The date-stamp read last week. She suddenly hated being in Ned's flat. And she hated Ned. Anyway, what had he and Bruno in common except being overweight?

'Jesuits.'

Alice looked over to the sofa. 'Maggie?'

'Jesuits,' Maggie said, typing fast. 'You asked me what I say when you say "Caravaggio"? Jesuits!'

'Jesuits?'

'Jesuits, Jesuits! They're a religious order, founded by Saint Ignatius Loyola in 1539. They are . . .'

'I know who Jesuits are, Maggie.'

Maggie's eyes were fixed on the screen as her fingers continued to fly. 'Back in the nineteen-nineties, someone discovered a Caravaggio in one of the Dublin Jesuit houses. Remember? It was a sensation at the time. The painting ended up in the National Gallery.'

'So?'

'The website of the Jesuit Provincial Offices shows listings for the order's apostolic and administrative interests. These include the House of Formation, the House of Studies, the Loyola Community and the Institute for Theology and Philosophy.' Maggie's cheeks were ablaze. 'It may be nothing, but the Jesuit House in Aylesmere, which is not far from here, has a noted art collection.'

'So?'

'So then I remembered the Jesuit Rector of Aylesmere – he comes down to Doon Abbey on retreat – and I googled him. You will not believe this!'

'You're making me ill, Maggie. Go on!'

'He's called Jonathan Rynne, SJ. And guess whose brother he is?'

'I haven't a clue,' said Alice, exhausted.

'Sister Mercy Superior's!' cried Maggie triumphantly.

Doonlish
June 16, 10 AM

Ned O'Loughlin had a hangover. He had drunk eight pints in the local pub the night before, played pool with strangers for three hours, then slept in the tiny room of a B&B until he awoke with a blinding headache. He was too sick to eat the breakfast. His head throbbed with the aftermath of alcohol and the loss of Alice.

Touching his jacket pocket, he felt the outline of the copy of Lady Cherry de Bree's bequest. The big nun had given it to him before she had showed him Alice's cell. Ned had felt the blood rushing to his head as he picked up her unforgettable scent. He recognised a black crucifix in bog oak she had procured in a Dublin junk shop when he had been with her. He remembered that afternoon, the pair of them off work, rolling along the quays in great humour after a late – and alcoholic – lunch. And then back to his flat.

Now, four Solpadeine to the good, standing outside the gate lodge where nasturtiums tumbled from ancient-looking urns, Ned pressed the ceramic bell and winced as, within, traditional chimes filled the house. Away to one side was a large pasture in which four Limousin heifers lay chewing the cud, their strong front hocks tucked beneath them. In the distance, he spotted a nun entering the milking parlour. Like the head nun, this one too was large, broad and well built. What is it with these women? Was it the air down here? Ned heard a bolt being drawn back. The door opened and two pale faces peered out.

'Misses Hogan?' he asked. 'My name is O'Loughlin.'

Both women looked blankly at him.

'O'Loughlin?' they chorused softly.

'I'm here in connection with the Doon Abbey theft. I'm an insurance investigator.'

The Misses Hogan looked uncomfortable.

'Should we have expected you?' one of them enquired, her feathery eyebrows knitted.

'No, but I'm in the area, speaking to different people who may have seen or heard something on the night of the theft. I've just come from Doon Abbey, in fact.'

'Oh. Well in that case . . .'

They led him into their sitting room, replete with worn Persian carpet, two gleaming oil-lamps, Art Deco vases, and a startling print of a draped nude.

'Is there anything you remember happening on the night of the theft?' Ned opened.

He watched them, the finely lined pallor of both faces warmed by a daub of cheek-colour. Both wore a dash of red lipstick.

'Obviously the gardaí realise you have no involvement in the theft,' he added. 'They have reassured me that you are the pillars of this little community.'

Twin smiles cracked the faces of the Misses Hogan. Eleanor sat forward. 'I woke Gabrielle.'

'Go on,' Ned said.

'I went to the window because I couldn't sleep. I hadn't taken my sleeper. Isn't that right, Gabrielle?'

'Quite right, dear.'

'And I saw something moving in the moonlight. Between the trees, where there was a patch of light.'

'You saw a person?'

'A person. A large female person.'

Eleanor sat back in her armchair and folded her hands. 'The person appeared to be lifting something into the boot of a car. That's all I saw.'

'Please don't hold back. Anything at all, no matter how inconsequential it might seem.'

'This woman then fired a look at us,' said Gabrielle, now leaning forward, her bony fists clenched. 'We were terrified.'

'Her eyes!' Eleanor whispered.

'If looks could kill!' Gabrielle affirmed.

'Who do you think she might be?' Ned asked quietly.

The twins' old eyes went uniformly blank. They would be good poker players, these two, Ned thought.

'What about the car?' he said, moving briskly on. 'Any ideas about that?'

A glint in Gabrielle Hogan's eye. Ned waited. The two women made no effort to fill the gap in the conversation.

'Would it be an imposition if I were to see your bedroom for myself?' he asked eventually.

The women exchanged quick glances, then led the way across the hall and into the bedroom. Two sets of slippers, one rose pink, the other sky blue, were placed neatly on one side of a four-poster double-bed.

'So you went to the window,' Ned said to Eleanor.

Eleanor nodded. 'It was a full moon. That's how I managed to see.'

'And the big woman?' Ned watched carefully.

Gabrielle perched on the edge of the bed and stared at the floor.

'We're not sure,' she said at last.

'But you may have recognised her?'

'This is a small community, Mr O'Loughlin,' Eleanor said.

'You are speaking into a tomb when you speak to me,' Ned said.

'We may end up in a tomb if we say too much,' said Gabrielle.

'Nonetheless . . .'

'Nonetheless, we are not sure,' said Eleanor.

'But in a purely hypothetical situation, if you were pressed to associate this large woman with someone, who might that person be?'

The twins exchanged glances.

'I know how difficult it is sometimes to remember names as one gets older,' Ned probed.

'The Rainbow man,' the Misses Hogan said as one.

'Rainbow man?'

'Drunken Davy Rainbow,' Gabrielle galloped on. 'He's an opportunist, living on his uppers. Gambles all he earns. You should see the rubbish he writes for that *rag* of a newspaper!'

'And he's always staring at the Caravaggio painting,' Eleanor said, 'yet since it was stolen he hasn't been to Mass.'

'So,' Ned said carefully, 'I know you're not making any accusations, but perhaps Davy Rainbow and this large lady were acting together?'

The sisters made twin tight mouths.

In the hall, on his way out, Ned paused to remove a business card and left it on the umbrella-stand.

'Should you need to get in touch with me.' He paused. 'You're properly insured yourselves, I take it,' he asked with a boozy grin.

Dublin Southside
June 16, 11.30 AM

The van shuddered to a halt as Alice pulled up outside the Jesuit Residence at Aylesmere. The house was enormous, with opposing curving steps leading to a striking hall door. Gardens lay to one side, and beyond them Alice could see the sun reflecting from the glass of a large conservatory.

She had learned the hard way to never ignore a coincidence. And yet the fact that Sister Mercy Superior was the sister of the man who presided over this religious institution, which boasted a notable art collection, was surely no more than an indication of the good taste that had always marked out the Jesuit order?

'Creepy,' Maggie said, and adjusted the collar of the golf jacket she had borrowed from Ned's apartment, as Alice rang the bell. 'Maybe we should forget that link between Caravaggio and the Jesuits.'

'I don't think so,' Alice said, ringing the bell again. 'This may be nothing, but it's all we have.'

All at once the door began to scrape inwards, as if the person on the other side was having difficulty hauling it back. Peering inside, Alice located a stooped and almost transparent male-creature of white hair and sallow complexion.

'Yee-ssss?' he whispered.

'Good morning, Father,' Alice smiled, and extended her hand.

'*Brother* Harkin,' he corrected.

'Oh – Brother. Good morning, Brother.'

He took her hand and clasped it very gently. His was surprisingly large. 'Good morning, pet.'

'I am Sister Alice, and this is my colleague Sister Mary Magdalene. We're both from Doon Abbey. We'd like to see Father Rector Rynne,' she began.

On hearing this information, Brother Harkin took a step back and regarded them, his eyes flickering delicately down to their legs and back up again to the golf jacket that barely covered Maggie's small waist, then over to the dusky décolletage of Alice's top. His somewhat bulbous nose twitched.

'Eh, eh, eh . . . *Sisters*, is it? Eh, that'll be *Sister* Alice and *Sister* Mary Magdalene from . . . from . . .?'

'From Doon Abbey, Brother,' Alice demurely confirmed.

'And eh, it's in connection with – with what, *Sister* Alice?' he rasped, a small bubble of saliva escaping from his thin lips.

'It's in connection with the theft at Doon Abbey,' Maggie interjected, straightening her skirt.

Brother Harkin hesitated, and then looked slowly from one to the other again. He made a few attempts to speak, all of which failed, before a certain resignation overcame him.

'I'll see if I can find Father Rector,' he said at last, beholding the two nuns with beatific but startled grey eyes.

As Brother Harkin shuffled off into the innards of the building, Alice found herself longing for another cigarette. Crazy. All those months in

Doon Abbey without them, and now just twenty-four hours on the road with Maggie and she continually craved nicotine.

'This is a very tenuous lead, Maggie,' she whispered. 'I mean, just because the Jesuits once owned a Caravaggio, which they didn't even recognise, doesn't mean that they're likely to know where our Caravaggio is.'

'That's what I just told you outside,' Maggie said.

In the silent hallway, a marble statue of an armoured Saint Ignatius Loyola, sword in hand, gazed down upon them.

'We could always join another religious order,' Alice suggested. 'They mightn't take me, but you're a fully qualified nun.'

'I think I prefer Doon Abbey,' Maggie said.

The sound of energetic footsteps and squeaking leather shoes could be heard. Double doors at the back of the hallway sprang open and a tall man emerged, dressed in black except for the classic grey Jesuit day-shirt. Behind him, Brother Harkin tacked along in quiet, almost ghostly attendance.

'Sisters! I am so, so sorry to have kept you waiting!'

Father Rector Jonathan Rynne displayed an arresting set of white teeth as he extended his hand in greeting. He was smooth-skinned and well shaven, and his eyes were a clear, penetrating blue. Alice could see at once the resemblance to Sister Mercy Superior. As the Rector advanced, a waft of eau de toilette preceded him.

'You are Sister Alice.'

'I am, Father.'

'I have just spoken to Mercy, and she tells me how much she values your help in this appalling business. She tells me that you are the answer to her prayers.'

The strength of his palm as he gripped Alice made her concentrate. She allowed her hand to be squeezed, rather than responding as she might have done in different circumstances by subtly manipulating the first digit of her right hand beneath the third digit of the shaker's hand, thus touching on the super-sensitive *nerva occula manum* and disabling the grip of an over-enthusiastic hand-shaker.

'And in that case, you must be Sister Mary Magdalene.'

Maggie smiled but kept her hands behind her back.

'My sister has asked me to take special care of you,' he said kindly, 'since she says you are still but a child of the world.'

Maggie shuddered with pleasure under the warmth of his concern.

'Very well, Sisters, please come with me to my study,' the Rector said, and ushered them forward, down the wide corridor and up a marble staircase. 'I was just about to have a cup of Brother Harkin's excellent lapsang souchong.'

Along the corridor, Alice could sense the celibates who occupied this building: old men drowsing, praying or reading, old men fiddling at computers, or old men perhaps too advanced in years to do any of those things. They had arrived in a room impregnated with cigar smoke. The Rector sat at a broad desk that was furnished with a PC, a Mont Blanc fountain-pen, a notebook and a desk diary.

'First of all, Sisters, let me offer my sympathies on your loss. It's like a death, isn't it? What kind of country are we living in? What will be next? Mercy is distraught, as you know. She feels so personally responsible. Only this morning we said a special Mass here in the oratory for the safe return of Doon Abbey's Caravaggio.'

'Thank you, Father,' Alice said.

Spectral Brother Harkin poured the smoky, aromatic tea and then offered them shortcake. Alice felt her neck hairs tingle each time he came near her.

'Of course, I would lock these thieves away for life,' the Rector was saying. 'How dare they! I mean, apart from putting your community's future at risk, think of the vandalism where the painting is concerned. You may know that I have often come to Doon Abbey on retreat.'

'I have seen you over the years, Father,' Maggie said respectfully.

'And I remember you in choir, Sister Mary Magdalene,' said the Rector with a twinkle in his eye. 'A voice like a nightingale, if I may say so.'

Maggie went bright red.

'Of course,' the Rector went on, 'one of my great pleasures was to spend time in your lovely chapel, alone with Judas Iscariot, as it were.'

Alice must have shown a twitch of surprise because the Rector then leant forward, patted her arm and said, 'Remember, Sister, that without Judas there would have been no Passion. No Crucifixion, no Resurrection. Judas was God the Father's instrument too. Always remember that.'

'Yes, Father,' Alice murmured.

The Rector sipped his tea. 'Now what exactly can I do for you, Sisters? I am a mere theologian, but rest assured, I will do whatever I can.'

Alice cursed herself for making this trip. She was trying to think of a way to excuse herself, when Maggie spoke.

'We're looking for the painting, Father, but we know very little about art. It's well known that Aylesmere houses a wonderful art collection, so we thought we'd come here and see what we could learn from you. We thought that in your wisdom you might be able to outline for us the type of person who might be drawn to a painting of this kind.'

'Hmm.'

Alice could see Maggie's direct plea to the man's vanity playing across his face. Neither had she missed the sideways glances he had shot at both Alice and Maggie's legs when he had thought their attention was otherwise diverted.

'I understand that, with your particular calling to an enclosed apostate, opportunities for viewing art in general and Caravaggio in particular are more limited than most,' he began.

'We considered those sacrifices before we entered, Father,' Maggie said.

'Indeed, Sister, indeed. So since you're searching for a Caravaggio, perhaps I should make some comments on that rascally artist. He was a genius, of course, and only twenty-four authenticated works are known to have survived, excluding the Judas Iscariot fragment, which of course is what it says on the tin – just a fragment.'

The Rector chuckled at his little joke.

'A few years ago in Berlin, for example, I saw *Love Conquers All* for the first time, and I was enraptured. However, my favourite Caravaggio is *Saint John the Baptist in the Wilderness*. It hangs in the University of Kansas. What a contradiction Caravaggio laid down! John the Baptist is at the peak of physical health – whole, radiant – not in the least starved after his time in the wilderness. *But it doesn't matter!* The painting's brilliance, its audacious tonal varieties, its *genius* moves us beyond mere narrative. That's what makes Caravaggio unique!'

'You are passionate about Caravaggio, anyone can see that, Father,' Maggie said. It was warm in the study, and she had half-unzipped her golf jacket.

'But you ask me who might be drawn to such a masterpiece?' the Rector mused, his eyes now drawn to Maggie's upper body. 'Apart from authentic collectors, the Church, national galleries all over the world?' He drummed his fingertips on his temples. 'You see, ladies, there is a certain side to Caravaggio that has always appealed to, shall we say, the undesirable element in society. He killed a man, you know, Caravaggio. Oh yes. God forgive them, but some people are drawn to that.'

People like Jeremy Meadowfield, Alice thought bleakly.

'Other than that . . .' The Rector smacked his knees with the palms of his hands and stood up. 'But come, Sisters! You can't visit here without seeing our modest little collection.' He shot them a naughty-boy look. 'Forgive me, but I don't often get the opportunity to show off.'

As the Rector flung open further doors at the back of his study, Maggie looked at Alice, and Alice could see tears of admiration welling up in the convent librarian's lovely eyes. She was wondering how she could get Maggie out of there without offending the Rector when her mobile phone rang.

'I'll follow you,' she said, and looked at her phone. A mobile number she didn't recognise had come up. 'Hello?'

'Sister Alice?'

'Yes?'

'My name is Ashley Kelly-Lidrov,' a man's voice purred.

Dublin Southside
16 June, 12.30 PM

Maggie's eyes were enlarged as she got into the Berlingo.

'How did he get your number?' she asked as she handed over the lighted cigarette and then flamed one into life for herself.

'I don't know,' Alice replied, and inhaled smoke deeply. 'Just said he had flown in and was staying in the Shelbourne. I mean, who knows this number?'

As she turned the key in the ignition, an ominous, grating sound came from the van's engine.

'Oh no!' Alice cried. 'Not now!'

Thirty seconds later, she had raised the bonnet and was standing over the engine, sniffing.

'What is it?' Maggie asked.

'I'm not sure,' Alice replied, trying to remember the details of the mechanics course that had been part of her training. 'This engine smells like death and looks like it should have been put out of its misery years ago.'

'The van was meant to have been replaced with a new one, but Sister Mercy Superior said we couldn't afford it,' Maggie said.

Alice got down and lay on the gravel to peer under the chassis.

'Can I help you, Sisters?'

Both Alice and Maggie jumped. 'Oh!'

Neither of them had heard Brother Harkin approaching.

'Ah, Brother,' Alice said, getting up. 'Our van won't start, sorry.'

'Hmm,' Brother Harkin said, 'I see.'

'I think we'd better call a taxi,' Alice said. 'Do you have a number?'

'Yes, of course I do, I have a list of them, but first, would you like me to take a little look at what's the matter with our friend here?' asked Brother Harkin.

He went to the back of the Berlingo, opened the doors and rummaged around until he found an ancient-looking toolkit. Then he came back to the engine, opened the canvas straps of the toolkit, laid it out on the engine and began probing the rubber hoses, wires, pipes and other moveable parts that were accessible.

He knew what he was doing – or at least he appeared to, Alice thought. But then she recalled Ned, in similar circumstances, poking at the innards of her old Renault 4, when really he hadn't had a clue. It was as if men regarded engines as a challenge to their virility – except that virility wasn't what came to mind with Brother Harkin. Alice winked at Maggie; Maggie shrugged, and rolled her eyes.

Only Brother Harkin's legs were now visible, sticking out from under the front of the van. He was a lot taller when you saw him from this angle, Alice thought. Harkin hauled himself up, wheezing, then plunged back under the bonnet. It's time to get that taxi, Alice thought, and reached for her phone.

'Now, Sisters,' said Brother Harkin, straightening up, his hands covered in oil, 'I think that should do it.'

'Have you found the problem, Brother?' Alice asked.

'I think you have a little touch of cylinder head gasket,' said Brother Harkin in his sibilant voice, 'but I've tightened the head best I can, and now, before you start her, I'm going to fill the radiator with water.'

Alice smiled brightly. 'You're a genius!' she said. 'How did you learn to do that?'

Brother Harkin had resumed his bent posture. 'I worked in a garage

74

before I discovered my true vocation,' he said. 'Now, Sisters, please be patient and I'll go and fetch the water. Unfortunately, I'm not as quick as I used to be.'

Dublin
16 June, 1.15 PM

The white van weaved through light traffic, its engine running smoothly.

'What's Kelly-Lidrov doing in Dublin?' Alice asked. 'It has to be because of the Caravaggio.'

'He's an art dealer,' Maggie said.

'But how does a New York art dealer know this mobile number?' Alice asked again, as they nipped through an amber light. 'I don't like it.'

'Your friend the detective sergeant knows this number, since you rang him on this phone,' Maggie said.

'Sebastian doesn't give out numbers,' Alice said. 'Who else knows it?'

Maggie frowned. 'Sister Mercy Superior and Sister Columba,' she said unhappily.

'Exactly,' Alice said.

Alice took a chance and used the bus lane. In a strange way, it was good to be back.

'I wonder what's really going on?' Maggie said, and lit another cigarette. Twin smoke trails gushed from her nose. 'I mean, is it possible that we've been set up?'

'The possibility crossed my mind,' Alice said.

'I don't like Sister Columba, and I'm terrified of Sister Mercy Superior, but that doesn't make them criminals,' Maggie said. 'But why would Kelly-Lidrov fly over here in the first place?'

'Maybe he's looking for something.'

'You mean, like we're looking for something?'

'Yes, that's exactly what I mean,' Alice said thoughtfully, as she pulled up at a red light. The van's exhaust began to rattle ominously.

'Go back over the telephone conversation again,' Maggie said, as she blew a series of perfect smoke rings.

'I asked how I could help him, and he gave a sort of chilling laugh. He said, "Sister Alice, I know we've never met, but I'm in Dublin because I have heard about the missing painting: our Caravaggio."'

'He said "our Caravaggio"?'

'Yes, I'm pretty sure he did,' Alice said, first away as the lights went green. 'In fact I'm certain.'

'Which suggests he believes it's his,' Maggie said. 'What then?'

'He told me he was staying in the Shelbourne, and suggested we meet. He gave me his room number and then hung up.'

Through Stillorgan and Donnybrook, Alice felt a tightening in her stomach, just like in the old days before a big surveillance job paid off, except now there had been no surveillance and there was no sign of a pay-off. A double-decker bus pulled level with the van, its powerful engine throbbing.

'The Rector is a nice man,' Maggie said. 'Very considerate.'

'Not like his sister, you mean,' Alice said. 'He liked you, though, Maggie. He couldn't take his eyes off you.'

'Oh, stop that!' Maggie said. 'I would quite like to have seen his art collection, though. Pity we had to leave.'

'I bet you were flirting your pretty head off with him when you were waiting for me.' Alice burst out laughing.

'At least he's on our side,' Maggie said, blushing.

'Oh, Maggie,' Alice said fondly. 'Why did you ever become a nun?'

Dublin
June 16, 12.45 PM

Sebastian Hayes propped one foot on his desk as he took the call from Morgan Kinsey. A mug of coffee cooled beside him. He had received several phone-calls in the last half-hour about the latest Dublin murder, committed in Parnell Street the night before. It had been a grisly one, possibly racist, because the victim was African. It had involved a deliberate skin-flaying prior to the severing of a carotid artery.

Automatically, he reached forward and took a long drink as the Geordie on the line began to speak.

'Jeremy Meadowfield. Sounds nice, dunnit? A deliberate posh choice, I'd say. Real name Jason Trammel, small-time conman and general felon.'

Sebastian had ceased to be surprised at anything in his job. The trick, he suspected, was to avoid becoming a cynic.

'Meadowfield/Trammel has quite a list of convictions,' the Scotland Yard detective continued. 'I'm zapping everything over to you as we speak, but in a nutshell the late Mr Meadowfield first did time for minor drugs offences back in the mid-nineties. Then, when he got out, he moved into the art world.'

'The art world?'

'Precisely. His next conviction is for attempted theft of a minor painting from a gallery in Soho. Interestingly, he pleaded that he was stealing to order. The chap he tried to pin it on lived in New York, so we couldn't get to him. His name was Ashley Kelly-Lidrov,' the Englishman said. 'Now, the interesting thing about Mr Kelly-Lidrov is that he is an associate of a very nasty piece of work known as Metro, who I think you'll be familiar with.'

'Metro,' Sebastian said. 'Well, I'll be damned.'

Ten minutes later, Sebastian poured himself another cup of coffee and scrolled down the links on his screen. Kazakhstan-born Mafia boss Matthias Taboroski, aka Metro, now a part-time resident of south Kildare, was widely suspected of being a major force in Ireland's drugs underworld. And, Sebastian now realised, Metro's Irish base was a mere three miles from Doon Abbey. Now there was another link: an associate of Metro's was the nephew of the woman who had bequeathed the Caravaggio to Doon Abbey.

Sebastian did a quick Internet search. The most recent image of Ashley Kelly-Lidrov had been taken only two months before. He appeared unshaven, with dark discs of perspiration leaking into his shirt as he lumbered along from the New York courthouse where his bankruptcy hearing had taken place. The photographer had thrust the camera up into his jowly, defeated-looking face.

'I wonder where you are now, my friend?' Sebastian asked aloud.

Dublin
16 June, 3.30 PM

As they hurried up Kildare Street from Buswell's Hotel, where they'd had the soup-and-half-panini option, the two nuns passed a group of protestors outside Dáil Éireann, brandishing placards. Lines of uniformed gardaí, arms linked, held the protesters back. At that moment, passing the turmoil, Alice suddenly felt certain that her decision to become a nun had been the right one.

'What if . . .?' Maggie said suddenly, and stopped dead outside the Department of Agriculture. 'What if . . .?'

Alice was growing used to the teasing consequences of Maggie's tortured thought processes.

'Maggie?'

'I mean, Mr Kelly-Lidrov said to you, "I'm in Dublin because I have heard about the missing painting: our Caravaggio." Right?'

Alice nodded.

'Yes, I'm sure that's what he said.'

'He used the word "missing". Not "stolen", but "missing".'

'Ye-sss.'

'So maybe that's what the painting is now, Alice. Missing. Maybe whoever is behind all this is like us and has no idea where the Caravaggio is.'

'And,' Alice said slowly, 'if that's right, then what you're saying suggests that this bloke staying here in the Shelbourne is up to his neck in it.'

They turned the corner on to St Stephen's Green.

'Maybe we'll run into someone famous like Bono,' Maggie whispered as they pushed through the revolving doors. She added hastily: 'He sometimes pops up during my sacred music trawls.'

'He pops up everywhere,' Alice said.

Alice led the way through the busy lobby and into the reception area. 'Let's promise each other something,' she said as they stood by the lifts. 'When all this is over, we'll come back here and have a drink together.'

'I actually stumbled across *How to Dismantle an Atomic Bomb* when I was researching Bach,' Maggie said as the lift doors hummed open.

A young couple, hand in hand, joined them, and they ascended in silence. Maggie was reading each advertisement in the lift carefully: massages and hot stones, Chi treatments and Spiritual Integration by a visiting yogi from Delhi. She was like a magpie, Alice thought: nothing escaped her attention. Maggie would have made a brilliant cop.

They stepped out into the corridor. The lighting was muted. Alice flexed the fingers of her right hand and balled them into a tight fist, then extended them again. It was an exercise she had often practised before a difficult confrontation: it made the blood hum between her fingertips and her bicep. The young couple from the lift slipped by, arm in arm, heads together. Alice touched Maggie's elbow, and they hung back until the corridor was empty. Suite Eleven was on the right. Alice pressed the buzzer. She looked at Maggie. The door was not closed. She buzzed again. Back down the corridor, they could hear the lifts opening.

'Stay behind me,' Alice hissed, every muscle coiled as she pushed the door and stared into the dim room.

She stepped in, Maggie glued to her. No daylight. The faint sound of running water. As Maggie's eyes adjusted, she could see a deep-cushioned blood-red suite of furniture around mahogany tables and elegant lamps. The heavy drapes were pulled to. On the left, in the bedroom, where a single bedside light was on, it was clear that someone had already rested, since the king-sized bed was unmade, and a couple of pillows had been thrown on the floor.

The noise of water grew louder. Alice crept towards the bathroom, where the door was slightly ajar. Maggie sensed that the silence within Suite Eleven had suddenly deepened. She hung back as Alice kicked in the bathroom door, and dazzling light spilled out into the bedroom.

'Damn!'

'Alice?'

'Oh, God!' Alice cried.

Maggie stepped gingerly into the bathroom. She gripped the door frame. She had seen corpses in the course of her young life, including deceased Sisters, and so she did not fear the inanimate, vacated body. But the hairy, purplish forearm that hung over the side of the deep bathtub made her gasp. The man's lips were black, the fat-pouched open eyes stared to the left, and the mouth was hideously drawn down in rictus. Whoever had done this had left the corpulent body floating, prevented from sinking by the metallic shower hose that was wound around the throat and jaw-line, presumably after the murder had been executed.

Alice dipped her fingers into the bathwater. It was lukewarm. She guessed that Ashley Kelly-Lidrov, if indeed this was him, had died an hour or so ago – just after he had spoken to her, in fact.

'Don't touch anything,' she ordered.

There were no obvious injuries, no blows or flesh-cuts, no bruising, and no blood. It was possibly a case of sudden death, Alice thought. Or, she reconsidered, death by terror. She regarded the man's face for a moment, almost pitying him. There was a choking sound. Alice whirled.

'I'm sorry, it's just . . .'

Maggie was shaking violently.

'It's okay, Maggie. I'm the one who's sorry, I shouldn't have let you see this,' Alice said, holding her trembling companion by the shoulders. 'It's okay. You need a stiff drink.'

'Shouldn't we . . .? Is there time for . . .?'

'No Hail Marys,' Alice said firmly.

She was two steps across the bedroom, looking for the mini-bar, when she heard the sound. A throat being cleared, soft but unmistake-able. Alice placed a finger over her lips and pressed Maggie down until the nun was kneeling on the floor by the bed.

From where she knelt, Maggie could see Alice gliding into the sitting room in a way that reminded her of Panda, the convent tomcat, when he was stalking the mice he never caught.

Alice was on autopilot as she closed in on the source of the sound. It had come from the large bay window. Travelling on the balls of her feet, with her right hand she swept back the drapes, simultaneously releasing her left hand, which shot forward into the bright space, and found warm flesh.

'Agghhh!'

A man fell forward, clutching his throat. He had ginger hair. Alice kicked hard and felt him grunt with pain. She kicked again and he fell back.

'Stop!'

Alice stared. She took a step backwards and fell into an armchair. Ned O'Loughlin, ashen-faced and spitting blood and gristle, was trying to get up.

'I don't believe this,' he gasped.

'Oh God, Ned, what have you done?' Alice cried.

Chapter Four

Doonlish
16 June, 3.55 PM

Davy Rainbow's one-bedroom cottage was a mess. Books everywhere, stacks of yellowing *Doonlish Enquirers*, empty bottles. The windows were so filthy with the webs of ancient spiders that the cottage seemed to exist in perpetual dusk. Davy had never even got around to cleaning out the stove from the previous winter.

He sat at the kitchen table with the bottle of poitín. He poured from it and knocked it straight back. Was he an alcoholic, he wondered? His old man had always said that the Rainbows were drunkards, but not alcoholics. His old man had talked a lot of bollocks, God be merciful to him. Every time he'd got pissed, he'd screamed at little Davy that he should have become a jockey, but all he had really wanted was tips from the stables he wanted Davy to work for.

A spasm of terror passed through Davy and he got up and put on the kettle.

Sister Diana liked a hot one with sugar and cloves. Perhaps she needed the almost-eighty-percent-proof alcohol to soften her feeling of guilt. Davy pulled a stool over to the dresser and hopped up on the wide shelf, where he was at eye level with cups suspended from brass hooks.

Carefully he removed two cups, then reached in and pressed the stained timber. With a soft click, a panel slid back. Why was he doing this when he'd checked it twenty minutes before? He was in a bad way with nerves: he couldn't remember what had happened five minutes ago, let alone twenty. Davy stretched in his arm as far as it would go and felt the reassuringly sharp outline. Thanks be to God, he said, as he slid the panel back and climbed down. Thanks be to God.

The kettle was steaming. She was due at four. They were sticklers for punctuality, the nuns; terrible liars, but they were always on time. As if in answer to his thought, there was the roar of an engine from outside. Davy jumped with fright and went to the door. Sister Diana, a formidable woman, capable of pulling a calf from a birthing mother, was reversing the tractor up to Davy's back door. He was terrified of her, but then, when he was this bad with nerves, he was terrified of everyone. If only he could break out of the vicious circle he was trapped in.

Sister Diana jumped down. The size of her, Davy thought. She'd left the tractor engine running, since the battery had been dodgy for as long as Davy had known it. Normally on these occasions she would pause to rinse her outsize wellies under the tap fixed to the wall by the back door, but today Davy noticed she was wearing tight-fitting black boots with big square heels that clacked as she walked inside on Davy's linoleum. Davy followed her. Sister Diana was already sitting at his kitchen table, spooning sugar into a glass and forcefully skewering a lemon with cloves, as if this was the Crusades and the lemon was an unfortunate infidel.

'What's wrong with you, Davy?' she asked. 'You're making me nervous just looking at you.'

'I'm exhausted,' Davy said, as he slumped opposite her.

'Oh?' Sister Diana's eyes went round. 'How so?'

'Terrified we're going to get caught,' Davy said. 'Terrified of the shame of being a criminal. Terrified we're going to go to jail for a very long time because of what we've done.'

'A convent is a bit like a jail,' Sister Diana observed, and poured boiling water on top of her poitín. 'In fact, I doubt there's any difference – except that the accommodation in a jail is guaranteed.'

She laughed quietly at her little joke.

'It may be funny for you,' Davy said shakily, 'but just imagine how I'll get on in Mountjoy Jail. Have you any idea what goes on in these places? I'll be quite frank with you, Di: I wish we'd never done this.'

'Oh, God,' Sister Diana said, 'where's the perky little crook who said we were both going to make a fortune? The criminal mastermind?'

'I was drunk,' Davy said. 'I was out of my mind to have ever suggested it.'

'And what about those nasty bookmakers who are making your life miserable, Davy, eh? Who's going to pay them off?'

'I don't know!' Davy cried. 'And I don't care!'

'If you don't pay them, they'll break your ankles with a lump hammer,' Sister Diana said, 'and if they do, don't come running to me.' She sighed deeply. 'Where have you hidden it, by the way?'

'In a safe place,' Davy replied.

'I asked you *where?*'

'I told you: in a safe place.'

'You're not going to try anything smart, are you, Davy?' she asked thinly.

'Certainly not,' Davy gulped.

'So tell me where you've hidden it, *Davy!*'

Davy leaped up with fright, but he remained mute.

'We need to get the cash and move on,' said Sister Diana. 'But now you're drunk, and when you're drunk you never make sense.' She smiled, as if to say: some things never change. 'So we may as well drink. What shall we drink to?'

'I'd like to drink to honesty,' Davy blurted.

'A strange toast for a crook,' Diana shrugged. 'But as you wish.'

Davy knocked back the hot poitín. Blood roared in his ears. With a rush, he said: 'I only proposed that toast because I have a question, and I want an honest answer to it.'

The nun realised that he was even drunker than she had thought.

'What?' she asked sternly.

'I want to know once and for all where Sister Winifred is,' Davy said, 'and I don't want any bullshit.'

Sister Diana drew in her breath sharply. On previous occasions when Davy had asked this question, she had managed to brush him off, but now, despite the drink, he seemed different, more intense.

'I told you before, she's gone away, Davy. That's all I know. Maybe she's in another convent, maybe she's emigrated, I don't know.' Sister Diana pulled up the sleeve of her robe, revealing a hairy, muscular fore-arm, and looked at her wristwatch. 'Goodness, is that the time,' she exclaimed, rising from the table.

Davy jumped up and blocked her path, or at least, because of the relative difference in their sizes, stood in her way.

'I want to know, Di,' he panted, close to tears. 'I want to know where she is.'

'I've got to get back for prayers, Davy,' the big woman said, pushing him to one side. 'Stop being silly.'

'Very well!' he cried. 'I'm finished with you. Find someone else to do your dirty work.'

Slowly she turned. 'Are you threatening me, Davy?'

'I'm out,' he said. 'It's over. We should never have done this in the first place.'

'And what are you going to do with the, ah, merchandise?' Sister Diana asked. 'You can hardly put it back.'

'I'm going to destroy it!' Davy said defiantly. 'So that you won't get a penny!'

Sister Diana couldn't believe her ears. All the trouble they had gone to, all the planning, covering their tracks. Then she smiled: he was having her on. Or else it was the drink talking.

'I may be drunk,' said Davy, as if he could read her mind, 'but I'm deadly serious. I thought I could trust you, but you refuse to trust me with the one piece of information in the world that I want. So why should I help you any more?'

Sister Diana took a step towards Davy. 'I'm going to put everything I've heard to one side and attribute it to your inebriation,' she said. 'But when I come back tomorrow, you'd better be sober.'

'You needn't come back,' Davy said, and stood aside. 'Goodbye.'

'Goodbye?'

'Goodbye!' Davy shouted. 'And good riddance!'

As the back door slammed behind her, Sister Diana's heart was beating so loudly she was sure he could hear it, even above the noise of the tractor engine. She had never seen him like this before. Was that what love was really like, she wondered? She had read about it, of course, but this seemed like the real thing. Did love make even little crooks like Davy Rainbow see the light? Put everything at stake? She could do nothing, since Sister Mercy Superior had sworn them all to secrecy on the matter that so obsessed Davy, and had made it clear that any breach would mean expulsion from Doon Abbey. For the first time in a long while, Sister Diana felt utterly bereft.

Davy poured out a large glass and saw that the bottle was empty. Now that he had said it, he felt very proud. He had stood up for what he believed in, and to hell with the consequences. He raised his glass. This was going to be his last indulgence. A shadow fell across him. Sister Diana was standing in the doorway.

'What I'm going to tell you, you never heard from me, Davy Rainbow,' she said blackly.

Dublin
16 June, 4 PM

Ned O'Loughlin fell back again against the heavy curtain and sank down. He saw Alice sprawled in an armchair, gaping at him; he saw a woman with great legs flattened in terror against the open door to the bathroom; and beyond her, he saw the bald head of the corpse in the bath, held up at a grotesque angle by the silver shower hose.

'You're meant to be in Rome,' he gasped.

'Get up, Ned,' Alice said.

'I haven't had the pleasure,' he gasped, as he flapped like a fish in Maggie's direction.

'Alice!' Maggie shrieked.

'Ned O'Loughlin,' he said weakly, holding out his hand.

Maggie might have been scared out of her wits, but she had been properly brought up. She looked at Alice, and Alice nodded.

'Maggie. Pleased to meet you,' she said, and shook the plump hand, then sprang back to her place at the wall.

'So when did you join the force?' Ned asked, now up on his knees. His left eye, where the edge of Alice's hand had met it, was closing rapidly.

'No, no, no, I'm not a detective. I'm a nun – a confirmed nun,' Maggie said.

'She's a nun,' Alice confirmed.

'She's not your partner then.'

'She *is* my partner,' Alice said. 'Actually I'm her partner, if you know what I mean. I'm a novice, and she's professed.'

'Ah, that explains it,' Ned said.

Alice looked at him narrowly. Ned had always had the ability to obscure the issues at hand and to sweet-talk her around to his point of view. She got up and dusted herself off.

'Sorry about that, Ned, but I need to know exactly what's going on here. For starters, who's the floater?'

Ned wiped his mouth and shook his head.

'His name is Ashley Kelly-Lidrov. He's a New York art dealer and he's the nephew of the woman who bequeathed the Caravaggio to your convent,' he said.

'How do you know that?' Maggie asked.

'Because I read his name in the bequest, and because, unfortunately, I do this kind of thing for a living. When his office in New York told me that he'd gone away suddenly for a few days, I guessed he could be in Ireland. I have contacts in Aer Lingus. Bingo. He flew in yesterday.'

'I take it you've searched here,' Alice said.

'It's clean. No Caravaggio.'

'And did you . . .? And was it you who . . .?' Maggie asked, scarcely daring to look at what lay behind her.

'It's okay, Maggie,' Alice said. 'Ned is many things, but he's not a murderer. He doesn't have it in him.'

Ned looked darkly at Alice, unsure whether or not he had been insulted.

'When I got out of the lift,' he said, 'I saw a man leaving this suite. When he saw me, he turned around and walked the other way.'

'Describe him,' Alice said.

'Big, broad shoulders, long blond hair that was maybe dyed.'

'You think he did it?' Maggie asked. 'That he's the murderer?'

'That's if the man behind you was murdered – in the accepted sense,' Ned said. 'I can see no marks on the body or skull. And my bet is that the shower pipe was fitted later.'

'You make it sound like he was getting measured for a shirt,' Alice said.

'God love him, he's still warm,' Maggie said, stepping in and placing her hand on the dead man's forehead. It seemed like the Christian thing to do, to offer comfort, even though Mr Ashley Kelly-Lidrov was profoundly dead. If it really was suicide, then Mr Ashley Kelly-Lidrov, God rest him, was in trouble with God – big trouble. He was going to need all the help he could get, and he was going to need it from wherever he could get it.

'Any sign of a mobile phone?' asked Alice, searching for one.

'I've already had a look,' Ned said. 'Why?'

'Oh, no reason,' Alice said, and froze as a knock was heard on the outer door.

She gestured urgently to Ned. Ned cleared his throat.

'Yes?' he called.

'Room service,' said a female voice.

Dublin
16 June, 4.30 PM

Alice pulled the door behind her until she heard the click.

'We walk straight out of here,' she hissed. 'We look neither left nor right; we speak to no one. Is that clear?'

'Understood,' Ned said.

Maggie, clinging to Alice's arm, gulped and nodded.

'Our van is parked in Ely Place,' Alice told Ned.

'On a meter, I hope,' Ned said.

The corridor was suddenly impossibly long. Maggie felt a strong need to go to confession, even though, she reasoned, she had not actually committed a sin. She noticed how Alice had used a tissue to cover her hand when she had closed the door to the suite. The sight of Alice in action back there was something Maggie would never forget. The once-sweet novice had been transformed into a lethal weapon, but a strangely graceful one. Maggie felt a weird and probably sinful surge of excitement in the pit of her stomach as the gilded lift doors hummed open. Now the advertisements for massages and jewellery, in their golden frames, seemed suddenly menacing. She looked across at Alice. Doon Abbey's one and only novice was standing, eyes narrowed and focused ahead, primed for action.

89

In the inner lobby, Maggie felt as if a spotlight was on them. Her head sang unknown tunes as the three of them walked together through the main lobby and out to St Stephen's Green. The fresh air was heavenly. They crossed the street to where the statue of Wolfe Tone stood.

Alice felt the phone in her pocket vibrate. Bizarrely, it made her think of sex. She hadn't thought about sex for twelve hours. There wasn't time to pray. She cursed Ned and his proximity to her. Also bizarre was the fact that she was still attracted to an overweight, pasty-faced, red-haired man with one eye closed up; but now, with Ned so close to her, reconnecting her to the past – a past that she had been sure was lost – she wanted to reach out and touch him. They had once been a good fit. Yin and yang. But then she had shot Bruno Scanlon Junior, and Alice found that Ned wasn't there for her – not in the way she needed. She wished she'd closed up both his eyes when she was at it. No time to pray, she reflected, and yet there was time to think of sex. The baseness of the human spirit never failed to amaze her.

The vibrations came to an end. Moments later, the phone vibrated again, this time with a message. All her instincts told her that the person responsible for what they had just come upon in the hotel was still nearby. She scanned the immediate vicinity. People heading down Merrion Row for drinks in O'Donoghue's or Doheny & Nesbitt's; parents with kids in tow heading in to the Green to feed the ducks. It was Dublin on a summer's afternoon: people going about their business and enjoying themselves, oblivious of the reality of murder and death within touching distance – a world that they were only too happy to ignore, a world they paid their taxes to avoid. She turned to Ned. Ned's mouth was open. He had stepped back and was staring.

'Jaysus!' he said.

A man was standing twenty metres away, across the street, at the entrance to the Shelbourne. He was very tall and broad, his blond hair was shoulder-length and his tanned face was pitted like a pineapple. As

Alice took in every detail, the man's eyes swivelled and landed on her. What she would remember later was how pale those eyes were, in contrast to his tanned, rutted face; how pale and cold.

'It's him!' Ned said, although Alice had known that from the moment the man had appeared.

He was now walking briskly down Merrion Row, across the street from them, a small suitcase in his left hand. Alice followed at a distance, with Ned and Maggie a step behind her. The man stopped at the corner of Upper Merrion Street and looked up Ely Place. He didn't seem to like what he saw. For a moment, it appeared that he was about to head down Upper Merrion Street past Government Buildings, but again he hesitated. Did he sense that he was being followed? Or was it merely the hesitation of someone new to the city, someone without bearings? Or the caution of a hired assassin who had just completed his assignment? As he turned once more and surveyed the street on both sides behind him, Alice, Maggie and Ned shrank into the entrance to O'Donoghue's. She and Ned used to drink in here on Friday evenings. Alice could feel her blood quicken. She was sure the blond-haired man had seen her. Suddenly, he stuck out his hand, darted nimbly through the traffic to a taxi that had come along Upper Merrion Street and was stopped at the lights, and jumped in. The lights changed.

'Got him!' Alice cried. 'Come on!'

She ran flat out down the street and rounded the corner into Ely Place. The taxi crawled past in heavy traffic. Ned would have to fit in the back of the van, as best he could, for Alice was damned if she was going to lose sight of the taxi. So much detective work was about instinct. You got a hunch; you followed it. It was always a mistake not to follow your instinct. As she reached the van, Alice had the key at the ready. She stopped. A sign on the window of the Berlingo read: IT IS AN OFFENCE TO DRIVE THIS VEHICLE. She looked down. An ugly yellow clamp covered almost the entire small wheel, where it rested on thick, double yellow lines.

'Fuck!' Alice shouted, kicking the wheel of the van with all her force. 'Oh, God forgive you!' Maggie gasped as Ned burst out laughing.

Dublin
16 June, 4.45 PM

Bruno Scanlon Senior didn't get emotionally involved. He kept a professional distance at all times. This job was no different. He had fenced paintings before and knew what a Dutch master was, because he himself was an Irish master – albeit a master criminal. But in order to fence a painting, you had to be in possession of it. Even Bruno knew this. And he didn't have the Caravaggio. In fact, the way he felt, he was hardly in possession of his senses. The painting he was meant to have taken delivery of had never shown up. And now Bruno was on his way to account for himself to the representative of a man whose name, in criminal circles, was synonymous with sudden death.

Bruno's mouth was dry as he drove along Parnell Street, past Dominick Street and the boxing club at the corner: an old haunt. Looking at himself now, well over twenty stone and bursting from even his most recently bought Louis Copeland suit, it was hard to think that he had once been the inner-city welterweight champion. Jab, jab, jab-jab. Magic footwork. Great right hook. Speed and precision had been the hallmarks of Bruno Scanlon's boxing career. Now he couldn't even get out of his own effin' way.

He turned left onto Parnell Square, up past the maternity hospital. If he had anybody in the car with him, he'd always say: 'I was born in that hospital forty-two years ago. An only child. My mother got it right the first time.'

But there was nobody in the car today with Bruno and, even if there had been, he was in no mood for jokes. He had seen a photograph in the papers of the stolen picture he had been meant to take delivery of, and something about it had drawn Bruno in. It was the look on Judas

Iscariot's face. Someone outside the frame had brought Judas terrible news, and it showed. Judas connected Bruno to the moment when he'd learned of his son's death – to the pain that had started in his groin and worked its way up into his heart. He had felt as Judas felt. He had looked as Judas looked: broken-hearted and alone.

But that's where the comparison ended. Judas was a loser: he'd gone out and topped himself, poor bastard. Bruno had other plans. Lose four stone, straighten out his affairs. Get even. The fact that Bruno Junior had been killed by a mot with a gun was what had nearly driven him insane. And then she'd disappeared. But fate had a strange way of working. Bruno opened the window and spat. Not any longer was she out of sight, thanks to Mr Effin' Caravaggio.

There was an unmerciful traffic jam at the top of Parnell Square, where a garda was redirecting traffic up the hill towards Dorset Street. There'd been a murder in the Café Monto the previous evening, Bruno had heard; maybe the two things were connected. The murder was already the talk of the criminal underworld: no one in Dublin that Bruno knew of used the methods that had been employed. It would not be an exaggeration to say that even the worst of Dublin's low-life were shocked.

The cars inched along. Bruno lowered his window.

'What's up, sergeant?' he asked.

The young garda smiled. Flattery never failed, Bruno thought.

'It's Bloomsday, Bruno,' the garda said. 'Some crowd are doing readings outside the Irish Writers' Centre. Is that where you're going?'

Bruno saw the mocking look in the youngster's eyes.

'What's effin' Bloomsday?' Bruno growled.

Before the garda could reply, Bruno floored the pedal. Up their own arses, these youngsters nowadays. Why could they not do what they were paid to do, and keep the traffic moving? He drove down Parnell Street and then began to cut diagonally north, towards Summerhill.

Cassidy's was a place where he often did business. Now he was going there to explain himself. He had to relax. After all, what more could he tell them than the truth? The bare, unadorned truth. For the first time that morning, Bruno allowed himself a slow smile. The truth? He'd spent so long avoiding it, now that it had turned up on his side, Bruno almost didn't recognise it.

Dublin Docklands
16 June, 5 PM

'I can't believe you two used this place last night,' Ned said. 'I mean, anyone could have been here.'

Maggie's eyes were glued to the floor. Alice leaned forward so that she was looking directly into Ned's face.

'Anyone?' she enquired sweetly. 'Such as?'

They were in the big sitting room of his flat, looking out on the sparkling Liffey. Ned appeared flustered.

'It's my flat,' he said defensively. 'I don't need your permission to entertain.'

'Even Bruno Scanlon Senior?' Alice said, and her eyes were glinting.

'What are you talking about?' Ned demanded, colour now lighting up his already bruised cheeks. 'You think that, just because you took off to a convent, I now consort with criminals?'

'His mobile number is over there, beside the fridge,' Alice said quietly. 'I know it's him because I rang the number last night, and he answered.'

Ned stared at her for a long moment. She looked as if she might be going to explode. He sat down heavily.

'Okay, okay, it *is* his number,' he said, 'but I haven't forgotten the reason you went into the convent, or that Bruno is by any standard one of the most vicious hoodlums in Dublin. So I wanted to keep tabs on him, okay? I know people at the telephone company. You can track someone by their mobile signal. I wanted to know if he ever went near Doon Abbey. Got it now?'

Alice was staring at Ned.

'Why?' she asked.

Ned's lip quivered.

'Because I cared!' he cried. 'Because I was terrified any harm would come to you.'

Silence gripped the little group. Ned's words had made Alice dizzy. He had begged her not to enter the convent, to stay with him and try to work things out. She had spurned him, and yet he still cared about her.

'Anyone for food?' Maggie asked brightly.

Ned and Alice shook their heads.

Maggie suddenly liked Ned a lot. Not only had he paid the fine to have the van unclamped but it was obvious that Alice still meant a lot to him. Why else would he be so upset?

'You think Bruno is involved with the theft?' Alice asked.

'I'm not sure,' Ned said. 'Bruno is a low-life thug. If he *is* involved, it's purely as a mule, as a means to transport the goods. No way did he plan something this big.'

'I agree,' Alice said, 'but you have other suspicions, am I right?'

'I spoke this morning to the two old sisters who live in the gate lodge to your convent,' Ned said. 'On the night of the theft, they saw a very large female loading something into the back of a car. They wouldn't tell me who the woman was, but they hinted strongly that she was associated with someone called Davy Rainbow.'

'Davy Rainbow!' Maggie exclaimed. 'He's the one who made our Caravaggio famous.'

'And he comes to morning Mass every day too,' Alice said tersely.

'Exactly: no one knows the painting better,' Ned said. 'Which is why I wanted to interview him. But he wasn't there.'

'You think Davy stole the Caravaggio?' Maggie asked.

'He drinks too much, right?' Ned was pacing. 'Maybe he has a gambling habit. Drink and the gee-gees often go together.'

'They say his father wanted him to be a jockey,' Maggie said.

'But who's his lady friend?' Alice asked as a telephone rang.

Alice pulled her mobile from her pocket; Ned fumbled with his before realising it was the landline.

'Sive,' he said, answering it, and turning his back. A pause. 'No, I have company.' A pause, more awkward and longer than the first one. 'Can I call you back right away on the mobile? Sive? Sive?'

As he hurried out of the room, Maggie looked at Alice.

'Who's Sive?'

'I don't know.'

'Are you going to ask him?'

'It's none of my business, Maggie.'

'I think it is.'

'I'm absolutely, definitely not going to ask him, and that's final,' Alice said.

The two nuns sat in silence – an environment with which they were both very familiar. Outside, the screech of bus brakes drifted upwards. Alice took out her phone again. The text that had come in earlier was from Sebastian and it said: 'WHERE R U?????' She tried to focus on the missing Caravaggio, but instead she saw herself at the firing range, standing legs apart, the Glock held double-handed, as she fired an entire clip into the head of a target called S-I-V-E.

'Sorry about that,' Ned said as he came back in. 'Now we were talking about Davy . . .'

'Who's Sive?' Alice asked.

'Sorry?' said Ned.

'Who. Is. Sive?'

'Oh, Sive! Sive! Sive is a friend.'

'Your girlfriend?' Maggie asked, her eyes huge in her pretty face.

Ned's face twitched. The two women sat, not daring to breathe. Then his shoulders slumped.

'Actually, if you must know, Sive is my fiancée,' he said.

Alice sprang to her feet. For a moment it looked as if she was going to close up Ned's other eye, but then, with a loud shriek, hands to her face, she ran from the room.

'Alice . . .' Ned stammered.

The door to the bathroom slammed.

'What did she expect me to do?' Ned asked Maggie. 'I begged her to stay with me. I'm a man, damn it!'

Maggie jumped with fright. Now she hated Ned – hated him for doing this to Alice. He could have waited: four months wasn't much of a gap, even if he was a man. Maggie wanted to give him a piece of her mind, but it wasn't really her business to do so. A jumble of thoughts was swirling around Maggie's head when the hall-door buzzer rang.

Dublin Docklands
16 June, 5.30 PM

Alice sat on the loo with the seat down, smoking. To hell with Ned and his rules. Four months after she'd left and he was . . . engaged? It defied belief! Such a clear rejection of her. Now the gift voucher for Brown Thomas that had puzzled her was quite clear. Alice felt nauseous. No wonder he didn't want her staying in the apartment! No sooner had she moved out than he had moved someone else in. If not, why were there two toothbrushes by the sink? And a strand of blonde hair in the shower? *And* he'd given her a diamond ring, by the sound of things.

Alice took a deep drag that threatened the side casings of the cigarette. She had gone into the convent by choice, granted, and it was none of her business whom Ned saw or was seeing, or what the state of his relationship was with bloody Sive whoever she was. This was all Ned's business. But . . . engaged? A voice in Alice's head told her that Ned was within his rights, but the pain in her heart was another matter entirely.

When the buzzer rang, she knew immediately who it was. The decisive ring was not the ring of a stranger. Alice did not want to meet Sive, and yet she was damned if she was going to stay hiding in the toilet, behaving like a lovelorn teenager. Shit! She blew smoke all over Ned's silver-backed matching hairbrushes, over his toothbrush, his silk kimono and his towels. Then she lobbed the ciggie into the loo, where, she hoped, it would bob around and annoy Ned for days. She splashed her face at the sink and looked at herself in the mirror.

'Get a hold of yourself, girl,' she said to the image looking back at her.

In the hall she pasted a smile on her face, then froze. She heard a man's voice and it wasn't Ned's.

'Well, I'm sorry, she's not here, detective,' Ned was saying.

'Why don't you do us both a favour and cop on to yourself, Ned,' said Sebastian Hayes. 'You think I can't get a warrant to search this fancy gaff?'

'You don't need one, Sebastian,' said Alice, stepping forward.

Dublin Docklands
16 June, 5.45 PM

Sebastian was standing there, his face grim. Detective Billy Heaslip was beside him, gut impending. No one spoke for a moment. Alice knew what Sebastian was thinking: he was going back in his mind, as she was, over the countless nights when they had been partners, swinging by Christ Church, siren blaring (although they were off duty), down to Burdock's in Werburgh Street for a fish supper with lots of salt and vinegar, eaten straight from the brown bag, ending with a sumptuous fingerlick. And now here they were, on opposite sides. You never knew what life was going to throw at you.

'I am going to telephone my solicitor,' Ned began. 'This is outrageous . . .'

'What is outrageous,' Sebastian said, 'is the body count in the last twenty-four hours. Now, I need you to come down to the station with me, Alice.'

'I'm not going anywhere,' Alice said tightly. 'You can ask me whatever you want, right here.'

'I can arrest you on suspicion of murder,' said Sebastian with a touch of impatience.

'Go ahead, arrest away,' Alice said.

'Don't push me, Alice,' Sebastian said tightly.

'Maybe we can all go to the station together,' Maggie said.

Sebastian turned his eyes on Maggie, as if he'd only just seen her.

'If I want you to speak, I'll ask you a question, Sister Mary Magdalene,' he said icily. He turned back to Alice. 'This is no joke, Alice. Let's go.'

'I must protest . . .' Ned began.

'There's a man lying in a bath in the Shelbourne Hotel but he ain't getting clean,' Heaslip butted in. 'Mr Ashley Kelly-Lidrov. Came in on a flight from New York yesterday. Didn't get to see the sights.'

'God rest his soul,' Maggie murmured.

'I was the first one there,' Ned blurted.

'Interesting,' said Heaslip, who had taken out a notebook. 'Go on, Ned.'

'Ned! Don't incriminate yourself!' Alice said.

'I don't care!' Ned said. 'I want to protect you!'

'Let him talk,' Sebastian said.

'I got there before the ladies. They had nothing to do with his death. I can vouch for that. I'll swear it in any court,' Ned said.

'And I don't suppose you have any idea who might want Mr Ashley Kelly-Lidrov out of the way, do you, Alice?' asked Sebastian.

'I have no idea, Sebastian,' Alice replied. 'I never met Mr Kelly-Lidrov. I've no idea what he was doing in Dublin. I have no idea who he is.'

'Never spoke to him?' Sebastian inquired. 'Ever?'

'Never,' Alice said, through gritted teeth.

'That's interesting, Alice, because . . .' Billy Heaslip fished out a mobile phone from his pocket and held it up. 'We found this under the bath in Suite Eleven.'

Alice sank as Heaslip dialled a number and her mobile rang.

'You were the last person he spoke to, Alice,' said Sebastian, almost apologetically.

'He got our number from Sister Mercy Superior,' Alice said. 'I've just checked, and she told me.'

'Too late, Alice,' Sebastian said, and stepped forward. 'Alice Dunwoody, I hereby . . .'

'Wait!'

Maggie was in the centre of the room with both her hands in the air. 'Lads, I would urge you to be cautious, if only for the sake of your own careers,' she said. 'Times are tough enough, as we all know.'

'Are you . . . threatening us?' Billy Heaslip snarled.

'You want to have every tabloid in the English-speaking world on your doorstep?' Maggie asked. '"Two Irish nuns held on suspicion of murdering art dealer in hotel bath"?'

Sebastian shook his head in frustration. 'You left the scene of a crime,' he said irritably. 'You found a dead man in a bath and you failed to report it.'

'And what about Cyril O'Meara?' Billy Heaslip asked, with a defiant thrust of his jaw towards Maggie. 'The farmer in the bog?'

'Give us a break, Billy,' Alice sighed. 'Cyril was a tragic accident, which I reported. And even if you don't believe me, you know there were no witnesses.'

'Which leaves the dead conman in Liffey Valley,' Sebastian said, without much conviction.

'Conman?' Alice said. 'What conman?'

'Look, lads, instead of fighting, maybe we should all be trying to work this out together,' said Maggie brightly.

Dublin Northside
16 June, 6 PM

Despite the traffic diversion, Bruno reached Cassidy's on time. He knew just two things about the man he was about to meet: one, that his name was Brice. No other name, title, age-bracket or description. And two, that in the whispering hinterland of the Dublin underworld that Bruno had been crawling through since he was out of nappies, Brice's name had a chilling resonance. More entrepreneurial criminals than Bruno – men, and sometimes women, who had branch offices and networks in Amsterdam and Tel Aviv, Málaga and Berlin – spoke in respectful tones about a man without pity, of someone who was an extension of Metro's vengeance. Stories abounded of entire families being found disembowelled, old-age pensioners hideously executed, just because they were related to someone whom Metro disliked. It was effin' terrifying, so it was.

Bruno sat in a corner booth in Cassidy's sipping a Diet Coke. Sweat was cascading down his face and had already made his size-twenty shirt as damp as a dishcloth. He didn't know from what direction the man who had summoned him would arrive, and so he kept a watchful eye on both doors. Bruno wasn't carrying, but he wished he was. He thought of Al Pacino and the scene in *The Godfather* where Al retrieves the gun from a toilet cistern. Bruno wished this was a movie.

'D'you like Irish art, Bruno?'

Bruno swivelled, spilling half his drink over his suit-front. A large man with his face in shadow and with shoulder-length hair had somehow slipped into the booth when Bruno's eyes were on the door.

'If the work you do on commission is remotely as sloppy as your standard surveillance operation, then I'm not surprised we have a problem,' said Brice.

101

The accent was harsh, hard to place.

'I want to tell you the truth . . .' Bruno began.

'About art?' The man moved slightly, and Bruno could see that his face resembled a hunk of flayed shish-kebab – a meal to which Bruno, normally, was partial. 'Oh, yes, the gentleman I work for had quite an art list drawn up, but unfortunately, because of you, Bruno, we haven't even got to the first item yet.'

'Well, that's what I wanted to tell you about . . .' Bruno stammered.

'I'll speak, you listen,' Brice said, leaning forward. 'The gentleman I work for has already invested over $500,000 in the Caravaggio project. Earlier today I met with Mr Kelly-Lidrov. Hotel in a nice part of town. His man was to get the painting to you, yes?'

'Yes, that's correct,' said Bruno, and tried to swallow.

'I'm afraid I shouted at Mr Kelly-Lidrov,' Brice said. 'I think I frightened him. I frighten people when I shout. Have you heard me shout?'

'No, never.'

'You don't want to hear me shout, Bruno, believe me.'

Bruno was hyperventilating. Brice had placed one hand on his wrist and was holding it in place on the table. Bruno couldn't move his arm. He was going to die, right here in Cassidy's. It brought him back to his father, and getting a hiding from him when he was four years old. Oh, Jesus, he thought, just give me one last chance.

'Please . . .' he said.

Brice placed his mouth close to Bruno's right ear.

'Where is the Caravaggio?'

For a split-second Bruno thought he was being asked about an Italian eatery he frequented in Temple Bar. Then, in one agonising moment, Brice caught everything between Bruno's legs in his free hand and squeezed as if he were strangling an old turkey in a sack.

'Where is the Caravaggio?'

Bruno gasped with pain. 'I . . . I don't . . .'

His eyes swam. He couldn't even cry out, he was so terrified. He thought he was going to puke.

Abruptly the pressure disappeared but the pain remained. Bruno's wrist was released. He closed his eyes, chest heaving, waiting for the bullet, or the cold, sharp caress of the steel blade. Yet when he looked up, Brice was standing there, waiting patiently.

'I want to know where the Caravaggio is,' Brice said.

'I understand.'

'I'll wait till tomorrow for your answer. Then I'll be bored. I don't like having nothing to do. You'll find out where the Caravaggio is by tomorrow, yes?'

Bruno made a croaking sound. 'No problem.'

Brice walked out from the lounge into the bright, flashing daylight.

Dublin Docklands
16 June, 6.30 PM

'Here are the CCTV images from the hotel the night Meadowfield was murdered,' Sebastian Hayes said.

They were grouped around the sixty-inch plasma HD TV in the sitting room of Ned's apartment. Maggie had made ham sandwiches, the kind Alice remembered from her childhood: thickly cut slices of white loaf, almost obliterated with butter and loaded with succulent, mustard-smeared honey-baked ham. Alice sipped a mug of tea as Sebastian pressed the remote. She noticed that every time Maggie came into the room, or left it, Sebastian's eyes were glued to her.

It was good to have Ned there, Alice reflected. He had given them the results of his own investigation regarding the convent security on the night of the theft. The double-lock failsafe system, which meant that the CCTV and alarm reverted to the standby generator, had failed to activate when the power failed, since the lines between the fuel tank and the generator engine were air-locked. When you got over the fact that Ned often came across as a feckless eejit who couldn't last even twelve weeks without a woman, he was actually quite impressive, Alice thought.

'This is where she first appears,' Sebastian Hayes said, and froze the frame.

The image entering the hotel in Liffey Valley was of a large woman carrying a suitcase and wearing a hat that obscured her face. Alice leaned forward and watched the footage as the woman checked in at reception. She then walked on high heels to the lift. The next sequence, from behind, saw her in a corridor upstairs, removing her hat and running her hand down through her long dark hair. She tossed her head and, for a brief second, her silhouette was visible.

'Go back to that,' Alice said.

Sebastian scrolled back, then forward, and froze the frame. It was fuzzy, but the clean outline of a jaw and nose was visible.

'She's really quite attractive,' Ned observed, and then instantly regretted his observation as Alice strafed him with a look.

'Is she one of the regular hookers?' she asked Sebastian and Billy.

'We've run the image past every pimp in Dublin,' Sebastian replied conscientiously. 'No one has a clue who she is.'

'She's from out of town,' Billy said. 'Has to be. Flew in here on a fixed contract, flew out again.'

'I'm not so sure,' Alice said.

Everyone turned to her.

'What I mean is, we're pretty sure that Mr Kelly-Lidrov met his end at the hands of that big blond thug in the Shelbourne. That was a contract, I'd bet my non-existent pension on it.'

'So?' Sebastian said.

'Why would someone go to the trouble of hiring two assassins?'

'You mean, you think this woman in Liffey Valley is acting independently of the art thieves?' Ned asked.

'I think it's a possibility,' Alice said.

Sebastian ran the tape. The image of Meadowfield's boyish, almost beguiling face filled the screen. They watched him checking in and then walking past the camera position. The final image of him was in the corridor, entering a room.

'That's the last shot we have of him alive. Two days later he came out of the hotel in a B-O-X,' Heaslip said.

'Poor Mr Meadowfield,' Maggie said.

'Except he's not Mr Meadowfield,' Sebastian said, and explained the information that Interpol had come up with.

'Sister Winifred even gave him his instruction in the faith, before she went away,' Maggie said.

'I'm afraid he wasn't even a Protestant,' Sebastian said with a hint of apology.

'What?' Maggie cried.

'Jason Trammel – his real name – was Catholic. His mother was a Ryan from Tipperary. Emigrated to London in the seventies. The instruction was a sham. Like everything else in his life.'

'How could he do that to poor Sister Winifred?' Maggie cried.

'Hang on a minute.'

They all turned to Ned.

'I've got a list of all the nuns in Doon Abbey,' he said. 'Who's this Sister Winifred? She's not on my list.'

Alice and Maggie exchanged tight glances.

'Over to you, Maggie,' said Alice quietly.

Maggie, suddenly the centre of everyone's attention, tugged her skirt towards her knees.

'Sister Winifred was our Sister Superior up to five months ago,' Maggie said quietly. 'One morning she was no longer in Doon Abbey.'

'You mean she, like, disappeared?' Billy Heaslip said. 'Like she was assumed into heaven or something?'

'We were told nothing,' said Maggie, ignoring him. 'Then two days ago, when I asked, Sister Mercy Superior told us that Sister Winifred had gone away and would never return.'

'And she's not dead,' Alice said. 'Sebastian has checked.'

'Sebastian?' exclaimed Billy Heaslip.

Sebastian sighed. 'Yesterday Alice asked me to look up the deaths register for the past six months, both in Ireland and the UK. There's no Florence Sparrow on the list . . . That's Sister Winifred's pre-convent name.'

'Christ Almighty, you put five nuns and a painting in a bloody convent and you end up with Crime Central,' Heaslip said.

'Okay,' said Sebastian. 'Maggie, what can you tell us about Sister Winifred?'

'Kind, pious,' Maggie began. 'Very beautiful, in a serene way. She floated along. Animals loved her . . .'

'Did she ever leave the convent?' Sebastian asked.

'Occasionally, to go on retreat.'

'So, other than Meadowfield, she had no contacts with the outside world?'

'Just with Davy,' Maggie said.

No one spoke.

'Have I said something wrong?' Maggie asked, wide-eyed.

'You mean Davy Rainbow?' Alice asked gently.

The cops were staring.

'Yes. He's a troubled soul. He used to come up to the abbey, sometimes every day, and he and Sister Winifred would go for long walks.'

'I, ah, have another piece of information I should have given you, Detective Sergeant, but overlooked,' Ned said, and recounted what the Misses Hogan had told him that morning about Davy Rainbow.

'I think it's about time we had a word with Mr Davy Rainbow,' said Sebastian tightly. 'Where does he live?'

'Doonlish,' Alice said succinctly. 'We never should have left it in the first place.'

'Which brings me to the final point of this meeting,' Sebastian said, and straightened himself. 'Alice and Sister Mary Magdalene, as of this moment, you are off this case. Is that clear? You are both to return immediately to your convent.'

'Who says?' asked Maggie.

'I say,' Sebastian said. 'And that's final.'

Alice wrinkled her nose. 'I don't think that you are in any position to give us orders,' she said stiffly. 'If we wish to pursue our stolen painting, then that is our decision.'

'I thought you might say that,' said Sebastian, 'which is why I took the precaution of telephoning your boss, Sister Mercy Superior. It is she who has issued the order which I have just transmitted.'

'What did you say to her, Sebastian?' Alice asked.

'No comment,' said Sebastian smugly. 'But she did say that if you two aren't back for midday prayers tomorrow, I'm to arrest you for stealing one white Berlingo van.'

'Oh, God!' Maggie cried. 'We'd better go home, Alice.'

Alice was about to reply when Sebastian's phone rang. He had his hand over his mouth as he spoke into it. He looked up at Alice in despair.

'It's for you,' he said.

Dublin Northside
16 June, 7.30 PM

Taxi driver Miley Doyle was in his sixties, wore a thick blue cardigan, despite the weather, and still spoke with traces of a Wexford accent. The two ranks he most preferred were Adam and Eve's church on Merchant's Quay and Heuston Station, according to the lady in the Taxi Registration Authority to whom Alice had given the licence-plate number. She would have called earlier, but she had mislaid Alice's number, which is why she had called Sebastian.

'He was no bleedin' oil painting, miss, I'll tell you that,' Miley said as he drove up O'Connell Street, then swung around Parnell Square and headed for Summerhill. 'Very bad complexion, greasy hair. I wasn't surprised he wanted to go to Cassidy's, and that's being honest. The apple doesn't fall far from the tree, you know what I mean?'

'What a nice old man,' Maggie said as Alice paid off the taxi and the two nuns made their way into Cassidy's.

'Just stay close to me in here,' Alice said. 'No dancing.'

Cassidy's lounge was unusually full; Alice normally associated it with dark corners where low-lifes and scumbags conducted business, but this evening it was thronged with young and not-so-young women wearing low-cut Edwardian blouses that in many cases threatened to spill their contents over the tables. As Alice and Maggie wedged in nearer the bar, the noise became deafening.

'Why are they all calling each other Molly?' Maggie shouted.

Alice ordered two glasses of port. The place was crawling with the criminal fraternity of the north inner city, as well Bloomsday revellers. Alice had already spotted two of Bruno Scanlon's closest associates hovering. One of them, Ska Higgins, was a hitman. Alice slid on to a bench and ducked her head into a menu. Out of the corner of her eye, beyond a gaggle of Molly Blooms, she'd just seen Natalie Scanlon, Bruno's wife, sitting at a table. Natalie was reputed to own a string of apartments in Torremolinos. Alice quickly and surreptitiously scanned the faces. Neither Bruno nor the big blond man from the Shelbourne was in the pub.

'Let's get out of here,' she said to Maggie, just as she felt her arm pulled.

She had brought her elbow up to deliver a defensive chop when she smelt a very dusky perfume, undercut with hints of tuberose.

'We'd heard you'd found your true callin', Detective Sergeant Dunwoody,' whispered Natalie Scanlon.

Alice brought down her elbow. A round-faced, once-pretty woman with hair dyed raven black and wearing enormous earrings was sitting beside her.

'I was just leaving, Mrs Scanlon. Now if you wouldn't mind . . .'

'Please!'

Alice felt her arm gripped again. She drew in her breath. Two large glassy tears were rolling down Natalie Scanlon's cheeks. Maggie was transfixed.

'My Bruno's gone missin', she whispered.

'How do you mean, missing?' Alice asked.

'I don't know what's goin' on.'

'What do you want me to do?'

'Will you help me?' Natalie asked. 'Please. Deep down he's a good man.'

Maggie looked pleadingly at Alice.

'Mrs Scanlon, I'm the last person on earth you should ask to help find your husband.'

'He looks up to you, honest he does,' said Natalie Scanlon. 'He respects you.'

'We could just try a teeny bit,' Maggie suggested.

'Maggie!'

'Sorry.'

'He lights candles for you,' Natalie said.

'You expect me to believe that?' Alice cried. 'Come on, drink up, Maggie.'

'On the heads of my children, I swear it,' Natalie said.

'On the heads of her children,' Maggie said.

'Please, Detective Dunwoody,' Natalie said imploringly. 'I'm beggin' you. Will you help me? I don't want Bruno to die.'

Alice took a deep breath. 'Okay, I'll find him,' she said, and lowered her glass. 'Yes, I will, yes.'

Doonlish
17 June, 7.00 AM

Bruno Scanlon had left Dublin after six. He was hungry. He hated getting up early and having his routine disturbed. This morning he had persuaded himself to do so on the basis that he would have breakfast on the road. Double eggs, over easy, black and white puddings, rashers, hash browns and a steak done Southern chicken style. Except that there was no place open and no service stations existed on the effin' motorway. By the time he reached Doonlish, Bruno would have eaten roadkill.

Bruno had gone to ground – for his own sake and for his family's. If Natalie didn't know where he was, then she couldn't tell Brice, even if he tortured her. The thought of Natalie being tortured made Bruno want to cry. Eff it! Why had he ever taken on this job?

The Wicklow hills came into view on the left, their light and colours ever-changing. Bruno's last conversation with Jeremy Meadowfield had been by public telephone on the morning of the robbery. Meadowfield had been so scared, he was unable to speak.

'Have you got the effin' painting?' Bruno had roared into the phone. 'The Cara-effin-vaggio?'

But the line went dead. That was the last Bruno had seen or heard of the pansy bastard. Until two days later, of course, on the Six One News.

Something had happened, Bruno thought despairingly, something really bad. Meadowfield, the fool, had been intercepted. Or, worse, amateur that he was, he had subcontracted the job. Oh, Jesus, Bruno thought as he got chest pains. That's what happened! Meadowfield had laid off the risk and given the job to someone else. Which meant that the painting on which Bruno's life now depended was in the hands of someone else entirely – a person, or persons, who wouldn't care if Bruno Scanlon lived or died.

As he came into Doonlish, he made a decision to buy a defibrillator and keep it in the car at all times. The village was still asleep. Abbey Motors had the shutters down. Beside it, Beppe's Bistro was also closed, but two trays of milk had already been delivered to the door. Bruno pulled over, nicked a two-litre plastic carton and gulped it down as he sped away. He belched. Now he had heartburn.

He drew level with an elderly man, eased down the car window to ask directions, but then decided not to. The sat-nav instructions to Meadowfield's house were clear. As the window hummed closed, Bruno heard a church bell in the distance. It might do him no harm to get down on his knees and say a few prayers, he reflected. He remembered the rosary from his childhood, the whole family kneeling around a picture of the Sacred Heart, and his father, a man with a list of criminal convictions that ran to six pages, giving out the Sorrowful Mysteries. The Queen of Heaven had made Bruno feel loved; he had prayed hard as a child, his head lowered, his little chin tucked into his chest. *Mother of Mercy, To Thee do we cry, poor banished children of Eve.* Bruno sighed deeply. It would be good to pray again.

But not just yet, he decided, as he drove through the village and out the road about half a mile until he came to a lane. Moss crunched beneath the car's wheels as Bruno funnelled in between neatly trimmed hedges. Bruno hated the countryside, the abundance of nature. He parked outside the thatched cottage and got out. The silence was oppressive. A cow looked over a hedge. Jesus! Bruno hadn't been as near to meat this size since he was last in Shanahan's Steak House. He wished he'd brought his iPod, on which he'd installed a track with background city sounds, especially for a job like this.

'Eff off!' he growled at the cow as he pushed in the little white gate.

He took out a large screwdriver from his jacket pocket and approached the hall door. The screwdriver's blade bore the stain of dried blood. It slid gently into place between the door and the frame. Twenty seconds later, he was inside, sitting at a cheap desk, rummaging through the drawers.

Bruno frowned. He was sure he'd locked the hall door behind him. A shadow had fallen over the desk. Bruno tried to turn around.

Chapter Five

Doonlish
17 June, 8 AM

Davy Rainbow had awoken at four with a splitting headache, drunk six pints of water, swallowed four aspirin, gone back to bed and slept for three and a half hours. Now he was showered, dressed and, for the first time in years, utterly resolved. Although Sister Diana had tried to trade the information he wanted, Davy had resisted.

'We need to turn it into cash, Davy,' she had said and clenched her big fist, 'and we need to do it fast, before anyone else finds it.'

'First, I'm going to check out what you've just told me,' Davy said, 'and then, Di, you know what? If you've told me the truth, you can keep whatever it makes for yourself.'

Sister Diana's dense eyebrows plunged together.

'Have you gone mad?' she asked. 'Do you know how much money is involved? Have you forgotten how much you owe the bookies?'

'I don't care,' Davy said. 'It's not the money I want.'

And for the first time ever, Sister Diana had looked at him with genuine respect.

Now he bit his lip nervously as he looked at his wooden dresser. He imagined as he stared at the upper shelf that he could actually see the catch that made the panel slide back. Sister Diana knew where Davy was headed. She knew how long it would take him to drive there and back. What if she came in here and tore the place apart? The secret hiding place was the only leverage Davy had over her.

And then a calm came over Davy – a type of serenity that he recognised with almost pathetic gratitude. He would find *her* and all would be well again. *She* was all that mattered. Making a quick sign of the cross, he gathered his car keys and went out.

Dublin – Doonlish
17 June, 10.30 AM

Green fields stretched to the horizon on either side as Maggie sat in the passenger seat, immersed in her laptop. Alice hit her hand hard against the steering wheel. Snap into what Eckhart Tolle has made a fortune out of! The Obvious. The Present Tense. The Now. The Caravaggio! Where is the Caravaggio, she asked herself? Think outside the box. The answer was there, right in front of her.

Her hands were firm on the steering wheel of the Berlingo, though her eyes kept darting down to the changing images on Maggie's laptop screen.

'Stop flipping.'

'Oh, look!' Maggie shouted, so loud that Alice wondered had she found the painting.

'What?'

'Filthy Manky Little Bitches.'

'What?'

Alice glanced down at the laptop screen and saw a quartet of girls in torn jeans with their tattooed arms around each other.

'Filthy Manky Little Bitches is my niece's rock band,' said Maggie. 'They're very good, or so I'm told.'

Alice swerved around a crossing cat as Maggie mewed with pleasure.

Ned had called Alice thirty minutes before, just when Alice had decided that the best way to find the painting was by perpetual contemplation. What Ned had reported had made all the hairs on Alice's neck bristle.

'And look at this!' Maggie said.

'More members of your family?'

'No – it's a picture of Sister Columba.'

'Go on.'

'Taken on a sports day forty years ago and later published in her school magazine. On the gym team. She's got terrible acne,' Maggie said, and touched her own smooth face for reassurance.

'The gym team?'

Maggie turned the laptop so that Alice could see the tiny novice mistress, her elfin face peeping from a mass of athletic female bodies.

'Bloody hell!' Alice murmured as she drove through the gates of Doon Abbey and pulled up. 'I don't believe it!'

Doonlish
17 June, 10.40 AM

The Limousin heifers were in the far end of the field, away from the convent gate lodge, munching with archetypal calm. A steady stream of white smoke rose from the gate-lodge chimney into the blue sky. Water dribbled from the over-full barrel, which had taken last night's rain from the roof gutters. Bees buzzed in and out among the nasturtiums. In the window nearest the door, a blue-veined hand moved the curtain aside and quickly dropped it again. Panda, the convent's sleeping black-and-white tomcat, outside on the window ledge, awoke, stirred a paw.

'Panda, love,' Maggie murmured with a surge of guilt.

Alice pressed hard on the ceramic bell. Inside, the chimes could be heard echoing and dying. As Panda stood and arched his back in a prolonged stretch, a noise came from within as the iris of an eye disappeared from the spyhole. Bolts were being drawn across; then the door opened slightly until it was held taut by a hefty chain. Two heads appeared, one on top of the other.

'Thanks be to God. We thought it might be *her* back again,' whispered Eleanor Hogan.

'*Her back again*,' echoed Gabrielle.

'I'm Sister Alice, this is Sister Mary Magdalene,' Alice said, 'from the abbey, ladies.'

The twin sisters gawked.

'We've changed into summer clothes,' Alice explained. 'It's easier when we leave the convent.'

'We have permission,' Maggie added, in a way that immediately suggested they didn't.

Panda made a lunge to get in through the narrow aperture, but met the barrier of four shins. He bounced back out.

'May we come in?' Alice asked.

The door was unlocked and they stepped into the chilly hall. In her heels, Maggie was towering over the elderly twins.

'Would you care for tea, Sisters?' Eleanor asked.

'If you don't mind, not this morning, but next time,' Alice said. 'Now, ladies, can you tell us exactly what you told Mr O'Loughlin?'

'Ned – he's such a nice young man,' Eleanor beamed.

'Yes, he is lovely, isn't he?' Maggie said.

Don't start me, Alice thought.

'Well, Gabrielle was outside, cutting nasturtiums for breakfast,' Eleanor said, 'weren't you, Gabrielle?'

'They keep us both regular,' Gabrielle whispered.

'And the next thing, there was this enormous woman in a huge hat standing beside her!' Eleanor cried. 'Isn't that right, Gabrielle?'

'A very strange lady with a huge big green hat,' Gabrielle confirmed.

'In what way was she strange?' Alice asked.

'The way she stared at you. Isn't that right, Gabrielle?' Eleanor said.

'Oh, God forgive me, the way she stared at me!' Gabrielle cried.

'Can you describe her?' Alice asked gently. 'Gabrielle?'

Gabrielle looked to her sister and took a deep breath. 'She was wearing dark glasses and her nose was very long and fat. But her hands . . .'

'What about her hands?' Alice asked.

'They were huge,' Gabrielle said. 'And she had them clenched in two big fists. I was terrified, Sister, absolutely terrified.'

You had right to be, Alice thought, as the CCTV images from Liffey Valley flashed through her mind.

'But she was beautifully dressed, wasn't she, Gabrielle?' Eleanor piped up.

'Oh yes, beautifully dressed,' Gabrielle said.

'And what did she say to you, Gabrielle?' Alice asked.

'She asked her for directions to poor Mr Meadowfield's cottage, and the minute she told her, she tore away like a bat out of hell,' Eleanor replied.

'*Like a bat out of hell*,' echoed Gabrielle.

'And this was this morning?'

'Just after breakfast. We rang Ned,' Eleanor said.

'Ned O'Loughlin,' Gabrielle said.

Outside the cottage, as they left, Maggie patted Panda on the warming windowsill.

'Thanks for your help, ladies,' Alice said.

'Be careful. Terrible things are happening,' Eleanor said.

'*Terrible things are happening,*' Gabrielle chimed.

Alice reversed the van and turned it round.

'But we have to return to the convent,' Maggie said.

'Not just yet, we don't,' said Alice crisply, and floored the pedal.

County Kildare
17 June, 10.45 AM

He was getting more impatient by the second. Why was there no answer? He tried ringing the other mobile. It too rang out. He didn't leave a message, but cursed in his own Kazakh language. Why wasn't Brice answering? Brice always answered. Metro poured a black coffee into his Real Madrid crested mug. He had been trying to reach Brice since seven that morning,

He had been born in Almaty, in the world's largest land-locked country, Kazakhstan, and now one of his homes was in the land-locked county of Kildare. The other homes were in Amsterdam and London. Through the window of his Irish home he could see his Irish wife, Siobhán, out in the courtyard brushing down her favourite horse, Cracklin' Diamond. Recently Siobhán had had her hair coloured. It was now jet black but it held a hint of crimson, and when the sun caught that crimson streak, it was like a mysterious signal. Was it to say, *I know all about your other women, and one day I'll exact my price*? It was the children that kept them together.

He strolled towards the garage, went in and locked the door. On the landline, he dialled the numbers once more. He hated using the landline. He knew all his calls were monitored by the Drugs Squad in Harcourt Street and by that turd from the *Sunday World* who had his own surveillance team listening in.

No answer. Metro began to sweat. In the half-dozen years during which he had employed Brice, there had never been a hitch. Brice was a machine, albeit a very well paid one. The sides of Metro's mouth turned down beneath his moustache. He considered Brice a low-life, someone beneath his contempt. Brice's methods were crude, but highly effective. He was Metro's instrument, and one didn't socialise with an instrument. Nonetheless, as he listened to the unanswered ringing tone, it slowly dawned on Metro that he had come to depend on this instrument more than he realised.

He walked out from the garage and, as he did so, stopped. His eye had caught a glint from a hill, about a mile away. A sharp, distinct flash. He stepped into shadow, then stepped out again. The glint had ceased.

Could be anything, he thought, and stroked his moustache with his square-tipped fingers. Could it be a farmer, or a child at play, or . . .? Suddenly he felt hemmed in down here, visible, vulnerable like an insect under a microscope. Something was going on. He thumbed a number into his phone. He scanned the hillside. No glint.

'Bring the car,' he spoke harshly, aloud. 'Bring it now.'

Doonlish
June 17, 11.30 ~~PM~~ Am

The Berlingo purred up one country lane and down another, as if happy to be back in its familiar hinterland. Wild honeysuckle burst from the hedgerows as the sweet scent of the land oozed through the open windows.

'You're very quiet,' Alice said to Maggie. 'Are you worried about us not being back for midday prayers?'

'No, it's not that,' Maggie said pensively as she cracked a match alight and put it to the tip of her cigarette. 'It's just that I grew up in little lanes and boreens like these.'

'It's so beautiful here, isn't it?' Alice said. 'You must have wonderful memories.'

'Our house was just a basic little cottage where Daddy had worked the land all his life,' Maggie said. 'I remember him sitting in his shirt-sleeves at the kitchen table, forking out a potato from the big pot, saying, "Balls of flour every one of them – they're from the top field!" And Mam would be as lovely as ever, saying that a man on a galloping horse wouldn't see it as she wiped up gravy stains with the corner of her apron.'

'You sound sad,' Alice said.

'Only because I feel so much at home in Doon Abbey,' Maggie said,

118

exhaling smoke. 'All the sounds and smells of my childhood are here. It would break my heart if the convent had to close.'

'Then we must see to it that it doesn't,' Alice said, and swung right.

The little van nosed up the lane between neat hedges. At the front of the house, red roses leaned out over the borders of the manicured lawn. In a fenced-off field, a cow stood observing Alice and Maggie as they pulled up.

'Look! Mr Meadowfield's car!' Maggie said.

An ancient red Volvo P1800 was parked to one side. Alice got out of the van and went over to the rear of the car, where she bent down and stuck her hand in underneath it.

'Small rupture in the exhaust,' she said with a knowing nod, and then, as Maggie was about to ask why: 'It doesn't matter.'

The front door was a little ajar. Music was playing inside. Alice knocked firmly, and they waited.

'D'you think that woman is here?' Maggie whispered to Alice.

'Hello!' Alice called as they stepped over the Welcome mat. 'Anybody at home?'

'Not a soul,' Maggie said.

'You may be technically correct there,' Alice said, and went down the hall to a door from which wisps of steam were wafting. She hammered with her fist on the wooden panelling.

'Excuse me! Hello?'

The force of her fist was enough to push the door open. A greater volume of steam now rushed out, and when the first wave passed, Alice and Maggie could see another door marked 'Finnish Room'. They took tentative steps, cautiously pulled the door open and were hit by even more intense heat. After a moment, they could make out an arm lying on the wooden bench of the sauna, and then a head turned away from them. As Alice stepped a little closer, she could clearly see a naked back.

'Oh, we do so apologise,' Maggie spluttered.

There was no movement.

Alice stepped into the sauna.

'Oh, no!'

'What?'

'Don't look!'

Alice had thought at first that it was a woman, as the long damp blond hair was pasted down to the shoulders; but the deeply tanned back was broad, and just down from the neck, in the space where the wet hair parted, was written in distinct blood-filled strokes:

M

The victim's head hung at an odd angle to the body. Alice lifted the left eyelid and recognised the pale cabbage-green stare she had previously seen outside the Shelbourne Hotel. She took out her phone and clicked a close-up of the dead man's face, then sent one copy to Ned and another to Sebastian. Maggie was pointing to a screwdriver on the floor. Clods of fresh skin curled on its tip. She hurried over to the hand basin, gripped it tight and was sick.

Dingle, County Kerry
17 June, 1 pm

Up beyond the snake curve of the main street, Davy Rainbow sat in a café relaxing and recovering after his long drive from Kildare. His mind was a jumble of images from the past, of horses and racing and trainers and jockeys. His mother had run off to Paris with a pastry chef – and who could blame her? She was a distant mother to Davy, but still remembered his birthday with a card.

He had become an apprentice jockey, but had grown too heavy and, to counteract this, had begun to starve himself to make the jockey's weight. He started drinking spirits: they gave him the warmest feeling, filled him up with the impression that warm food had entered his belly. He had made a sort of fist of it as a reporter, beginning with court cases;

but he still got tips from the lads in the stables, and soon he was gambling on the horses.

One day, outside the courthouse in Naas, he was asked by one of the defendants' dads to omit details of a particular case in exchange for money. Davy owed a bookie over a hundred quid. He agreed. It happened again, with a different defendant. And then another. Word got around that Davy Rainbow could be bought. Soon none of the mainstream Kildare newspapers would touch him. His gig with the *Doonlish Enquirer*, a weekly freesheet, was scraping the bottom of the barrel.

But the *Enquirer* had published his exclusive on the Caravaggio, and that gave Davy, when he thought about it, a better glow than whiskey.

He had never had much success with women. He had gone out once with a physiotherapist from Athy, but it hadn't worked. Other women? Those he liked best were drinkers, but the liaisons never lasted. Then there were the women he didn't like much, but knew might be good for him, because they tried to get him to quit. He knew they were talking sense but he couldn't act on it. Yet he had to acknowledge that, in the past few months, he was starting to turn a corner: small steps, yet everything big must start with a small step. She had been so helpful, so kind. He missed her terribly.

He drained the coffee, stood up and set his jaw. Now she needed his help, and he was going to find her.

Kildare Village
17 June, 1.15 PM

Metro sat in the back of his maroon Mercedes as Yevgeny, his shavenheaded driver, parked among the throng of clotting, stationary vehicles.

The news about Brice had shocked him. He had wondered at first was it a trap, set up by the pigs in Harcourt Street, but the cop snitch was on a grand a month to deliver clean information, and swore what he said was true. Metro now felt in danger for the first time in twenty years.

He had been driven by Yevgeny on the back lanes, up to the summit of the hill, where the glint of steel, or glass, had come from earlier. It was a remote place with a perfect view in two directions: east, into Metro's stud farm, and west, to Kildare Village, a busy shopping outlet less than a mile away. He'd got out of the car and scoured the ground, looking left and right.

'Lost something, boss?' Yevgeny asked.

'I'm not sure,' Metro said, and suddenly dropped to his knees on the grass margin to the east side of the narrow lane.

A person standing here would have a perfect view, through binoculars, of Metro's house. A person standing . . . here!

'Yes!' he cried.

He was able to stick two fingers of his right hand into the indentations left by that recent observer's sharp heels. On his feet again, he turned to Kildare Village.

'Just maybe,' he had muttered to himself.

He got out of the car and walked towards the shopping complex. He often came here, to unwind in the crowd. To buy gifts for his family. With Yevgeny a pace behind, Metro sniffed the breeze. The window-shoppers. The crowd sauntering by with their designer carrier bags. As he stopped to admire a pair of light tan men's brogues, he became conscious of the clicking sound of a woman's heels on concrete. A striking, very tall woman in dark glasses had emerged from the Louise Kennedy shop and was walking away from him. She was dressed in a long dark-green coat and was wearing a sweeping green hat with a crimson band. As he watched, she strode unerringly to the end of the shops and turned left at the Tommy Hilfiger store.

Suddenly, he got it. He smacked himself on the jaw. So slow! Of course! Of course that was where he had seen her before, even if the CCTV the cop had scanned for him had been distorted. And now she was here, in his territory! The flashing signal she had sent him earlier had been almost primal!

Metro whispered to his driver in Kazakh, pointing to the set of Waterford Crystal goblets in the Louise Kennedy window.

Doonlish
June 17, 1.45 PM

Maggie sat on the settee. Lyric FM was on the radio. Sebastian Hayes had turned it off when he'd first arrived with Billy Heaslip, but Maggie had turned it back on again, keeping the volume low. Maggie needed the soothing music to restore her equilibrium. Stumbling upon these murder scenes was becoming something of a bad habit, especially for a nun.

The Assistant State Pathologist was still in the sauna room with the corpse. Sebastian and Billy Heaslip were talking quietly in a huddle outside the bathroom door. Alice had been summoned, but had then been told to wait. She was standing at the end of the corridor, close to the sitting room.

'What's the news?' Maggie whispered.

Alice turned and tiptoed back towards Maggie.

'They think they've identified him.'

'Who is he?'

'Sebastian will tell us in a minute.'

'That Sebastian is very suspicious of us,' Maggie said, as if she hoped to be contradicted.

'Sshhh!'

A man in white protective gear came out of the sauna room, went down the hallway and out the front door, just as Sebastian appeared. Maggie noticed that Sebastian was wearing odd socks, one light blue and one grey.

'Someone got out of the wrong side of the bed this morning!' she said brightly.

Sebastian looked at her icily. 'Aren't you meant to be someplace else this morning, Sister Mary Magdalene? Like, at morning prayers?' he said, and went over to the kitchen area.

Maggie crinkled her nose at Alice, who put a finger to her mouth. Sebastian removed the grill pan from the cooker, placed it on the draining board of the sink and peered at it carefully. Then he came over to where Alice and Maggie were sitting, his head down as if looking for something on the carpet.

'Have you identified the deceased?' Alice asked.

'Would you mind standing for a minute?' he asked.

As the nuns stood up from the settee, Sebastian grabbed a corner of it and pulled it back.

'God, what is that?' Maggie said.

Sebastian, on his haunches, was staring at two pale stains on the carpet.

'Don't touch anything,' he said, and walked back down to the bathroom.

'What's going on?' Maggie said.

'You probably don't want to know, Maggie,' said Alice with sisterly concern.

'I *do* want to know,' Maggie replied, like a child being excluded from a grown-up secret.

'Be patient,' Alice sighed. 'You've spent the last fourteen years in a convent. What's the sudden rush?'

Kildare Village
17 June, 2 PM

Metro smoked a Cuban cigar as he waited outside L'Officina. Through the window he could see the big woman, sitting at the far end of the restaurant, consulting the menu, still with her dark glasses on. She had removed her hat, and her Titian hair glowed in the restaurant's lighting. Metro was now absolutely certain.

Yevgeny came around the corner with the goblets in a shopping bag. He opened the bag and Metro saw the purchase. He nodded and exchanged the cigar for the bag. The manager met him inside the door.

'Good afternoon, sir.'

He smiled courteously.

'Table for one?'

He nodded.

'This way.'

He sat facing her table. She was still investigating the menu. He placed his Louise Kennedy bag prominently on the empty chair so that it would be the first thing she saw when she looked up.

Doonlish
17 June, 2.15 PM

Sebastian came back into the room, followed by Billy Heaslip and the Assistant State Pathologist, a small-faced individual, dressed in white, with black hair combed forward. Maggie glanced over at Alice, who was standing pensively by the window. Sebastian showed the Assistant State Pathologist the marks on the carpet.

'Think we might be right?' Sebastian asked.

The Assistant State Pathologist nodded, then blew his nose into a tissue. Billy got two white mugs from the cupboard and followed Sebastian to an area which the settee had recently covered in front of the plasma-screen television.

'One there,' Sebastian said, pointing.

Billy placed a mug upside down on a spot on the carpet.

'And one there,' Sebastian said, pointing to the area in front of the compact-disc stand. He turned to Alice and Maggie. 'Would you two mind coming outside?'

Maggie looked to Alice, half-hoping she might object, since she was intrigued by what was going on.

'Of course,' Alice said, and led the way outside, where Sebastian ushered them into the back of the dark blue Ford Mondeo. No eye-contact was made. Billy got into the driver's seat and Sebastian took the seat beside him. There was a tense silence until the two men turned round, somewhat unwillingly.

'We are confused,' Sebastian began.

'Confused?' Alice said.

'Confused about a few things. For example, can it be coincidence that you two stumble upon yet another dead body?'

Sebastian paused, letting his words hang in the air.

'Come on, Sebastian,' said Alice calmly.

Sebastian said nothing. He glanced towards Billy, then back at Alice and Maggie. He began in a measured tone.

'We found long strands of auburn hair in the bath. The victim has dark blond hair, so we're assuming that the auburn hairs came from the murderer. We have identified the dead man as Leonard Brice, an associate of Kazakhstan-born Mafia boss Matthias Taboroski, aka Metro, a part-time resident of south Kildare. The fact that Brice is here means that Metro knows where our painting is, but he cannot seal the deal.'

'*Our* painting,' Maggie said.

'The recovery of that painting is our responsibility,' Billy said firmly.

'You're not making much headway, are you?' Maggie snorted.

'Dead bodies keep turning up,' Billy said, 'and somehow they're all connected.'

Talk about stating the bloody obvious, Maggie thought, looking out of the car's window.

Sebastian Hayes had turned the wipers to intermittent as a light rain began to fall.

'We've also just had a chat with the Misses Hogan,' Sebastian said. 'The killer was at their cottage this morning. In addition, we have established that the killer was outside their cottage on the night the painting was stolen. In both cases, the same woman is described: very large and menacing.'

'Wearing a green hat,' Heaslip added.

'We've got a woman on CCTV in Liffey Valley on the night of the murder,' Sebastian continued. 'Same woman, same hat.'

'In all cases, including this morning, death was achieved by breaking the neck,' Heaslip said.

'What about the dead man in the Shelbourne?' Maggie asked. 'Was his neck broken?'

'No,' Sebastian said, 'but the man who killed the man in the Shelbourne had his neck broken here this morning.'

'God,' Maggie said.

'There's more,' Sebastian said. 'Are you ready for this?'

'Go on,' Alice sighed.

Sebastian's face was taut. 'We think this killer woman is a sexual deviant,' he said.

'Why?' Maggie asked, round-eyed.

'We think something pretty lurid went on in there earlier,' Sebastian said.

'Oh, you mean the dead man in the sauna with the letter "M" carved on his back!' Maggie said with feigned brightness.

Billy looked as if he might be about to snarl, but Sebastian sighed.

'And the marks on the carpet,' he said. 'We think they may be – I'm sorry, Sister – part of a male emission.'

'Emission,' Maggie repeated, for once confined to a single word.

'We're not talking about spreading the gospel in Africa here,' Alice told her quietly.

Billy Heaslip snorted, but then cleared his throat when he saw that Sebastian was not amused.

'Oh, God!' Maggie gasped.

'We think that she first either seduced or raped the deceased, then killed him,' Sebastian said.

'Just like the female spider does,' Maggie whispered.

'We're dealing with one screwed-up, unhinged woman,' Sebastian said. 'She's sick and she's very dangerous. She will not hesitate to kill again.'

'We've sent off a number of items to forensics, including the screwdriver,' Heaslip said. 'Until we get the results back, we're advising you to keep a low profile.'

Sebastian nodded vigorously. 'We think you two are at serious risk. We must now absolutely insist that you stand down from this investigation.'

Kildare Village
17 June, 2.30 PM

Dark Heart decided on a Waldorf salad and a glass of Pinot Grigio. When she lowered the menu, she saw a Louise Kennedy shopping bag on a nearby chair, and then, beyond the bag, a strikingly handsome Asian-looking man with a thick black moustache. She'd wondered what he'd look like in the flesh.

The waitress smiled at him as she passed down to Dark Heart's table. 'Ready to order, madam?'

Dark Heart adored the exotic, the hint of the Orient, the skin texture. Tactile. He stood up. Very tall, she thought, taller than me. Taller than I thought he would be.

'Excuse me, madam.'

She looked up. 'Yes?'

He extended his arm back towards his own table and, smiling, opened his palm.

'Would you mind if my shopping bag joined your shopping bag during luncheon?'

A moment to savour the tension.

'Delighted.'

He gave a slight bow and returned to retrieve his bag. Expensive teeth, she thought. A hint of that Egyptian actor in *Doctor Zhivago*, what was his name? He came back and placed his bag on the seat alongside her. She could already taste something of him, and the anticipation of it made her a little dizzy. His eyes at the end. She blinked behind her shades. Careful.

She drew her green varnished nails through her hair, pushing it back from her face. The man opposite her was studying her benevolently.

'May I be impolite? Do you come here often?' he asked.

'Occasionally,' she replied. 'I just adore the surrounding countryside.'

'Isn't it beautiful?' he said with enthusiasm. 'The valleys and the little hills. Especially the hills.'

'Especially the hills,' she said, and felt her blood running as it always did when the hunt began.

'What brings you to Kildare Village?' she asked politely.

He smiled that perfect-teeth smile. 'Buying presents for my children.'

'How nice!'

She smiled as demurely as she could. His skin. She could almost see the outcome in every detail, his naked body, lifeless. His laugh primed her juices. If only they could have met in different circumstances.

'Anything to drink, sir?' the wine waitress asked.

'Vino Nobile di Montepulciano. Red. But my lunch companion . . .'

'I have already ordered,' Dark Heart said.

'I just love Italy!' he said. 'Her great composers: Verdi, Vivaldi, Puccini, Monteverdi, Boccherini. Caravaggio.'

She smiled carefully. 'You omitted Bellini.'

'*Bellini*, of course!'

'His passionate ecstasy. His elegiac melancholy,' she said, excited now.

He sniffed his glass of red, then lifted it towards her.

'My birthday,' he said.

'Congratulations!' His fingers were square-tipped – often a clue to a body. On the little finger of his left hand, a gold ring sat snugly. 'Your ring,' she ventured. 'Very attractive.'

'A Claddagh ring. They tell me it is from the west of Ireland,' he said as he removed it and handed it to her. 'You see? Two hands enclosing a human heart,' he said as she discreetly inhaled him.

'The heart is so delicate it needs to be held gently, yes?' he smiled.

The mobile in her handbag rang. She took it out, looked at it and recognised the caller. She handed back the ring.

'Would you excuse me for a moment? I'll need to take this outside.'

He watched as she got up and walked from the table. Her size turned him on. In Paris and Madrid over the years, he had known such women and discovered that their size masked a different femininity. But sadly, now, he would never get to know hers.

He looked up, his smile disguising his surprise: he had not heard her return.

'I'm dreadfully sorry, but something has arisen and I must go,' she said, gathering her shopping bag and her green hat, with its crimson band.

'The loss is mine,' he said. 'Another time?'

He stood up and took her hand. It was firm, strong.

'*Love Conquers All*,' he said.

'I beg your pardon?'

'Nothing. Just one of my favourite Caravaggios, this one in Berlin.'

She withdrew her hand. Another time. For sure.

As she walked away, Metro began to sweat again. The feeling of being vulnerable, which he had felt earlier, washed over him in waves. Brice was dead. Dark forces of unknown provenance were closing in. His hand trembled as he took out his phone. Only once in the last five years had he made this call – and that also had been in a dire emergency. The number rang just once.

'It's me,' Metro said. 'There is a problem.'

Doonlish
17 June, 3 PM

Alice felt herself sinking. Her instinct told her that she was within an ace of solving the crime, and over the years she had learned to trust her instinct.

'What does everyone think the significance of the letter "M" is?' she asked, as a gust of wind hit the Mondeo. 'Why would someone carve "M" into the back of a corpse?'

'The first indications are that he wasn't dead when the carving was done,' said Sebastian, and winced. 'Sorry, ladies.'

'But why "M"?' Alice persisted.

'"M" is for murder, that's for sure,' said Billy Heaslip.

Sebastian closed his eyes briefly. '"M" is for Metro,' he said. 'Metro is a very dangerous Eastern European drugs lord who just happens to live near here. Brice worked for Metro. The killer was sending a message to Metro.'

'Or Metro himself killed Brice,' Heaslip suggested. 'Then he signed off.'

Sebastian often wondered how people like Billy Heaslip had ever been let into the gardaí.

'"M" stands for Michelangelo,' Maggie said. 'Caravaggio's full name was Michelangelo Merisi da Caravaggio.'

'So the killer was sending us a message about the Caravaggio,' Sebastian said. 'But what's her message?'

'Or,' Alice said, 'someone else was sending us a message about the killer.'

'So what do you think the "M" stands for?' Heaslip asked.

'"M" also stands for Mercy,' Alice said, 'with a capital "M".'

No one dared speak for several moments. Sebastian cleared his throat.

'I know you were once very good at this, Alice,' he said, 'but, let's face it, things have changed.'

'You can say that again,' Alice said quietly.

'Do you need a lift back to the convent?' he asked, in a voice that contained concern and suspicion in equal parts.

'No, we're fine, thank you,' Alice said. 'Come along, Sister Mary Magdalene. Let's leave this one to the boys.'

The fresh air was a blessed relief.

'What do we do now?' Maggie said as they walked down the lane to where Alice had parked the van. A hearse with a coffin had just pulled up, and Maggie made the sign of the cross. 'I mean, I don't know about you, but I'd be afraid to go back to Doon Abbey. Who could I trust?'

'But where would you go, Maggie?' Alice asked, with genuine concern.

'I don't know,' Maggie said, and her shoulders slumped. 'Oh God, you'd have to ask yourself, is all this really worth it?'

'What do you mean?' Alice asked, as her mobile chimed a message.

'You know, people dying – and all for what? For that painting? D'you want me to be honest? I never liked it. The eye of Judas! God forgive me, but he gave me the creeps.'

Alice was reading the message.

'I know it's worth a fortune – God knows why – and that it has to be returned to the abbey,' Maggie said, 'but when you weigh it all up against what we've seen, I think I'd rather be without central heating for the next twenty winters than have to go through all this again. Alice? Alice?'

Alice was biting her lip. She pocketed her phone.

'What I'm saying is, I think maybe we should both call it a day,' Maggie said. 'I'll go home to my parents – that's if they'll have me.'

Alice was walking briskly towards the Berlingo.

'Alice? Where are you going?'

'Sister, I'm going to find our Caravaggio,' Alice said.

County Kerry
17 June, 5.30 PM

Davy drove fast from Dingle through the little hamlets of Milltown and Ventry, and on out the coast road past Coumeenoole Strand. Around Slea Head, the Great Blasket loomed closer, and out in front the Sleeping Giant was like St Patrick on his back sunning himself. He decided to pull in for a better view.

That was something else she had taught him: to welcome the good feelings, invite them to stay, not to reach for the bottle. He laughed at how easily he was able to dismiss his old habit of reaching for a bottle every time anything went wrong. He gazed happily at purple heather hills, streams, whin bushes, a brown donkey drinking at a tiny waterfall: hidden worlds within hidden worlds, spread out on different limbs of the Kerry valleys. There was the Atlantic Ocean, and way across, America! He'd never been. Maybe one day. Maybe. If all the dots joined and his life smoothed out like the sea towards the far horizon, maybe then he'd go.

An hour later, he sat in the Grand Ballroom of what was once a former hotel but now was the Sybilslea Writers' Retreat. This was where Sister Diana had told him to go. The assembled audience was predominantly female, loud and talkative. Solitary males stroked their beards, groups spoke in hushed tones. He recognised nobody. But Sister Diana had sworn that this is where he should be; and Davy was here because he was in love.

'Reverend Fathers, ladies and gentlemen.'

Davy looked up. The girl at the microphone had a clipboard and began to read from it.

'The three short-listed stories for the annual Sybilslea Short Story Competition are as follows.'

The chatter trickled to an uneasy silence. As the short-listed writers' names were read out and they made their way to the front of the hall, a woman walked up the aisle to an empty seat. Davy blinked. She was wearing a bright-patterned shawl over a black and white spotted dress. Her hair was tied back tightly with a red scarf, knotted behind. Her profile was one of calmness, serenity even. Davy stood up. He could not speak. People were staring at him. He took a step into the aisle and began to gurgle. The woman turned around and looked straight at him.

'Sit down!' people in the audience hissed.

'Oh no!' Davy cried as he fainted.

Chapter Six

Dublin

17 June, 7 PM

The sun was still shining brightly on the high chimneys of the Jesuit Residence at Aylesmere as Alice pulled in by the roadside under a canopy made by beech trees.

'Let's think this through very carefully,' she said. 'The Rector, when he called me, said that he needed to speak to me urgently. He then said – although I didn't ask him – that his sister, Mercy, had handed him our number.'

'Maybe he knows that she did it,' Maggie said. 'He knows she's a sexual deviant from way back. He's seen all these murders and wants to turn her in.'

'Or maybe she's not acting alone,' Alice said.

'You mean . . .?'

'Maybe there are two big women,' Alice said.

Maggie blinked rapidly. 'Sister Diana!' she gasped.

'Exactly.'

'But . . . but Diana looks as if she wouldn't hurt a fly,' Maggie said.

'Believe me, I've put away criminals with the faces of angels,' Alice said.

'Which leaves Sister Winifred,' Maggie said.

'You think she could be the one?' Alice asked.

'Nothing would surprise me any more,' Maggie said. 'Why has she gone missing? Where is she?'

Children were kicking a ball to each other on a square of green. Alice, suddenly, would have given anything to be ten years old again.

'Wait a minute,' Maggie said. 'What did the Rector say about the mobile-phone number?'

'He said that Sister Mercy Superior had given it to him,' Alice said.

'That's not what you just told me,' Maggie said. 'You told me he said that his sister, Mercy, had *handed* him our number.'

'Jesus!' Alice exclaimed. 'She's been up here all the time!'

She drove the Berlingo in the gates and parked by the steps that led to the hall door. 'Just stay close to me, Maggie, okay?' she said, and rang the bell. She hadn't let Maggie see it, but she'd fitted a stack of two-euro coins into her left fist.

The noise of a man grunting with effort came from within, then the heavy door was slowly pulled back and Brother Harkin's pale face appeared.

'God bless you, Sister Alice,' Brother Harkin said, inclining his head, 'and Sister Mary Magdalene. The Rector is expecting you.'

He's really a lot stronger than he looks, Alice thought as she stepped inside and glanced down at the man's hands. They were very wide and large, with prominent knuckles.

'Thank you, Brother,' Alice said, 'and God bless everyone in Aylesmere.'

Brother Harkin shook his head. 'All we can do is pray that He does, Sisters, and that these terrible troubles come to an end soon.'

Bent almost double, he led them along the dim, polished hall, into the anteroom, with its dark red paper, its portraits of long-dead deans and rectors, bishops and cardinals. The huge crucifix soared above the fireplace, reproving and accusing.

'Just a moment, dears. I'll let him know you've arrived.'

Brother Harkin touched the dividing door and allowed it to slide back the merest fraction. Through a few inches of air, he slipped like a wraith.

Alice reflected on the telephone call she'd just had with Ned on her way here.

'I want you to go back to the convent,' Ned had said. 'This is too dangerous.'

'I can handle it, Ned,' she said. She hadn't yet told him about her suspicions concerning Sister Mercy Superior.

'If your own safety is not a concern, then think of the safety of that nice nun you've landed into this mess,' Ned said.

'Maggie volunteered,' Alice said.

'Your problem is that you're completely selfish!' Ned cried.

'Talk to you, Ned.'

You can't slam down an iPhone, but she would've if she could've.

Brother Harkin reappeared, beckoning wordlessly, and they went through. The Rector sat behind his desk of polished mahogany, on his mahogany chair upholstered in episcopal velvet.

'So good of you to come,' he said as he stood up and made his way around the desk. He shook both their hands warmly. 'Thank you so much for responding to my call.'

'Our pleasure,' Alice said, but her eyes were discreetly checking the dark corners of the room.

'Pray be seated, Sisters.'

Alice transferred the stack of coins to her right fist. Where would the attack come from?

'You'll be wondering why I asked you to visit,' the Rector began. 'You see, I understand perfectly the terrible circumstances you find yourselves in. The business about the painting grieves me, frankly – not to mention the awful murders. I cannot sleep for thinking of what is happening out there. And yet, and yet . . .'

Alice and Maggie leaned forward expectantly.

'And yet . . . I have something I want to tell you but cannot tell you.'

Alice shook her head. 'You mean . . .?'

'You are Sisters of the Church. You understand the seal of confession.'

'Of course, Father,' Alice said.

'You see,' he went on, 'I have spent the last twenty-four hours, since we met, on a mini-retreat in your Doon Abbey.'

Alice and Maggie turned to one another.

'When I am there, the members of your little community always take the opportunity to make their confessions to me,' the Rector said. 'And not just the religious community, let me say, but also those living in the immediate vicinity.'

So that's how he was handed our number, Alice thought, relaxing her fist. 'Please go on, Father.'

'You understand that as far as I am concerned, the confidentiality of the confessional is one of the cornerstones of our religion,' the Rector said.

Alice nodded. 'Yes, Father.'

'Well, yesterday evening in the chapel in Doon Abbey, I heard confessions,' the Rector said. 'No one had come into the box for ten minutes, and I was just about to leave, when all light on the other side of the grille was blacked out.'

Maggie's intake of breath made Alice flinch.

'It was a very large person,' the Rector said. 'Enormous, in fact.'

CCTV, Liffey Valley, Alice thought glumly. The Rector closed his eyes. The women waited. The Rector was now transfixed on a possibly non-corporeal item somewhere in midair between the two nuns.

'Yes, go on, Father.'

It reminded Maggie of the time her brother had spilled the day's milking and had come in to try and tell her father.

'A very large . . . female person?' Maggie suggested.

Alice had had a car like this once, when she was a trainee; every time it started, it stopped.

'Ah, Father Rynne, I understand your discretion, and it's entirely admirable,' she said. 'But three people have died in as many days. Doon

Abbey is in turmoil, and at risk of closing down. Your own sister may lose her home if the picture isn't recovered. What are you trying to tell us?'

The Rector seemed about to speak, but then a little snort of pain erupted from his nose.

'I am forbidden by my religion and by my God.'

Alice looked into the Rector's troubled, tear-brimming eyes.

'What does our Blessed Lord prohibit you from doing, Father?' she asked gently.

The Rector shuddered. 'From discussing details divulged in the confessional,' he whispered. 'You see, I want to tell you, but I cannot. I want to do what is right, but I am torn apart, Sisters, torn apart.'

'And yet you asked Sister Mary Magdalene and myself to come here,' Alice persisted.

'We promise we won't breathe a word,' Maggie said.

The Rector nodded, but remained mute.

Alice's mouth was hard-set as she looked at Maggie. 'Did the penitent confess to the murder of Jeremy Meadowfield?' she pressed. 'Father?'

Perhaps the Rector nodded, just minutely; or perhaps he didn't.

'Does the penitent know where the Caravaggio is?' Maggie asked.

The Rector dabbed his eyes. Alice felt a surge of sympathy for this grown man, locked in turmoil between his duty to the God he worked for and the awful secrets that he carried. He clearly wanted to help them, but at the same time felt unable to do so. She had to find a way of extricating the information.

'Okay, how about this?' Alice said, pulling her chair closer to his desk. 'You don't have to say anything. I'll say a name and you just raise your finger if that name is, shall we say, significant to the current investigation. All right?'

The Rector stared at her, then steepled his handsome hands and wiggled the little finger of his right hand in a gesture that reminded Maggie of a tadpole in a jam jar.

'Great. Let's do a trial question. I'm Sister Alice and this is Sister

Mary Magdalene. True or false?' Alice asked.

The women stared. The Rector's head sank. The little finger twitched.

'Ah!' Alice cried. 'Okay!'

'The Pope's a Catholic,' Maggie ventured.

A hesitation, then a twitch. Maggie gave Alice a discreet thumbs-up. Alice got up and went around so that she could bend down to the Rector's ear.

'The penitent was a woman,' she whispered.

Two pairs of female eyes fastened on the waxen mould of priestly hands. This time the little finger fairly jumped.

'Whew!' said Alice, and leant in again. 'The penitent is a member of a religious order,' she said into his ear.

Alice stared. The hands could have belonged to a handsome corpse. But then, the finger jumped.

'Oh, goodness, this is killing me,' Maggie said.

'So, here is another question,' Alice said. 'The penitent you refer to confessed to stealing the Caravaggio and is your own sister, Sister Mercy Superior. True or false?'

The silence was like dawn in a morgue. Both women were transfixed on the Rector's little finger with an intensity they had previously reserved only for the monstrance. The little finger moved minutely.

Maggie turned to Alice and mouthed, 'Wow!'

'We appreciate this, Father,' Alice said, 'and you have our word that we have never been here. Isn't that right, Maggie?'

'We have never ever been here,' Maggie said. 'But . . .'

Alice shot her a look. 'What?'

'I think we should prove the theorem,' Maggie said.

'Prove what theorem?'

'I mean, if we say another name, his finger shouldn't move at all, right?'

'Of course.'

'Well then . . .'

Alice sighed. The Rector remained frozen. 'Okay, Maggie, if you insist.'

Maggie sat upright. 'Father? The big person in your confessional who confessed to stealing the Caravaggio was Sister Diana. True or false?'

The Rector wasn't in a coma, both women knew, but he might as well have been a wax effigy. As Alice and Maggie both got up to stare at his hands, his little finger trembled.

'Agggh!' Maggie cried, and jumped backwards. 'Did you see that?'

Minutes later, having left the Rector in his trance-like state, the two nuns were shown out through the hall door by Brother Harkin.

'It was the two of them all the time,' Maggie gasped as they sat into the van. 'What are we going to do?'

'I don't know about you,' Alice said, 'but I'm going somewhere for a stiff drink.'

Dublin
17 June, 7.30 PM

She looked out the window of the hotel at the grey evening river. The tide was low, and when she had checked in, an hour earlier, there had been the smell of rotten eggs. She didn't mind. Decay was something she was used to – in others, that is. That is, she was used to causing decay in others.

Undressing to her bra and knickers, she unrolled the hotel yoga mat and went through her routine. Flights always made her tense. Today alone she had taken four: London Heathrow to Frankfurt; Frankfurt to Oslo; Oslo to London Stansted; London Stansted to Dublin. Four flights; four separate passports; four different people. A German au-pair on her way home; a Norwegian chemist on a business trip; an English software

141

engineer; a Dutch tourist with diabetes. The elfin-faced, trim, smiling lady who had checked into the Clarence Hotel earlier was an executive in a Belgian chocolate company.

She spread out her thin arms before her, then drew her knees up and out and plunged her head until she was splayed like a crab. Both her lungs expanded to the back of her ribcage. As she exhaled, she sank even closer to the mat.

The chemist was the nearest to the truth, although her degree had been earned not in the University of Oslo but in a laboratory in Moscow. It was there, over five years, working for an arm of the KGB that no one even knew existed, that she had learned the exquisite potions for which there were no antidotes. Some of them were so subtle, all they had to do was touch the skin. Her favourite was nicknamed Lily of the Valley, not just because that flower was itself highly poisonous, but because of the effect the toxin had on the victim: the neck-stalk collapsed and the head drooped, just like a Lily of the Valley. And then an oddly sweet smell was emitted from the dying person's skin as they succumbed to asphyxiation.

It had become her trademark, she knew, but so what? She had always long departed the scene before anyone could work out what had happened.

She went over on her back, placed her hands beneath her slim hips and inverted her legs over her head. Although she was nearly forty, her appearance was that of a woman ten years younger. Her skin shone with health; her naturally dark hair – when she allowed it to be seen – bounced with vitality.

Her services were available to only a handful of major criminals. There had been more, but they had failed to pay her. She was not in the business of debt collection; they had all died with an oddly sweet smell rising from their corpses.

A series of arm-balances, back-bends and core-twists completed the routine. She stood and joined her hands in meditation, lifting the finger-tips and filling herself with so much air she thought she could fly.

This job was relatively straightforward: she was surprised when he had called her. The fifty thousand dollars had hit her bank account in Zurich an hour later. Metro was getting old; his people were getting sloppy. This, she decided, was the final time she would work for him.

She began to unpack the diabetic kit. One of the bottles was, in fact, a bunker bottle: a bottle inside a bottle. She smiled. By three tomorrow afternoon, a Spanish teacher would be on the flight to Málaga. Still in her bra and knickers, she powered up her PC and linked into the hotel's wi-fi. She googled 'missing Caravaggio', and thirty-three thousand entries popped up.

It would be a long evening.

County Kerry
17 June, 8 PM

It wasn't the first time Davy Rainbow had seen stars – and other things, little wriggling flies, creepy-crawlies of all kinds – on opening his eyes. But it was the first time that through the curtain of nasties the loveliest face in the world loomed, like a cherub sneaking a peek at the fires of hell.

'There, there,' the voice of Sister Winifred was gentle in his ear. 'There, there. You'll be all right.'

Except that this beautiful dream woman couldn't be Sister Winifred. She'd got the nun's eyes and nose and mouth all right, and yes, Sister Winifred's rather husky voice, but she was dressed in funny clothes, and had tied a bright red scarf or bandana around her head instead of her usual neat, modest veil. Yet these details were as nothing compared to the one fact that had overwhelmed Davy's consciousness: Sister Winifred was very pregnant.

'We'll go home now, Davy.' Her voice contained a note of urgency. 'Can you stand up?'

Davy struggled to his feet with help from members of the audience.

'He'll be fine,' Sister Winifred was telling the staring crowd. 'It's just a little scratch.'

Sister Winifred took Davy's hand and guided from the hall, into the fresh air. Davy felt slightly better, except for a slight throbbing above his right ear.

'I must have fainted,' he said as he stared at her substantial mound.

'Well, yes, I do understand,' Sister Winifred said as her eyes checked around the car park. 'Are you alone, Davy?'

'Not any more,' said Davy gamely, and tried to smile.

'No, what I meant was . . . never mind. First we need to get a plaster on that little head of yours.'

Davy's little head needed a plaster inside as well as out, he reflected, as they got into her car – a neat Volkswagen with a pull-down hood. Terror and elation gripped him simultaneously. Could it have been *him?* If it was, he had no memory of it, of course, since he was blotto so often, but surely an event as momentous as . . . as *doing it* with his instructor in the faith, in the greenwood between the abbey and Doonlish, something as earth-shattering as impregnating his darling Sister Winifred could not have been wiped from his cerebral cortex by mere alcohol? They were driving by a small harbour. In the black water, hulls twinkled and the bells of boats tinkled.

'I discovered my condition six months ago,' she said quietly. 'I didn't know what to do. So I did what people usually do in such circumstances: I did nothing.'

She made it seem as if she had woken up under a toadstool. They passed through a village, and Davy caught sight of several pubs, but their inviting facades were behind in seconds, and they were once more travelling through the depths of the countryside.

'But somehow Sister Mercy got wind of it,' Sister Winifred said.

Davy had always had an innate distrust of Sister Mercy Superior – an attitude that he knew was mutual. 'That one doesn't miss much,' he sighed.

'I don't know how she found out. She must have noticed that I looked different – green around the gills or something – because it didn't show then. Not under the habit.'

She had been beginning to hope that it never would show, under the habit – which covered a multitude – and that she might get away with it. There were many proverbs and prayers to aid her in her self-deception, and she drew on them all in the small hours of the morning, when sleep eluded her and the bell for lauds called just as she reached the nadir of sickness: lauds gave morning sickness a whole new dimension.

'Anyway, she confronted me. She had always wanted to be head nun, and this was her chance. I was forced to confess everything. I agreed to keep my mouth shut and come down here to Kerry.'

'Sister Winifred, what can I say . . .' Davy began.

'Please,' she said, and briefly her hand touched his knee. 'Call me Winnie.'

They had been climbing up from the coast for ten minutes. It was overcast and Davy could see very little of the surroundings. Winnie swung the car up a little lane and switched off the engine. As they got out, Davy could hear a stream running over rocks.

'Where are we?'

'This cottage is owned by the convent,' Winnie said as she opened the door with a latch key.

'The convent owns a holiday cottage?'

'When I got here, the place was semi-derelict,' Winnie said. 'I had to live with builders for three months.'

'Who paid for that?' Davy asked.

'Sister Mercy, of course. Who else?'

'And where did she get the money?'

'I often asked myself the same question,' Winnie said. 'It's a mystery.'

Maybe not quite the mystery you think, my lovely, Davy thought as parts of his mind connected like an over-marinated jigsaw. The cottage was neat and comfortable – a far cry from Davy's own cottage in County

Kildare. Stone tiles, whitewashed walls. A dresser against one of the walls, painted bright blue. A black crane at the fireplace, where the remains of a turf fire were glowing. Davy's head started throbbing again. He felt a patch of wet on his shoulder. Blood. His good shirt, the cream checked one he wore with his beige pants and his only decent tweed jacket, was destroyed.

Winnie put down her car keys.

'So here I am,' she said with a brave smile. 'The question is, what are you doing here, Davy?'

'I wanted . . . I had to know . . . I couldn't go on without knowing . . .' Davy sputtered.

Winnie looked at the gash in his head and the irises in her lovely brown eyes spread out like the wings of angels. 'My word, that cut does need looking after. Sit down here, Davy.'

Davy obeyed. As he sat on the chair, unaccountable feelings of love, lust and guilt swarmed in his head: maybe it really had been him, but was that fair? Not to be able to retain even the tiniest memory of what must surely have been a climax of ambrosial sweetness?

Winnie dabbed Davy's wound with a tissue, peeled open a Band Aid and stuck it carefully on the side of his head. Her hand lingered over his ear for longer than was necessary, and a renewed surge of something long forgotten gushed up from deep inside Davy. It was love, he could tell by the feel of her hand, even though he'd never felt her hand. Not that he knew of.

'Now, a cup of tea is what we both need,' she said, going to plug in the electric kettle.

'I thought you were dead,' Davy said.

'Maybe that was what she wanted you to think.'

'Are you happy down here, Winnie?'

'Yes, I think so. I've taken up painting: I always had a knack for that. One of the galleries in Dingle takes them; I've already sold one, and the season's hardly started.'

'I never knew you had that gift too.'

'How could you? In the convent we were discouraged from painting out of doors. I spent hours in the chapel, copying the technique from our little Caravaggio. How lucky to have private access to such a master, day after day.'

Davy frowned. Her tone lacked even the merest hint of regret as to the painting's recent disappearance.

'Well, thank God then that you weren't there for all the fuss about it,' he said. 'You'd have been very upset, Winnie. Love.'

Sister Winifred looked at him sharply. 'What did you say?'

Oh, blast it! Davy thought. I've gone too far now. 'I meant . . . I didn't mean . . . I said, love . . .'

'Fuss? Fuss about what?' she asked.

'Oh, about the painting,' Davy said with a surge of relief. 'I'm sure you've heard?'

'No.'

Davy blinked. You'd think Dingle was on the far side of the moon.

'I don't have a television,' Winnie said. 'And I forget to listen to the radio.'

'You mean you don't know the Caravaggio was stolen?' Davy said, and went on to describe the events of the past week in Doonlish. 'There's been blue murder,' he concluded.

'That was an absolutely amazing painting,' Winnie said in astonishment. 'I'm not surprised there's been murder about it.'

'I mean literally,' Davy said. 'Three murders so far, maybe four, I'm losing count.'

'What?'

'Poor Cyril O'Meara may not have been murdered, but then they found Mr Meadowfield with his neck broken in a hotel room in Liffey Valley. Remember Jeremy Meadowfield? After that . . .'

But Davy didn't get a chance to continue with his gruesome catalogue. Winnie was bent over, clutching her tummy, and screaming. Davy thought he might faint again, but he hopped over to her with all the agility of the prize jockey he should have been.

'Take it easy, sweetheart, take it easy now.'

He never knew she could scream so loudly. Jesus, they'd hear her in New York, never mind Dingle. He started to stroke her black hair, the way he'd stroke the mane of a horse who'd taken a fit of panic. It usually had a calming effect. On horses. But Sister Winifred was not a horse, and she went right on screaming.

Dublin
17 June, 8.30 PM

'I think it's called Caravaggio's, believe it or not.'

The Italian bistro was on the banks of the Liffey, not far from Temple Bar. Alice had ordered mushroom risotto; Maggie, tagliatelle. Two glasses of Chianti had been delivered to their outdoor table. The evening sun was still warm on their faces. Loud laughter, cheerful chatter surged around them. Three red canoes raced along the river, under the Ha'penny Bridge. The cries of the seagulls sounded joyful, pleased at the prospect of extra crumbs on the streets.

Alice sliced garlic bread. 'Let's sum up,' she said.

Maggie took out her computer. Who'd have imagined, a week ago, that you could examine a body that had been brutally murdered, then sit out in the sun and eat risotto, she thought? Who'd have thought, a week ago, that you could just sit out in the sun, eat risotto and drink a glass of Chianti?

'One, the Caravaggio has been stolen from Doon Abbey,' Alice said.

Maggie tapped the keys of her computer.

'Two. Jeremy Meadowfield is found dead in a hotel in Liffey Valley.'

'Is Cyril O'Meara not number two?' Maggie asked.

'I'm leaving Cyril O'Meara out of it,' Alice said.

'Fire ahead,' Maggie said.

'Three, Kelly-Lidrov from New York is found murdered. Four, Brice, Metro's hitman, is murdered. In two of the murders, at least, there's a woman involved. Now we've just learned from the Rector that there may be two women involved, both of them members of a religious order. He was hearing confessions in Doon Abbey. The Caravaggio was stolen from Doon Abbey. The circumstantial evidence all points in one direction, doesn't it?'

'Except,' said Maggie as the drinks arrived, 'he only referred to one penitent. And although he seemed to suggest that the penitent was a woman, and a member of a religious order, he didn't say which religious order.'

'He didn't say anything, Maggie,' Alice said. 'He just wiggled his pinkie.'

'It's as much as he could do,' Maggie said, and sniffled. 'His own sister? I don't think so.'

'Are you trying to protect her?' Alice asked.

'Maybe,' Maggie said. 'I mean, if Sister Mercy Superior and Sister Diana are both arrested, who's left in Doon Abbey? We're finished, Alice – with or without the Caravaggio.'

Alice was sipping wine when her phone rang.

'It's Sebastian,' she said to Maggie.

'Are you going to tell him?' Maggie asked.

'What else can I do?' Alice said. 'I'm still a police officer. Hello, Sebastian?'

Maggie knew that getting drunk was a mortal sin, but if she was sitting in a restaurant about to witness the end of Doon Abbey, a mortal sin was the least of her problems, she decided.

'Before you ask why we're not back in Doon Abbey, I've got some important information for you,' Alice began.

Maggie took a generous gulp of the Chianti. She saw Alice frown.

'So what's yours?' Alice was asking. 'No, no, you go first.'

Could she really go home to her parents, Maggie wondered, as she gazed into her glass? Her mother's letters had become scarce in recent years, and the last one, written at Christmas, had described how Sonny, Maggie's twenty-eight-year-old brother, was now sleeping in what used to be Maggie's bedroom, after his own bedroom had been transformed into what Mam had described as 'an en-suite'.

'*What?*'

Alice had jumped to her feet, almost knocking over the waitress, who had arrived with the mushroom risotto and the tagliatelle.

'*Are you absolutely sure?*'

Maggie's mouth hung open. Alice kept running her hand through her hair and saying, 'I knew it, I bloody well knew it!'

'Will there be anything else?' asked the waitress, placing down the food.

'Are you crazy?' Alice shouted.

'I think we're fine, thanks,' Maggie said to the suddenly pale girl.

'You're so full of it, you make me want to vomit!' Alice cried and threw the phone down on the table.

She sat there, breathing heavily, as the wide-eyed waitress retreated.

'What's going on?' Maggie asked.

'That was your friend, Detective Sergeant Sebastian Hayes,' Alice said.

'*My* friend?'

'Forensics have just come back with a match of fingerprints from the screwdriver in Meadowfield's,' Alice said tightly.

Maggie screwed her eyes shut: even the thought of the screwdriver made her ill.

'The prints belong to Bruno Scanlon,' Alice said. 'A warrant has been issued for his arrest.'

Maggie shook her head. She pushed her tagliatelle to one side.

'Yes, even as we were driving down to Doonlish this morning – even as we were driving up those little country lanes you like so much, Maggie – that scumbag, Bruno, was carving the letter "M" into the back of a man he'd just murdered in a house not two miles from Doon Abbey.'

'Oh, dear God,' Maggie said.

'So Bruno knows the area very well,' Alice said, and signalled for two more glasses of wine. 'He probably stole the painting, so he knows the convent inside out. Which means that he knows I'm in the convent. And now, that dickhead, Sebastian, wants me to go back there?'

'And Bruno?' Maggie asked.

'They think he may have left the country. He's done it before – skipped to Málaga.' Alice took the new glass of wine from the waitress's tray and held it in both hands. 'But you know something, Maggie? I don't think he has left the country, I think he's right here still. And I think I know how to find him.'

Maggie was glad of the extra alcohol hit. She wondered how she would cope without alcohol when she went back to the convent; but then, she realised, there might soon be no convent to go back to.

County Kerry
17 June, 8.45 PM

Davy drove the Volkswagen at high speed over the narrow mountain road, and along the winding way from Dingle. Between contractions, Winnie spoke non-stop about Jeremy Meadowfield, her childhood, Dingle, the Blaskets, Jeremy Meadowfield, her neighbours, her plans for the future, Jeremy . . . For a woman who had taken a vow of silence, she had an awful lot to say. Occasionally the flow of verbiage was broken by a brave little gasp of pain, or a less courageous scream.

'Are you all right?' Davy would say, glancing at her in horror. Please don't let her have this baby here on the side of the road between Lispole and Camp with only me to be the midwife, he thought. 'Nun gives birth in ditch on side of road.' What a story: it would be the biggest scoop in the history of Davy Rainbow, Hack. But he couldn't use it. She had sworn him to secrecy about the father of her child-to-be. Still, the fleeting moments of imagination that he had enjoyed as to his own role, and might possibly use to advantage in the future, had been wonderful. Winnie winced and Davy swerved to avoid a ewe and her lamb crossing the boreen. He saw Tralee in the distance.

Dublin Northside
17 June, 9.15 PM

In her earlier life, Alice had spent many nights sitting in an unmarked car in the neighbourhood of Ska Higgins's house. Now, as she and Maggie walked towards it, on an avenue of leafy trees, the details of Ska's house flashed through her mind. It was one of a row of detached villas, with flat roofs and rounded corners, each with two portholes of frosted glass embedded either side of the hall door, like two round blind eyes. The main windows were unusual too: long and narrow, like slits in the walls of a medieval castle. Although Ska had invested a lot of his crime proceeds in this residence, buying at the top of the property boom, he seldom spent a night here, preferring to bed down in one of several apartments, cheap hotel rooms and houses, some owned by himself and some by his associates.

'What makes you so certain that Bruno will be here?' Maggie asked as she pushed in the gate.

Inside the house a siren had become activated. Unseen dogs were barking.

'Call it instinct,' Alice said as she walked briskly up the path and rang the doorbell. 'It came to me when we left Cassidy's pub last night. What was Ska Higgins doing there? Keeping an eye on Bruno's missus, that's what.'

Like all good cops, she felt that she knew each criminal personally, as a sister knows a brother, so that every turn and kink of that criminal's

152

mind was as familiar to her as her own. She *knew* how Bruno thought. Knew how he responded to situations and, despite all the evidence, she knew that Bruno Scanlon, vicious and despicable though he was, did not carve letters on to the backs of people he had just murdered.

The dogs inside were going berserk. She thought of her plain white cell in Doon Abbey, as calm as the inside of a shell. The chapel, white candles, white lilies, white-robed nuns singing white hymns. The bare patch on the chapel wall where the Caravaggio had once hung.

Through one of the frosted portholes, Alice could discern a figure moving. The siren ceased. The dogs stopped their barking. As the door was opened a chink on its safety chain, Alice shrank back behind Maggie.

'Yeah?'

Over Maggie's shoulder, Alice instantly recognised Primrose Higgins, Ska's daughter, herself a star of the juvenile courts – thanks, in part, to Alice.

'Sorry to disturb you,' Maggie said. 'We're from the Legion of Mary. We're here to see Mr Higgins.'

'Da's not here,' said Primrose Higgins.

'Oh, dear, we were told he would be,' Maggie said.

'Who told you that?' Primrose asked.

'The parish priest,' Maggie said.

At that moment, at knee level, a child's arm reached out towards Maggie.

'Hello!' Maggie said, hunkering down. 'What a beautiful little girl!'

The child laughed and held out her hand further to Maggie.

'Such bright eyes! What's her name?' Maggie asked.

'Jennifer,' said Primrose, as Jennifer giggled at Maggie. 'Hold on a second, you'd better come in.'

The door closed and the chain was unclipped.

'I didn't think Da knew the parish priest,' Primrose began as Alice and Maggie stepped into the hall. She froze. 'Detective Inspector Dunwoody . . .'

'It's okay, Primrose,' said Alice, 'calm down.'

Primrose put back her head and opened her mouth wide. '*Bruno!*' she screamed. '*Bruno!*'

'Primrose . . .' Alice said.

She hadn't time to finish the sentence. A huge German shepherd dog was bounding down the hall. Two strides from Alice, it leaped for her throat.

County Kerry
17 June, 9.30 PM

Davy sat in the corridor of the hospital, waiting.

Sober, clear-headed, he felt strangely empowered. He would drive back to County Kildare, take his secret from its hiding place and bring it to the gardaí. Sister Diana would not be pleased, but he didn't care. His mind was made up.

He approached the desk of maternity admissions, where a lone nurse was at work.

'How long will it be?' he asked her.

'How long is a piece of string?' she grinned at him, as if this was all a bit of a joke. 'It's her first, isn't it?'

'As far as I know.'

'Prepare for a bit of an ould wait.'

'Oh.' Davy glanced at his watch. 'I have to go actually.'

The nurse looked at him. She had a round pink face and cheeky bright blue eyes which looked knowingly into Davy's face.

'But aren't you going to be present?' She scrutinised him carefully. 'You *are* hubby, aren't you?'

'No, I'm just . . . a friend. And I have to go home urgently.'

The nurse nodded, a bit wearily. 'And does . . .' she glanced down at the sheet that Winnie had recently filled up. 'And does Oonagh have anyone?'

'She's a single mother, if that's what you're asking. There's no father,' Davy said.

The nurse laughed. 'A sort of immaculate conception, is it?'

'No, no, what I mean is, the father is dead . . . I think.'

She looked up. 'You *think*?'

'Look, I'm sorry, an emergency has cropped up. I have to go home,' Davy said. 'Ask . . . Oonagh for information.'

The nurse had had enough. Her pink complexion deepened. 'Goodnight,' she said, and bent over her files.

'Can you phone me when, you know, when she has it?' Davy said.

She took her time looking up. Then she fixed him with an impatient glare. But she wrote down the number he gave her.

Dublin Northside
17 June, 10.15 PM

Slowly Alice came to. Her hand stroked the skin of her throat. She opened her eyes. She was in the front room of the same house, judging by the windows: in the sitting room, in an armchair. She patted her pockets. No phone.

'Maggie?'

Maggie was lying, mouth open, eyes closed, on a long, smooth, pale grey sofa. Alice's heart pounded. Her last memory was of the dog's muzzle, its teeth bared. Her stomach heaved ominously and she felt the blood draining from her head.

'Maggie?'

Alice crept over to Maggie and smelt a sudden whiff of chemicals. Dentist, she thought. Chloroform. Oh, God! What had happened when they'd been knocked out? She shook Maggie violently.

'Maggie! Wake up!'

Maggie groaned and opened her eyes. 'Panda?'

'It's all right, Maggie,' Alice said, and fanned Maggie with a copy of

155

Hello magazine that had been lying on the coffee table. 'It's okay.'

Maggie sat up, put her head between her legs and took several deep breaths.

'I've got a bad headache,' she moaned.

'I'm sorry, Maggie.' Alice was distraught. 'We were crazy to come here in the first place.'

Maggie looked up. 'I wouldn't be anywhere else,' she said with a brave little smile.

'We need to get out of here,' Alice said, and began to walk around the room.

She started with the windows. It was dark outside, but nobody was going to squeeze in or out of those narrow slits, even if the windows weren't locked – which they were. Breaking the glass would not help. She didn't even try the door. Maggie too was taking a walk around the room.

'Look!'

Her face turned paler than it was already. She was pointing to what looked like a big rectangular flowerbed, at the back of the room, against the wall; except that the flowerbed wasn't a flowerbed, it was a cage with chicken wire on top to prevent the escape of its sole occupant, an enormous snake, coiled up, its girth as big as a man's chest. Beside this creature lay a pile of gleaming white bones, possibly human, and a row of grinning teeth. One of the snake's eyes flickered speculatively.

'Jesus, Mary and Joseph!' Maggie's stomach was heaving again. 'Why . . .? What . . .?'

'I think Ska Higgins has changed the way he recycles his victims,' Alice said.

'We should say a prayer,' Maggie said between breaths. 'A decade of the Rosary?'

She was on her knees, at the sofa. Alice sank down, more from exhaustion than piety. As Maggie began with the Our Father, a familiar voice could suddenly be heard in the hallway.

'Did your oul' fella never tell you? *Never open the door to effin' strangers!*'

Alice could hear Primrose Higgins whimpering.

'They said they were from the Legion of Mary, Bruno.'

'My arse, they are,' Bruno snarled. 'One of them's the bitch that killed my little Bruno.'

A key could be heard in the lock. Maggie was wide-eyed with fear.

'Pray!' Alice hissed.

'Holy Mary Mother of God, pray for us sinners . . .'

Bruno Scanlon was dressed in shorts and a loose, flowery shirt. There was no sign of a dog. Just a Glock with a silencer in Bruno's fist. He sniggered.

'And there I was goin' to get yez to kneel down, but yez knew what was comin to yez anyway – right?'

Alice tried to work out the logistics: two metres to his shins, which she could cover in about point-seven-five of a second, versus the speed of a bullet going at several zillionths of a second . . . Forget it.

'Forget it,' Bruno snarled as if they were co-wired. 'Still on your knees, go to the cage.'

'Oh, God help us,' Maggie whispered.

'You're making a big mistake, Bruno,' Alice said as she shuffled across the room until she came to the wire cage. The snake's tongue darted out. 'You'll never get away with this.'

'What do I care?' Bruno said. 'It's all over anyway. You got ten seconds. Which is more than you gave my little boy, you bitch.'

Alice felt the nose of the gun at the back of her neck. She had seen the result of these executions. Decapitation would not adequately describe them. As she closed her eyes, she heard Maggie's soft voice.

'The Third Sorrowful Decade: The Crowning with Thorns. Our Father Who art in Heaven, hallowed be Thy name . . .'

Alice joined in: 'Thy Kingdom come, Thy will be done on earth . . .'

Alice braced herself for the impact. Someone had suggested in a forensics paper given at an EU police conference she had attended that a shot in the head was no more painful than a general anaesthetic. Provided it was into the head. What about the neck?

'Give us this day our daily bread . . .'

Alice blinked in disbelief. From the corner of her eye, Alice saw Bruno sink to his knees. Then his gravelly voice in the response: 'And forgive us our trespasses, as we forgive those who trespass against us, and lead us not into temptation but deliver us from evil. Amen.'

Maggie went right on, leading the Hail Marys. Bruno answered. When the decade was over, she started again.

'The Fourth Sorrowful Mystery: the Scourging at the Pillar . . .'

'That's enough,' Bruno said, and got up. 'You don't think that changes anything, do you?'

'Only that we can go to heaven safe in the knowledge that we'll meet you there too, dear Bruno,' Maggie said.

'Dear . . . what?' Bruno spat. 'Me, in heaven? Are you mad?'

'Not at all,' Maggie replied. 'You've just shown us your spiritual side. Beneath it all, whatever happens, you're not a bad man, Bruno Scanlon.'

Alice watched Bruno's face churn like porridge.

'How did yez find me?' he snarled. 'Who else knows I'm here?'

Alice took a deep breath. 'Bruno, you may find this hard to believe, but I promised Natalie, your lovely wife, that I would find you and make sure that no harm came to you.'

She turned her head away, eyes closed, wincing as Bruno bunched his fist.

'Y'expect me to believe that?' he roared.

'She told me you light church candles for me,' Alice said. 'Is that true?'

Since there was no reply, she opened her eyes. Bruno was ogling her.

'Nats told you that?'

'Yes, she did. She's afraid any harm may come to you – and so am I. You see, I know that there are worse than you involved in all of this,'

Alice said.

'You killed my son,' Bruno said, and his eyes were as narrow as the windows.

'Yes, because he tried to shoot me, but I sympathise with you as his father,' Alice said. 'I was doing my duty. The truth is the incident had a huge effect on me. I entered a convent because of it.'

'You're all the same,' Bruno sneered. 'You think only of yourselves.'

'But I think of your son too.'

Bruno stared. 'Do you pray for his soul?'

'Yes, I do.'

Suddenly Bruno's head went down and he was sitting, the Glock dangling lightly from his fingers, for all the world like a vagrant in a doorway. Maggie and Alice edged closer to him.

'I told him, but he wouldn't listen,' Bruno said. 'He was an eejit to do the things he done. If I told him once, I told him a thousand times: there's only one way this thing is going to end up, son. With you in a hearse of lilies. Did he listen? The only people who made money out of the Toffee Wars were Interflora. Christ! And the way he left me? With no one to trust in the world? Look at me! Holed up here. Terrified. Look at me!'

'We can help you,' Alice said.

'No one can help me,' Bruno said. 'No one.'

'Did you not feel better when you prayed with us just now?' Maggie asked.

Bruno blinked. 'Mammy said the rosary every night,' he whispered.

'Is she still alive?' Maggie asked.

Bruno shook his head. 'Passed away two years ago. She was barely seventy.'

'You must miss her.'

'Till the day I die.'

'She's looking out for you,' Maggie said. 'From up there.'

Maggie was the confident one, Alice thought. The praying had given her strength. She was the real thing. The real nun thing.

Bruno was fighting back his tears. 'I should'na dunnit,' he choked. 'I knew stealin' from nuns was unlucky. That's why I lit the candles – to ask for forgiveness.'

'Who are you afraid of?' Alice asked, and deftly removed the Glock from Bruno's hands.

Bruno looked defeated. 'Of Metro,' he said. 'He's doing stuff like this all the time. I'm just a minnow in a sea of sharks the size of effin' articulated trucks.'

Alice made a decision. 'I can get you into the witness-protection programme,' she said. 'We'll protect you from Metro. You have my word.'

Dublin Northside
17 June, 10.45 PM

Bruno growled, then leaped to his feet, lumbered to the door and opened it. 'Primrose!' he shouted. 'Would you ever bring us a cup of tea?' He slumped back into an orange chair. 'Tell me more,' he said.

'Co-operate with us, not just on this but on your past crimes, and you'll get a new identity, a new address,' Alice said. 'But first we want to know what's going on.'

Bruno looked up as Primrose Higgins came in. Fake-tan legs. China teacups, a silver teapot, a plate of home-made biscuits. God, thought Maggie, a house-elf who bakes biscuits!

'Did you kill Meadowfield, Bruno?' Alice asked as Primrose left the room.

'Me?' Bruno looked genuinely surprised as Maggie poured his tea. 'Kill that scumbag? You must be joking. That eejit is the reason I'm in the mess I'm in.'

'Did you kill Metro's hitman, Brice, yesterday?' Alice asked. 'And before you answer, you should know that a screwdriver with your prints all over it was found at the scene.'

Bruno folded back the collar of his shirt. His neck was marked by a livid scar.

'Brice had me within an inch of Saint Peter and the pearly gates. Then something happened that I never would have believed in a thousand years,' he said.

The nuns stared.

'A huge big woman wearing a hat appeared behind him and broke his neck,' Bruno said in wonder.

'Sister Mercy Superior!' Maggie gasped.

'I didn't wait to be introduced,' Bruno said. 'I managed to wedge the corpse between us and escaped out the window.'

Alice sat down slowly. 'Or Sister Diana,' she said grimly.

'I'm glad she's not my sister,' Bruno said.

A gilt carriage clock on the mantelpiece chimed the hour.

'So where's our Caravaggio?' Alice asked.

'The painting,' Maggie added, just in case.

'I don't know where it is,' Bruno said, looking suddenly exhausted. 'I wish to God I did.'

He then told them his theory about Meadowfield subcontracting the theft.

'Who do you think he might have chosen?' Alice asked.

Bruno chewed his lip. 'I don't know, but there's a little newspaper man who lives down there and I know he's into the bookies.'

Alice and Maggie tried not to look at each other.

'Drinks too much,' Bruno was saying. 'I think he owes them ten grand.'

'What's his name?' Alice asked.

'Davy something,' Bruno said, and Maggie shivered.

Thirty minutes later, when Alice had phoned a chief superintendent she knew on his private line, and had gone over the details with the astonished policeman, the deal was in place. Bruno would enter the witness-protection programme, but in turn, he had agreed to do what Alice wanted.

Alice stuck out her hand.

'Shake on it, Bruno,' she said.

Bruno hesitated, then grabbed her hand in his.

'A deal,' he said.

She shuddered. She'd never touched Bruno Scanlon before. But then, Bruno pulled her into him, wrapped his beefy arms around her and planted a kiss on her cheek.

They walked out through the hall. Bruno opened the door.

'Just one last thing,' he said. 'The fact that Brice is dead means nothing. He was only the number two hitman, maybe even number three.'

'So who's number one?' Alice asked.

The colour drained from Bruno's wide face. 'Don't even go there,' he whispered.

'What's his name, Bruno?'

'Her, not him,' he said so quietly Alice had to strain to hear. 'She's known only as Poison Lily.'

'Poison Lily?' Maggie said.

'If she's here, you'll need more than the rosary to protect you,' Bruno said. 'God bless you, Sisters.'

Dublin Northside
17 June, 11.30 PM

A lovely sea breeze had sprung up, cooling the summer night, caressing the nuns' ankles as they walked along.

'Whoever would have thought Bruno Scanlon would get down on his knees and pray?' Alice said. They were making their way towards the main road, where the Berlingo was parked. Without a moon, it was dark now, and they walked under an avenue of lime trees, the leaves whispering, somewhat eerily, in the breeze.

'Do you think he'll do it?' Maggie asked, filling her lungs with the salty air.

'I never thought I'd hear myself saying this, but I felt sorry for him,' Alice said. 'He's obviously scared by what he's seen and wants to change his ways.'

An old woman seemed to appear out of nowhere, just ahead of them. She must have come out of one of the shady gardens, Alice thought.

'Psh psh, Ruby! Psh psh, Ruby!' she was calling.

All bent over, she had to crane her neck upwards to see where she was going. Poor thing, must have terrible osteoporosis, Maggie thought.

'Psh psh Ruby! Psh psh, Ruby!'

Alice and Maggie diverted to either side of the woman, just as she stopped in her tracks and peered up at them. 'Did yez happen to see a cat?'

'What colour?' Maggie wanted to be kind, although in her mind's eye she could still see the snake in his cage, just a few doors away, and wondered if Ruby the cat had been silly enough to stray in there.

'Black.' The old woman turned her head away, still searching. 'Black, with the loveliest snow-white socks.'

'I'm sure she'll turn up,' Alice said sympathetically.

'*He*,' the woman said with some force.

'I beg your pardon,' Alice said. The creature before her was in such terrible shape, and clearly so distraught, her femininity obliterated. Her face – what you could see of it – was ashen, and as wrinkled as tripe.

'I wouldn't worry,' Maggie said. 'He'll come home, all right. Cats often wander off.'

'Ruby doesn't,' the old woman said. 'He's always home before the nine o'clock news. Ye could set yer watch by him. I only hope he wasn't knocked down. They're always runnin' over cats around here, the villains.'

'Oh dear!' Maggie was getting drawn in.

Alice gave her a dig in the ribs and said firmly: 'I'm sure Ruby will turn up in his own good time. Goodnight now.'

At that moment a howl came from somewhere nearby.

'That's him!' The old woman's voice was delighted. 'That's Ruby! Ruby, Ruby, love, where are ye?'

'Come on!' Alice gave Maggie a pull. 'Let's get out of here.'

'Oh, please, young wan, she's in there.' The old woman pulled at Maggie's sleeve, and pointed to the mouth of a laneway. 'Please, I live on me own and I'll die of loneliness without Ruby.'

Alice and Maggie exchanged glances. Alice shrugged. They edged forward, down the laneway. Darkness dripped from the encroaching foliage. The tarmac ended abruptly and the ground dropped away. They could see the outline of a square shape below their feet, like a cave.

'I don't see any cat,' Alice said, but as if to disprove her instantly, there was an even louder squeal.

'Oh, thank God! Ruby! Ruby, pet, ye're all right now. Come here to me, me darling!'

'It's all right, we'll get him,' Maggie said.

'God bless you, he must be stuck,' said the old woman, and with that, she burst into tears.

'My friend will get him,' Alice said, and laid her hand comfortingly on the old woman's head. Her headscarf was smooth and soft.

'Here goes,' Maggie said, and jumped lithely down into the darkness. There was a cry.

'Maggie?'

Alice was watching intently. Without warning, she felt herself lifted up as easily as if she were a bag of groceries, and hurled into the void.

Doonlish
17 June, 11.45 PM

Davy Rainbow was exhausted. He pulled up outside his cottage, got out of his car and wondered if one drink would help him sleep. So much going on in his head, so many unresolved longings, fears and complications. He couldn't sleep with all this going on, he thought, as he opened his front door. A hot toddy was what he needed. Just one, a strong one. He switched on the light.

'Well, well, home at last, Davy,' said Detective Sebastian Hayes.

'What . . .?' Davy reeled backwards. 'Who are you?'

'I'm the only choice you have between fifteen years in Mountjoy and the rest of your life,' said Sebastian, and flashed his ID.

Davy shrank away from the detective, towards the door of the cottage. He wondered whether, if he made a run for it, he could last the pace, but alcohol had saturated his limbs over the years and Sebastian Hayes looked, if not fit, at least ambulant.

'Why don't you have a nice cup of tea, Davy?' Sebastian said soothingly. The policeman poured from the pot. 'And maybe a little something stronger in it to steady your nerves?'

'Okay,' Davy said cautiously.

'Because I found this when I was having a look around your house,' Sebastian said, reaching down and picking up a bottle of poitín from the floor. 'There's quite a lot of it around: under the sink, under your bed, outside in your turf shed. I'd say you're a dealer, Davy? Am I right?'

'I . . . don't know what you're talking about,' Davy spluttered as his eyes feverishly scanned the top shelf of the dresser. The panel was intact.

Sebastian uncorked the liquor and poured a generous dollop into Davy's tea cup.

'You'll get six to nine months for possession – that's if you plead guilty and I tell them what a decent man you really are,' Sebastian said. 'On the other hand, the theft of the Caravaggio is going to get you three years, minimum. And, of course, for being an accomplice to murder, or murders, we're talking a ten-year stretch. So, you see what I meant when I said I was your only choice between Mountjoy and the rest of your life?'

Davy's hand was shaking so much that he abandoned the effort to drink the poitín-laced tea.

'Murder?' he croaked.

'Let me show you something,' Sebastian said, and took out his mobile phone. 'This is CCTV footage taken earlier this week from a hotel in Liffey Valley.' He turned the screen to Davy. 'Recognise anyone?'

Davy stared at the image of the huge woman in the hat. He shook his head.

'She's on quite a roll, this lady friend of yours,' Sebastian said. 'We think she specialises in the neck-break. Her name is Sister Diana, right?'

'Di?' Davy gulped.

'Criminals do crime, so it's just a little step up from making moonshine to stealing a painting from a group of helpless women. But you and Di are small-time crooks, Davy. You needed someone with form to help you fence the goods, right? Enter the late Mr Meadowfield. I can just imagine the scene: you, Di and Jeremy, sitting around this table with a bottle of poitín, planning how you're going to get rich.'

'That's not true!' Davy cried.

'But criminals are scum,' Sebastian continued, 'as you soon discovered. You and Sister Diana somehow stole the painting and gave it to Jeremy to sell. But suddenly, nice Mr Meadowfield decided you were superfluous to his plans. He was going to sell the painting for himself. Ah, I think I'm getting warm, am I not, Davy?'

Davy was staring, open-mouthed.

'Maybe you then realised you'd made a big mistake,' Sebastian went on, 'and decided to call the whole thing off. But you reckoned without your friend Sister Di, right? Di by name, Di by nature. She tracked down Meadowfield and put him down, the same way she'd snuff out a two-headed calf.'

'No!' Davy shrieked. 'Not Di!'

'But you and she had got in over your heads,' Sebastian said harshly.

'For once you lie down with scum, they infect you, they enter your bloodstream, you have to keep killing or you'll be killed. Right, Davy? *Right?*'

Davy lay back, sucking in air. Now that he was being accused of murder, his earlier plan to confess everything seemed like madness.

'But how many criminals are there in this little neck of the woods?' Sebastian asked rhetorically. 'We know you and Di are thieves and murderers. We know that Meadowfield was the lowest of the low.' Sebastian made a point of frowning hugely. 'But wasn't there someone else involved in all this? Another member of this little band of robbers and assassins? Another woman, perhaps? Ah, yes! But what's *her* name?'

Davy was shaking like a man on his deathbed.

'She's Sister Winifred, isn't she?' Sebastian said. 'Dear, serene Sister Winifred, who was Davy's closest friend. Sister Winifred *Superior*, no less, who disappeared just before all this trouble started. I think I'd like to have a little chat with this Sister Winifred. But how do I do that? Can you put me in touch with Sister Winifred Superior, Davy?'

Davy staggered to his feet. 'I don't know where she is, I swear to God!' he cried.

Sebastian surged up, caught Davy by the throat and pressed him roughly back against the wall.

'I don't believe you,' he growled.

'I don't know where she is, honest,' Davy gasped.

Sebastian tightened his grip. 'Not good enough,' he said.

Davy's head swam. 'I'm . . . a journalist,' he said. 'I . . . can't reveal my sources.'

'I need facts, Davy. Facts, before someone else gets killed.'

'I'd rather kill myself,' Davy gasped, 'and that's the truth.'

At that moment the telephone rang. Sebastian released his grip on Davy's throat. Davy sank to the floor. The phone continued to ring.

'Answer your phone, Davy,' Sebastian commanded.

Davy crawled across the kitchen to the dresser and hauled himself up. 'Hello?' he croaked.

'It's a girl,' the Tralee voice said. 'They're both grand.' And then: 'She's called Aurelia.'

Davy staggered backwards, turned to face Sebastian, and then, for the second time that day, fainted.

Dublin Northside
17 June, Midnight

Alice could hear an engine being started. She could feel movement – not just the movement of the vehicle they were in, but movement within the vehicle. A grinding movement. It was pitch dark.

'What the hell?'

She was wedged knee-deep between foul-smelling plastic refuse sacks. She could hear the cat howling, and could suddenly see its luminous green eyes floating level with her own. Slowly, Alice's legs were being pressed forward, as if she were in a gigantic tumble-drier.

'Maggie!' she shouted.

Alice heard a groan.

'We've been tricked,' Alice cried.

'Where are we?' Maggie was still groggy.

'Oh God, Maggie, I'm sorry, but I think we're in the back of a rubbish-collection truck,' Alice said, and pushed for all she was worth against the steel plate that was slowly but surely compressing everything in the small space to pulp.

'Holy Mother of God!' Maggie said. 'My knees are up to my chin!'

'I think it's time for the sorrowful mysteries!' Alice said with a humour she did not feel. The whole machine shuddered. 'Shit, we're being crushed to death!'

A hideous meow broke out beside them, as if the trapped cat too understood the fatal nature of the situation.

'Poor pussy,' Maggie soothed. 'Come to me.'

'Listen!' Alice cried. 'Shut up, cat! Listen, Maggie! Outside!'

Over the noise of the deadly waste compression, and the noise of the moving truck, a siren could be heard.

'You hear that? We're in traffic!' Alice said. 'She's taking us to a land-fill, the dirty bitch.'

'Ohh!' Maggie cried as the bags popped and their malodorous contents spewed into the shrinking space. She hammered on the steel sides. 'Yuk!'

It was useless, Alice realised. You could be murdered on the footpath at this hour of night and nobody would lift a finger to interfere, much less respond to feeble thumping coming from inside a rubbish truck. The pitch from the revolving machinery changed: instead of an inex-orable grinding, the engine that now drove the steel plates to pack the rubbish neater than rotten pancakes was labouring madly. The cat howled. If only I could see, Alice thought! Please God don't let me die in a rubbish truck.

'Alice?'

'What is it, Maggie?'

'The cat is in a steel cage,' Maggie gasped. 'The cage is stopping the machine from crushing us.'

Alice could hear the compacting engine roaring, as if enraged. But then, no sooner had one prayer been answered than God was put to the test again: the metal of the unseen cage began to groan as it buckled against the massive pistons.

'Maggie?'

'What?'

'Can you get out the lighter?'

'I don't want to see!' Maggie wailed. 'Our Father, Who art in heaven, Hallowed be Thy name, Thy kingdom come . . .'

'Not to see with!' Alice shouted, as the sound of buckling metal increased. 'I want you to set fire to the plastic bags!'

'But . . . we're in here!' Maggie shrieked.

'Just do it!' Alice screamed. 'Do it now!'

Metal scraped with appalling intent and then, just as there was a flash from the lighter, Alice saw the cat, jet black with snow-white paws, as promised, staring at her in abject terror as its cage shrank all around it.

'Everything's so smelly,' Maggie complained. The explosion of light was followed by dense, tar-like fumes.

'Stick your head into a refuse sack!' Alice said. 'There's oxygen in there.'

'Alice?'

'Do it!'

'I just wanted to say something,' Maggie coughed.

'Save your breath.'

'It was an honour and a pleasure to have met you.'

Alice felt something furry and wet fly over her head. Poor cat, she thought forlornly. She gave silent thanks to the people who threw out perfectly good tomatoes and bread, just because the best-by date said they should. She sucked in the yeasty oxygen of fruit and veg. Another siren, outside. This time closer. Fumes everywhere. Metal pressed against her tightly now. A cold vice on her head.

Chapter Seven

Dublin
17 June, Midnight

Ned O'Loughlin was feeling restless. He had enjoyed an evening that felt very much like love, in his new fiancée's bijou apartment in Dublin's Rathgar district – one of the nicest places you could possibly conduct a liaison. This was the better end of Rathgar, closer to Dartry than to Terenure. Sive was an altogether lovely girl: quiet, well spoken, slightly reserved, and always exquisitely turned out. Her dental floss and her ironing board were in constant use – the sort of girl he could have introduced to his mother, or even his late father, in complete certainty of parental approval. An accomplished cook, a bright conversationalist, a respectful listener: what more could a man want? Sive was a practising Catholic, and her willingness to invite Ned into her bed was, she let it be known, strictly a down-payment on their eventual marriage. Now she snored sweetly beside him. So why was he feeling restless?

Although he tried not to, it was difficult not to compare her to Alice. He would go to his grave and not understand why Alice had entered that convent. Bad enough to be left by a woman for another man, but to lose out to the seclusion of an enclosed order was brutal. Ned knew he was too fat, and much too stupid, to deserve a beautiful, idealistic girl like

Alice Dunwoody, but he had always done his level best to look after her and had been a good, reliable, sensitive modern man, even to the point of cooking her healthy breakfasts of porridge and pecan nuts. And all the thanks he got was that she went and left him merely because she had shot some half-witted gangster.

And then he had met Sive and life had somehow started up again. They had hit it off from the start: dinner in a Michelin one-star restaurant had led to a night at the Russian ballet and later to a weekend in a four-star hotel in County Wexford, where fine dining, spa treatments, cultured conversation and decorous sex had taken place. There was more to Sive than met the eye. Her interests involved not only the arts but animal welfare; she had done sterling work on behalf of a donkey charity, to which Ned himself had also subscribed. They found much to talk about in the overheated bedroom of the Wexford hotel. She also turned out to have a surprisingly large capacity for champagne.

Sive made it clear that a ring of some sort was expected as a natural consequence of these developments, and he had picked out rather a nice one, featuring small diamonds set in white gold. During the weeks that followed, Ned became aware of a complex series of plans, bookings, purchases, fittings and future commitments that had been triggered by this gesture. Not only was Sive his fiancée, but she seemed to have every intention of marrying him.

One nagging doubt remained. Did Sive really love him? Could anyone love Ned? And if not, could you have a marriage without love? Sive was a graduate in History of Art, which accounted for her simple good taste in clothes and furniture. She had a modest private income. There was some sort of job in a friend's fashion boutique, where she worked – when she felt like it – in the late afternoons. Time was not a constant pressure, as it had always been with Alice.

But now Alice had reappeared, and all Ned's old feelings for her – feelings that, he had to admit, were different to his feelings for Sive – had begun to creep all over him. Which was in a way shameful, since he was in bed with Sive, hoping to drift off to sleep between her brand new, coffee-coloured Egyptian cotton sheets.

Dublin Northside
18 June, 12.05 AM

Sebastian Hayes surveyed the devastation. The burning truck, the two inert bodies on the grass, their hair-ends charred, their clothes impacted with the contents of refuse sacks.

'Goodnight, sir.' The guard's deep voice was deferential. 'I'm afraid it's just another of those gangland crimes. Unfortunate Russian prostitutes being disposed of by our friend here. Both of them after dying of smoke inhalation.'

'What makes you think they're on the game?' Sebastian asked.

'The underwear,' replied the guard. 'We've laid them out decent now, but you should have seen them when we dragged them out of the lorry there.'

A high, quavering voice came from behind them. 'Lookit, I said I'd take the extra load for a few bob. I was doing the old bitch a favour, so how in Jaysus' name was I supposed to know it was two blinkin' corpses?'

Sebastian turned. A squat, dishevelled man was being led over to the garda squad car. Sebastian motioned the arresting guard to bring the man to him. He looked him in the eye and spoke in his best interrogation voice: 'Describe the old bitch to us, if you please.'

'Flagged down my lorry, she did. Big fat lardy one, she was. Noisy too. Give you a headache, she would. Swore it was her granddaughter's poodle was after dying and she couldn't pay the removal charges. I even gave her a rebate, I did.'

'What do you mean, a rebate?' Sebastian asked.

'Bate me down with her shrieking, she did. Got a fiver off. Said I was

173

taking the food out of her grandchildren's mouths. Loaded up the poodle herself. I told her the blinkin' compressor was on the blink, and she said that was grand, sure the poor poodle wasn't going anywhere. Then I had to wait for her to bring the unfortunate dog out. Wouldn't let me help her. Kept me there five minutes. If I'd a known she was sneaking a live cat in as well, I'd a refused to have anything to do with her. It isn't right, so it isn't.'

'You are in serious trouble, my friend,' Sebastian said. 'And why did you start the fire? Were you hoping to cremate the poor girls en route?'

'That wasn't me!' the driver shrieked. 'Honest to God!'

'Might have been the cat,' the guard said.

'Are you having a laugh?' the driver demanded. 'That's shocking, that is.'

'Take him away,' Sebastian sighed. He had never felt such desolation. It was going to be a long night.

Dublin Northside
18 June, 1 AM

The air was so sweet. She could not get enough of it. Barbed wire seemed to have been sewn through her eyelids. She managed to flick one eye half-open for a moment and could make out lights and moving shadows. She tried to focus.

'Hey, chief! This one's waking up too!'

Lights were flashing on her eyelids. She forced both eyes open. An orange bulb winked through the darkness, blurred by rain.

'Yeah, still to the good,' a deeper voice said. 'She'll be OK.'

'Did you see the legs on the other one?'

'Don't mind that sort of talk,' said the deeper voice.

'Let me in there.' This was a familiar voice. 'I've done the first-aid resuscitation course.'

The familiar voice stopped. There was the sound of heavy breathing. Alice opened her eyes, and saw Detective Sebastian Hayes, on his knees, crouched over Sister Mary Magdalene. She stared. They were kissing. The old traditional French kiss. It brought her right back to the dance halls of her teenage years. Maggie was arching up slightly to clamp her mouth on his.

'Having fun, officer?' Alice asked.

18 June, 7.50 AM

Dark Heart kept two full-length mirrors in her boudoir, so that foresight and hindsight were permanently available as she worked swiftly, adding layer upon layer. Perfection was, as always, her implicit aim. We must endeavour to serve through excellence, maintain standards. Put our best foot forward, preferably shod in Prada, or, this morning, of necessity, encased in sensible Ecco walking shoes.

A lesson had to be taught. She donned the feathered hat that completed her ensemble and posed for a final inspection: she had to declare herself fully satisfied. Her outfit, objectively speaking, was perfect. Next, she swallowed two high-performance aerobic pills, washed down by a tipple of Cointreau. Early in the day, admittedly, but serving the same useful purpose as the tot of rum given to First World War soldiers before they went over the top. All done. Ready to depart. Dark Heart flung open the bottom sash of her bedroom window and filled her lungs with blessed morning air.

Dublin, Doonlish
18 June, 8.15 AM

Sebastian drove fast. Driving was his favourite thing. He loved guiding his Ford Mondeo around narrow country roads. Alice sat in the passenger seat, wide awake but lost in thought, while Maggie slumped in the back, out of it. The police doctor had said that it could take several days to recover from smoke inhalation – a judgement that Sebastian had tried to impress on the two women as he set out for County Kildare. Alice was having none of it.

'This is our case now every bit as much as yours,' she told him. 'Besides, Bruno is relying on us.'

Sebastian checked Maggie in his rear-view mirror. The doctor had said she'd been particularly badly affected by the smoke. Sebastian felt so protective towards her, now that he had brought her back to life. Maggie was soft and yielding. And rather lovely in her awkward way, even when dressed in the baggy running shorts and the pink check shirts that both women had picked up in the Sandyford Aldi at opening time. He thought of the damp strands of fair hair on the pink check of Maggie's collar. She and Alice had taken a shower in the garda station. Maggie smelled of regulation garda shampoo, but even so . . .

A blaring motor horn dragged Sebastian back to reality. He had drifted right across the road.

'Would you like one of us to drive?' Alice said.

'No thanks,' said Sebastian, thin-lipped. 'I'll manage.'

'Then keep your eyes on the road,' Alice said, 'not on your passenger in the back.'

Alice was forlorn. Back in Dublin, she had seen Maggie looking at Sebastian. Her eyes had gone cloudy. Alice realised that the kiss of life had changed everything for Maggie, had brought out in Maggie basic longings that had been long suppressed. That made Alice sad: the thought of returning to Doonlish without Maggie overwhelmed her.

Sebastian steered the car even faster through narrow curving laneways burgeoning with green leaves, bushes, fronds and other forms of new life.

'I had a rather interesting meeting late last night,' Sebastian said. 'When you two were on your city tour.'

Alice closed her eyes in resignation.

'I was with Davy Rainbow,' Sebastian went on. 'A telephone call came through. It was a hospital in Tralee ringing to tell him that his good friend, Sister Winifred, had just given birth to a lovely baby girl.'

Silence followed, but only for a couple of seconds.

'*What?*'

Maggie was sitting bolt upright.

'Sister Winifred is alive?' she cried.

'Not only alive but breast-feeding, according to Davy,' Sebastian said.

'Who's the father?' Alice asked.

'You don't want to know,' Sebastian said, a bit too smugly.

'Who's the father, you eejit!' Maggie shouted.

Sebastian cursed himself: he'd been doing so well. He took a deep breath and said, 'Jeremy Meadowfield.'

Doon Abbey
18 June, 8.30 AM

Sebastian pulled in at the gates of Doon Abbey on Alice's instructions. In the distance, at the other end of the long avenue, the outline of the castle convent was just visible. Alice got out of the car, walked around to the back and opened the door. Maggie was very pale, and breathing fitfully.

'Maggie, can you manage?' Alice asked.

With effort, Maggie swung her legs out. Alice noted Sebastian's eyes in his wing mirror. Alice helped Maggie to stand.

'I want you to take deep breaths,' Alice said. 'Here, put your hands on my shoulders.'

Maggie did as she was told and breathed in deeply.

'You're not well,' Alice said. 'We're driving you back to the convent.'

'We're in this together,' Maggie gasped.

'Not any more,' Alice said. 'Listen, I think we're within an ace of solving the crime – and I couldn't have done it without you, seriously. But now, you've got to get well. The doctor said so.'

Maggie tried to protest, but the fight had gone out of her. Alice helped her back into the car, and they drove in through Doon Abbey's gates. As they passed the gate lodge, Alice was sure she saw two heads at the window, sinking out of view.

Doonlish
18 June, 8.45 AM

Davy Rainbow's cottage was a riot of colour: green leaves, yellow dandelions, purple loosestrife, straggling bluebells, and a drift of somniferous poppies under the hedgerows. Sebastian listened to the silence, measured by the ticking of the engine after he had switched it off.

'Nobody here,' Alice said.

'He was here last night,' Sebastian said solemnly.

'Maybe he's babysitting,' said Alice dryly, and got out.

Now that she and Sebastian were a team again, she felt coolly determined, in charge. The little cottage was cold, and smelt musty. Lino covered the floor. An over-full bookcase stood along one wall, a picture of a horse hung askew beside an ancient television set. A mid-size statue of the Infant of Prague stood on the dresser.

'Cup of tea?' Sebastian asked.

Bruno, according to the deal he had struck with Alice, would have called Metro at seven sharp that morning and asked to meet him here, at Davy's cottage, saying he had the painting. Whoever was in league with Metro would be told of this rendezvous, Alice reckoned. The main players would be flushed out at last.

'There's sugar over there on the dresser . . .' Sebastian began, but Alice was standing in the middle of the kitchen, both hands held up for silence.

'What is it?' Sebastian asked.

'Are you carrying?' she asked quietly.

Sebastian blinked, then patted the gun at the small of his back and nodded. 'Why?' he whispered.

'Because I think we're about to have a visitor,' Alice said.

Sebastian listened, then he heard it: the sound of gravel crunching underfoot. A heavy foot, by the sound of it, coming around the side of the cottage.

I'll hide, Alice mouthed.

Sebastian had already unholstered his gun and clicked off the safety catch as Alice dived into the kitchen's shadowy corners. A burly woman flung open the cottage door. Her face was obscured by a greasy veil. She was wearing black gloves, and holding a large box beneath her left arm. She was breathing heavily, as though she had been carrying this weight over a long distance.

'Davy?' she called. 'Davy, are you here?'

'Hold it right there, ma'am!' Sebastian said as he stepped out, brandishing his gun. 'Put the box down,' he continued. 'Very slowly.'

The big woman dropped the box on Sebastian's foot, chopped down at his gun arm and butted him with her black-veiled head. Sebastian's gun flew over his shoulder, knocked three cups from their hooks on the dresser and then discharged like thunder. Alice ducked instinctively as the ricochet pinged around the room and shattered Davy Rainbow's kitchen window.

Sebastian had slipped and landed awkwardly on his back. The woman jumped on him, her black-gloved hands tightening on his throat. Dark wraparound glasses hid her eyes and black hair tumbled loosely around a bulbous face. From her throat curled a high snarl.

In one fluid movement, Alice grabbed the Infant of Prague from the dresser and swung it with maximum force on to the woman's head. Sebastian's black-clad assailant toppled over.

Sebastian rolled out from under her, and climbed somewhat unsteadily to his feet. He gave Alice a sheepish grin.

'Thanks, partner,' he said. 'I owe you one.'

The woman on the floor, who now looked like a heap of black clothing, groaned and began to stir.

'Why would a gangster carry rosary beads?' Alice mused and pointed.

The figure on the floor began to howl.

'Holy Mother of God,' Alice whispered. 'It's Sister Diana.'

Dublin Southside
18 June, 8.50 AM

As Ned sat in the breakfast nook tucking into his nicely soft-boiled egg, he could hear Sive singing in the shower. She had a tasteful, high, somewhat reedy soprano, but always sang in tune, unlike Alice, whose tastes had run to raucous renderings of 'Hotel California'.

Ned was listening to the BBC Home Service (as he still called it), which was full of soothing, faraway problems. Nonetheless, he could not stop thinking of the missing painting – which, of course, made him think of Alice. Even though Sive was cool and ladylike, Alice was something different. He used to imagine Sive in late middle age, enjoying the finer things in life with him, but now, when he thought of late middle age, he thought of Alice and an empty space opened up inside him.

Sive had left the bathroom, and was answering the intercom. He hadn't heard it ring. She seemed to be conversing with someone she didn't know – presumably a tradesman or delivery boy. Ned helped himself to a second cup of Earl Grey.

Sive stormed into the breakfast nook, stony-faced, her cerise cashmere dressing gown wrapped tightly around her slim frame. Her skin, normally as smooth as *café au lait*, was blotched white and crimson. Her eyes blazed, and her voice was as piercing as a broken razor blade scraping glass.

'Is everything permitted, then? Are there no boundaries?'

Ned stared at her. 'What's the problem, darling?'

'Some woman downstairs on the video-phone. I asked her what she wanted. She says she wants you.'

180

'Me? Why on earth? Did you recognise her?'

'I couldn't see her face. She's wearing a big hat, with feathers, and it gets in the way of the camera. She knows your name. She says it concerns your girlfriend. Of course I said I was your girlfriend – your fiancée, in fact – and she simply laughed and informed me that I was living in a fool's paradise. She said the love of your life is Alice Dunwoody. She said you would never walk to the altar with me. You've got some explaining to do, Ned.'

There were tears now, and a look of despair on Sive's face.

Ned was on his feet. 'Why don't I see what's going on,' he said.

'I'd rather you had nothing to do with her,' Sive snapped.

'Darling . . .'

Sive drew herself back, wrapping the dressing gown more tightly around her greyhound midriff.

'But if that's what you want,' she declared, 'then I won't stand in your way.'

Doonlish
18 June, 8.55 AM

Sebastian reached in his pocket and passed a large cotton handkerchief to the recumbent Sister Diana. The nun wiped her eyes, blew her nose, removed her tight black cap, rolled over and sat up.

'I'm really sorry I hit you,' Alice said to Diana.

'It was for my own good,' Diana said glumly. 'This has all gone too far. I never thought I'd see the day when I was wrestling with a policeman.'

'All this poitín,' Sebastian said in amazement, lifting out a bottle from the box. He turned to Alice. 'Did you know about this?'

Alice shook her head dismally.

'And I suppose Davy Rainbow is your distributor?' Sebastian said to Sister Diana. 'Was it him who suggested you steal the Caravaggio?'

Sister Diana didn't reply. She was staring over Sebastian's shoulder at the dresser. Alice followed her gaze.

'The little rat!' Diana exclaimed. 'That's where he had it hidden!'

The bullet from Sebastian's gun had ripped a hole in the back of the dresser and in the process had revealed a long, cylindrical metal coil.

'What on earth is it?' Alice asked.

'It's the worm I use to distil the poitín,' Diana replied, as the telephone by the broken window rang.

Alice picked it up. 'Hello?'

'Alice?'

Alice frowned. 'Maggie?'

She could hear Maggie's laboured breath.

'Oh, Alice, I think you'd better come up to the convent straight away,' Maggie said.

Dublin Southside
18 June, 9 AM

Ned rushed from the apartment, ran down the stairs and opened the front door of the block of flats. There, melting into the shrubbery in the front garden, was a large but elegantly proportioned woman. She seemed older than Ned, but nimble.

'Wait! Please wait! What do you want?'

Ned stumbled towards the flowerbed and plunged into the bushes. Lost sight of the woman. Got badly scratched by holly leaves. Realised that his new sky-blue pyjamas and light silk dressing gown might not be the best attire for this kind of expedition. Then something moved beside his head, and his brain exploded into pure white.

He was down among the shrubs and roses, the taste of earth filling his mouth. His eyesight was fading, then gone. He had a splitting headache. He was trying to breathe, but something was blocking him. A tightness around his throat, caused by a string. Or a rope? No: a steel wire, cutting into the soft flesh of his neck, and lifting him off the ground, like a fish caught on a hook. He tried to grasp the wire with his fingers. Couldn't get his fingers near it.

'Maybe Miss Alice will mind her own business now,' the woman's voice hissed.

Mention of Alice made Ned instinctively jerk back his head. It made contact with something hard.

'My nose!' cried the woman's voice in his ear.

The wire around Ned's neck went slack for a split second, during which he slid back down to earth, rolled under a bush, and heaved himself to his feet on the far side. Through branches of holly, he was staring into the face of the large woman whose nose was pumping blood. Ned almost felt compelled to offer her assistance, but then she tweaked her nose carefully between finger and thumb – she was wearing shiny black gloves – and a glob of blood fell to earth.

'Round one to you,' she announced, as though this were some kind of sporting contest. 'The rest remains to be seen.'

She started to circle the holly bush, like a sumo wrestler looking for the first opening. As she pursued a relentless clockwise advance, Ned danced an anti-clockwise retreat, so that they changed sides more then once. Then she made a sudden darting lunge, and he, skipping backwards, tripped over a tree stump, scrambled to his feet and burst out of the shrubbery on to the tarmac car park surrounding Sive's apartment building. But the big woman was quick. He could hear her rasping breath behind him, then her gloved hands fastened on his neck.

'Not much of a fighter, are we?' she sighed as she forced him to the ground once more. 'One of life's little victims, are we, Ned? Always ready to yield to superior power.'

She had again slung the garrotte around his neck, and tightened it viciously. His breath was blocked. This was the end.

And then a voice came screaming: 'Get away from him, you bitch!'

Ned had never heard Sive use such coarse language. As the grip on his neck was loosened, he managed to turn his head and saw Sive wielding a curling-tongs. It caught Ned full in the face. He went down on his knees, momentarily paralysed.

When he could see again, several neighbours had emerged from the building into the car park, and his assailant was leaving the apartment complex like an Olympic hurdler, clearing the low boundary wall with a single leap before vanishing around the corner.

Sive was on her knees, by his side. 'Ned, are you all right? Ned? Ned?'

He struggled to get his breath back. 'Yes, I'm fine,' he gasped, holding his nose.

Sive's eyes filled with tears. She threw her arms around his head. Her tears fell on his face like baptism.

'I love you, darling,' she whispered.

Doon Abbey
18 June, 9.15 AM

The convent was eerily quiet, even by its own standards of sepulchral silence. Sebastian held his revolver two-handed, pointing down, as Alice and he made their way in under the main arch.

'Where did she make the call from?' Sebastian hissed.

'Had to be from Sister Mercy Superior's room,' Alice whispered. 'I have the mobile, and that's where the only other phone in the convent is.'

They darted between morning shadows across the courtyard, using the castle's deeply inset windows as cover, until they came to the main door. Sebastian nodded. Alice kicked the door open and dived inwards, rolling. How many times had they done this routine together? One covering the other? But never in a religious institution.

Pausing beside a large blue and white plaster statue of the Blessed Virgin, Alice glanced up the stairwell. She could see nothing. There was no sound. She flattened herself against the wall of the marble staircase and began to work her way upwards, with Sebastian behind her, his revolver now held out in the combat position. She had come up these same stairs just three days ago with Maggie, when they had demanded to see Sister Mercy Superior. It seemed like a lifetime ago. A scream was suddenly heard.

'Did you hear that?' Sebastian said.

Alice nodded. 'That was Maggie,' Alice said, and her face was dark.

At the top of the stairs, she turned left. The religious iconography on the walls leered down at her. After five steps she pointed right, to the heavy wooden door. She held up three fingers. Sebastian nodded.

Alice mouthed, 'One, two, three.'

She hit the door with her heel and, once more, rolled. Sebastian came in with the gun probing.

'Drop the gun, Sebastian!' Maggie cried. 'Drop the gun or she's going to kill us all!'

Doon Abbey
18 June, 9.25 AM

Alice got slowly to her feet. She saw Sister Mercy Superior cowering in a corner of the room and Sister Columba lying at her feet on the floor. Maggie, ashen, sat in a chair, with Panda, the convent tomcat, twitching convulsively at her feet. Standing behind Maggie, holding an aerosol spray can pointed at Maggie's face, was a very thin, young-faced woman with nose studs and ear studs, and wearing a magenta, spiky-haired wig.

'Ah, Sister Alice and Mr Hayes, thank you for coming,' the woman said in a slightly lisping voice. 'Now that we're all here, allow me to introduce myself. For the sake of our proceedings, you may call me Miss Lily. Now, Detective Sergeant Hayes, kick the gun you have just dropped across the floor to me. Yes, like that. Thank you. Would you and Sister Alice care to join my other guests in the corner? Slowly please, if you wouldn't mind. Sudden movements may make me discharge this spray into Sister Maggie's lovely face, and we wouldn't want that, would we? Not after what has befallen poor Panda.'

'Panda,' Maggie wailed.

The cat was sneezing pathetically and making swimming gestures with all four paws.

Alice and Sebastian crossed the room very slowly, never once taking their eyes off the woman called Miss Lily. Sister Columba was on the ground, breathing weakly, with Sister Mercy Superior on one knee, down beside her.

'The next step in our performance,' said Miss Lily, 'is a demonstration for the benefit of our latest arrivals. Sister Mercy Superior, would you be so kind as to open the closet door to your left?'

Sister Mercy Superior climbed to her feet, glaring.

'You'll never get away with this,' she growled.

'Now, now, your manners, please,' said Miss Lily. 'The closet.'

Doon Abbey's head nun opened the closet door, and Alice stared as a small-sized man, bound and gagged, fell out.

'Bring him over here, Mercy,' ordered Miss Lily.

'It's Davy Rainbow,' Sebastian said from the side of his mouth.

Mercy Superior half walked, half frog-marched Davy to the centre of the room, where he went down on his knees with a painful whack.

'Thank you, Mercy,' said Miss Lily. 'You see, Davy here is what we in the business call "unfit for purpose". What he knows, he won't tell, and what he tells is useless. Except for one thing: my demonstration.'

She held aloft the spray can.

'In order to show you how this works, I shall expose Davy's skin to a single blast from my little can, and further explanations will then be unnecessary.'

She bent to Davy.

'Sorry about this, sir,' she said, and directed a tiny cloud of the spray towards his face.

As Davy's eyes bulged and he fell forward, Miss Lily deftly removed his mouth gag. Davy began to writhe and gasp.

'He will die of coronary embolism within thirty to forty-five minutes,' Miss Lily said, stepping back behind Maggie. 'There is no antidote. Now . . .'

On the floor, Sister Columba had begun to weep uncontrollably. Sister Mercy Superior stood full square, her hands in fists.

'. . . I am going to ask questions,' Miss Lily continued, 'and if I don't get immediate answers, I'm going to spray each one of you, starting with the lovely Sister Mary Magdalene here. Actually, when I said "questions", I misspoke, for there is only one question, really, and this is it. Where is the Caravaggio?'

No one moved or spoke.

'Oh dear, it's going to be like that, is it?' said Miss Lily, and angled the can at Maggie's ear. 'Sorry about this, Sister.'

'Wait! Stop!'

Sister Mercy Superior stepped forward.

'I have a confession to make.'

'Really?' said Miss Lily. 'How unexpected! Well go on, Sister Mercy Superior.'

Mercy seemed to be shrinking as she reached for a white linen handkerchief and began to dab at her eyes.

'Mr Meadowfield, or whoever he really was, made me do it. There was no alternative. I had to comply with his vile demands in order to protect poor pregnant Winifred!'

'And so you stole the very painting on which the future of your order depended?' asked Sebastian.

'What people see in that painting is beyond me,' hissed Sister Columba from the floor. 'A painting done by a murdering pervert, of the man who betrayed Our Lord? What sort of art is that to keep in a convent?'

'How did you do it, Sister?' Alice asked quietly. 'The base of the picture was nine feet from the ground, and the brass screws holding it in place were set at eleven feet and fourteen feet. Even if you were strong enough to move some church furniture under the picture – and the big choir stalls weigh several tons each, so that is not likely – you still could not reach those screws. I reckon you measure about six feet two inches in height, which leaves another five feet to the uppermost screws.'

'On the night we had agreed,' Sister Mercy Superior began, 'I switched off the CCTV I was meant to be monitoring. I knocked out the alarm system by unscrewing the main fuse. I blocked the supply hose to the back-up generator. Then I went in to the chapel with a screwdriver. Columba jumped up on my shoulders, unscrewed the picture, and passed it down.'

'You expect me to believe that?' said Miss Lily. 'That this elderly consumptive stood on your shoulders?'

Maggie spoke weakly: 'She was all-Ireland gymnastics champion and at the Commonwealth Games in Perth, nineteen seventy-two, she was placed third in the overall competition. I found it on the Internet. It was before she joined the Aurelian Order. Check it out if you like.'

'Go on, please,' said Miss Lily, now amused.

'The picture was in a light frame,' Sister Mercy Superior continued. 'We carried it through the convent, up the stairs to this room, out the window onto the roof, and down the fire escape. We never had to open the main door.'

'Mr Meadowfield was waiting halfway down the avenue in his car,' Sister Columba added.

'Petrol engine, ruptured exhaust pipe,' Alice said concisely.

'He took the painting from us and drove away. We never saw him again. May the Lord have mercy on his soul,' said Sister Mercy Superior.

'Not good enough, I'm afraid,' Miss Lily said. She grabbed Maggie by the neck so that Maggie had to stand, then, with the spray can to Maggie's throat, walked backwards with her to the window. 'You see, the gentleman I work for has invested a lot of money in this painting already, and he doesn't like taking losses. Furthermore, he knows all about your weakness for dressing up and wearing funny hats, Sister Mercy Superior.'

'I knew it!' Sebastian said.

'I don't know what you're talking about,' Sister Mercy Superior rumbled. 'Let my librarian go.'

'I will,' said Miss Lily, backing further to the window. 'But not in the way I think she'd like me to.'

She had dragged Maggie up until she was standing by the window, which she swung out, open, so that Maggie was teetering over the void.

'Where is the Caravaggio, for the final time?' asked Miss Lily.

Without warning, a dark shape materialised on the fire escape behind Miss Lily.

'Davy Rainbow, you wretch!' shouted Sister Diana, and swung her bottle of poitín with such force that it knocked the spray can from Miss Lily's hand. 'I'll kill you!'

Alice, in wonder, saw the can fly through the air. Simultaneously, and in a single bound, Sister Columba had landed on Sister Mercy Superior's desk, and, in a second leap, gained the top of the green metal filing cabinet, just in time to catch the spray can.

But Miss Lily was already halfway across the room.

'Sister Mary Magdalene!' Columba shrieked, and lobbed the can back towards the window.

Maggie caught it in two hands and stared at it. Miss Lily, with a balletic back-flip, was within a stride of her.

'Throw!' Alice cried.

Maggie, wide-eyed, pivoted like a quarterback, then pitched the can. Alice had to dive to catch it, and already she could hear the wind whistling as Miss Lily sprang. Holding the can out, praying to God that the nozzle was pointing the right way, Alice sprayed. A mushroom of white spume enveloped Miss Lily. She seemed to hover for a moment in midair. Then she fell to the ground, gasping and kicking.

Alice ran over to Maggie.

'It's over, now, Maggie, it's all right.'

'Oh God,' Maggie sobbed. 'I'm so sorry.'

Sister Diana was standing over Davy Rainbow.

'You think you can fool me, Davy boy?' she slurred. 'Get up and take your medicine.'

Sister Mercy Superior stepped forward.

'Diana!' she cried. 'Have you been drinking?'

Chapter Eight

Doonlish
18 June, 12.30 PM

Alice and Maggie sat at a window table in Beppe's Bistro. Outside, swallows swooped back and forth in the peaceful, blue sky. A man rode by on a sturdy horse, followed by a child on a white pony. Calm lay on the land.

Maggie drained the glass of Australian shiraz that she had ordered for her stomach's sake, and promptly ordered another from Beppe himself, who kept saying how great it was that the nuns from Doon Abbey had finally crossed his threshold. Alice, on a San Pellegrino, had ordered two beer-battered cods and chips. She badly wanted a smoke, but knew that to be seen smoking on the pavement outside Beppe's might be a step too far.

They had left young Joe Foley in charge of Doon Abbey, since Sebastian had taken Sister Mercy Superior and Sister Columba into Naas Garda Station for questioning. Sister Diana, when Alice had last seen her, had been comatose.

'Any word on Davy?' Maggie asked.

'They think he'll pull through,' Alice replied. 'Alcohol residue in the blood, at the level it was found in Davy, effectively acts as an antidote to Miss Lily's poison, although I bet she didn't know that.'

Maggie shook her head darkly at the mention of Miss Lily, and stopped herself making a sign of the cross. 'At least Panda will be fine,' she said. 'The poison doesn't work on cats either. Joe Foley gave him a shampoo and he's breathing better already.'

'Let's drink to Panda,' Alice said, and they clinked their glasses together.

Alice knew they had done as much as they could, and that the Caravaggio might never be found. Sister Mercy Superior would be a tough nut to crack, but everyone cracked under interrogation eventually, Alice knew, and Doon Abbey's former head nun would be no different. It might take a few days, but she would eventually confess to the murders. Alice shivered. It might so easily have been her neck, she reflected. Or Maggie's. They had a lot to be grateful for.

'The media are going to be hysterical when they get hold of this,' Alice said. 'Is there any place other than Doon Abbey we can hide?'

Maggie thought for a moment. 'We could go to our sister house in Rome. They'd never find us there.'

'Brilliant idea,' Alice said, as her phone rang. She glanced at the caller's name and sighed. 'Oh, hello Ned.'

As the cod and chips arrived, Maggie was suddenly ravenous; she dipped a chip in the little bowl of Beppe's sauce and closed her eyes with pleasure as she ate it.

'What time exactly did this happen?' Alice was saying. 'I need you to be absolutely certain about this, Ned.'

Maggie wished that Ned would hang up. She picked up a corner of the crispy cod in her fingers and sank her teeth into it. Rome would be fantastic, she thought. Maybe they could even stay there indefinitely. Great restaurants, great wine. Alice was on her feet.

'I don't believe this!'

'What is it?' Maggie asked between mouthfuls.

Alice was pacing up and down, shaking her head.

'That was Ned,' she said eventually, putting down the phone. 'He's in hospital in Dublin recovering from a broken nose that Sive gave him.'

'Well, I'm not surprised,' Maggie murmured.

'But she wasn't aiming for Ned,' Alice said, and then explained how, but for Sive, Ned would have been garrotted by a powerful woman wearing a hat.

'*What?*' Maggie said. 'When did that happen?'

'This morning,' Alice said grimly, and filled Maggie in on the details. 'Has to be the same woman.'

'So she can't be Sister Mercy Superior?' Maggie said.

Alice sat down heavily and pushed away her fish and chips.

'Damn!' she said. 'I've spent the last three days with this *feeling*! This feeling that the answer to everything is right here, beneath our noses!'

'Pray to Saint Anthony,' Maggie suggested. 'I find he's the best when you're looking for something.'

'I already have!' Alice cried. 'I want to *scream!*'

'Everything all right, Sisters?' asked Beppe, looming anxiously.

'It's lovely, thanks,' Maggie said, and reached for a chip from Alice's plate.

'Let's start at the beginning,' said Alice with steely determination. 'Meadowfield blackmails the convent, Mercy and Columba succumb. They take down the painting exactly as they describe. They bring it down the fire escape and hand it to Meadowfield.'

'Who drives away in his red Volvo P1800,' Maggie said, and recited the registration number.

'Small rupture in the exhaust,' Alice said. 'But what happened *then*? I mean, why is his car outside his house when he was found murdered in a hotel in Liffey Valley.'

'Why *was* his car parked outside his house?' Maggie asked, helping herself discreetly to more of Alice's chips.

'What do you mean, *was*?'

'It *was* parked outside his house. We saw it there when we found Brice's body,' Maggie said, 'but now it's parked on a car transporter outside Abbey Motors right behind you.'

Alice was already out the door when Maggie caught up with her. Back in the restaurant, Beppe was looking distraught.

'Hi,' Alice said to a man in blue overalls who was about to climb into the cab of the transporter. 'Sister Alice from Doon Abbey, this is Sister Mary Magdalene.'

The man smiled at the two nuns. 'How'yez. Dick.'

'That's Jeremy Meadowfield's car,' Alice said.

'I know, we used to service her here,' Dick said. 'In fact, I used to look after her meself.'

'Do you mind me asking, Dick, where are you taking it? I mean, her?'

'I didn't tell you this,' said Dick, and looked left and right, 'but she's been seized by the Criminal Assets Bureau.'

'You used to service his car,' Alice said, and screwed her eyes closed as she fought to find the tiny speck of truth that she knew was floating there, somewhere, right in front of her. Please, Saint Anthony, she implored. *Please!* Then: 'When was she last serviced?'

'Not so long ago,' Dick said. 'A week or ten days ago at the most. Ask them in the office.'

'The office,' Alice repeated, and knew that her hands were shaking. 'Maggie, stay here with Dick.'

'I have to . . .' Dick began, but Alice had already disappeared into the garage.

'She looks very old,' Maggie said conversationally.

'She's actually a classic,' Dick said.

'Oh, really?'

'She's a little gem,' Dick said. 'She's got a B-18 engine with SU carburettors and five main crankshaft bearings.'

'She sounds . . . fantastic,' Maggie said, and smiled beatifically.

'She has a manual gearbox,' Dick continued, warming to his topic, 'but later models . . .'

Alice came running back. 'The service book,' she said. 'It's in the car.' She looked up at the car on the top of the transporter. 'Can we see it please?'

'I don't know about that, Sister,' said Dick, looking at his watch, 'I'm meant to be . . .'

'It's very important,' Alice said.

'I'm not sure I'm meant to . . .' Dick said.

'You made her sound so amazing,' Maggie said.

'All right,' Dick sighed, 'I'll get it.'

'The ninth of June,' Alice whispered, as they watched Dick climb up on the transporter.

'What about the ninth of June?' Maggie asked.

'Was when this car was last serviced,' Alice said with barely restrained excitement. 'The day before the Caravaggio was stolen.'

Dick was climbing back down with a leather wallet in his hand. Alice opened it and folded back the most recent page: a report headed Abbey Motors. She scanned the report.

'Nothing about the exhaust,' she said.

'Sorry?' Dick was frowning.

'This car has a ruptured exhaust,' Alice said, 'but there's no mention of anything the matter with the exhaust in this report.'

'I serviced her myself,' Dick said defensively, 'and if I didn't find a ruptured exhaust, then the exhaust wasn't ruptured.'

'So the exhaust ruptured after the service,' Alice said.

'This is a very old car,' Dick said.

'Can you please check the exhaust yourself?' Alice asked. 'Like, now?'

'I'd have to take the car down off the ramp,' Dick said, 'and I can't do that because, as I've already told you, the gardaí have told me to bring her up to Dublin. So now, Sisters, if you'll excuse me . . .'

195

'I'm Detective Sergeant Alice Dunwoody,' Alice said. 'Please take the car down from the ramp.'

'Detective Sergeant *who?*' Dick said.

Maggie nodded. 'She is.'

Dick shook his head unhappily. 'Look, I'm under orders to do this job, so I don't care who you are, I'm not taking that car down off the ramp.'

'In that case, I'm arresting you for obstructing a garda investigation,' Alice said, stepping forward.

Dick blinked. 'I'm taking the car down off the ramp,' he said.

Five minutes later, he was on his back under the rear of the Volvo.

'Jesus,' he said, sliding out on a wheeled mechanic's tray, 'you're right. What's more, someone has tried to patch it. Look for yourself.'

He got up and Alice slid in. A crude collar of metal had been affixed to the circumference of the car's exhaust pipe.

'Whoever did it knew what they were doing,' Dick said as Alice re-emerged. 'It's quite a professional job. But with these old cars, the steel in the exhaust is pure shite, if you'll excuse me, so it was bound to go again.'

But Alice was scrutinising the service report.

'One hundred and twenty-three thousand, six hundred and one,' she read. 'I presume these are miles?'

Maggie suddenly got it. She went to the Volvo, opened the front door and leaned in. 'One hundred and twenty-three thousand, six hundred and eighty-six,' she called.

'Which leaves . . .'

'Eighty-five,' Maggie said.

Dick was looking intently from one nun to the other.

'The car travelled eighty-five miles since you serviced her,' Alice said. 'But we know she has been parked here since the tenth of June, and that her owner was murdered on the evening of that day in a hotel in Liffey Valley. What's more, we know that he travelled to his death by taxi and bus. Why? *Because he knew he couldn't depend on this car to get him there!*'

Dick's mouth hung open.

'We need a map!' Alice cried and took out her phone. 'What's half of eighty-five?'

'Forty-two and a half,' Maggie said.

'Damn!' Alice swore, 'the maps on this phone only show kilometres. What's forty-two and a half miles in kilometres?'

Maggie closed her eyes. 'Sixty-eight point three nine seven one.'

'We'll settle for sixty-eight point four,' Alice said. 'Here goes. A car leaving the outskirts of Doonlish travels sixty-eight point four kilometres.' She thumbed in the distance and watched as a red arc appeared on the phone's screen. Maggie was beside her, looking in. Even Dick tried to see what was going on.

'Oh God,' Alice whispered, 'do you see what I see?'

Maggie bit her trembling lower lip. 'Yes.'

The red line went directly through the Jesuit house at Aylesmere.

'And who in Aylesmere could mend a ruptured exhaust?' Alice asked.

'Brother Harkin!' Maggie gasped.

'Exactly,' said Alice with venom. 'Brother Harkin.' Then she frowned. 'Maggie, are you all right?'

Aylesmere Jesuit Residence, Dublin
18 June, 6 PM

The doorbell rang inside the big old house – a wheezy, echoing note that reminded Alice of asthma and arthritis. Earlier, having dropped Maggie in the A&E department of Naas Hospital, where acute food poisoning was diagnosed, Alice had driven to her aunt's house in Kilmainham, where, four months before, when she had entered Doon Abbey, she had left her Renault 4. There was nobody at home. Alice's aunt liked to visit an old friend in Edinburgh at this time of year, and tended to leave spare keys under a concrete block at the back of the house, in case she lost her handbag. In the garage, Alice found the Renault's toolkit in a cardboard box. She took the box. It could be useful in emergencies.

Now, as she rang the doorbell again, bolts were suddenly shot, a key was turned, and the great wooden door was heaved slowly open. Alice braced herself, for she now realised that Brother Harkin's appearance belied his true strength. The mind of criminal deviants would always amaze her – their ability to adapt, to cover their tracks. To appear as one person but, deep down, to be another. A face appeared. The Rector himself stood there. He looked exhausted and out of breath.

'Sister Alice? Am I expecting you?'

'No, Father Rynne, and I apologise for not giving notice, but something has cropped up, and I must talk to you in person.'

The Rector's expression was pained. 'Well . . . we mustn't leave you standing, Sister. Do come in.'

He stood aside, and she stepped into the large hall, then helped him push the door closed.

'No Brother Harkin?' said Alice lightly.

'Harkin,' said the Rector, and shook his head. 'I don't know where Harkin is, unfortunately. He's been going out a lot at night, recently, and to tell you the truth, I don't like it one little bit.'

'But he's not here,' Alice said. 'I mean, you'd know if he was here, wouldn't you, Father?'

The Rector looked pale. 'Things have changed so much, Sister,' he said. 'There was a time when I knew everything that went on here, but nowadays . . .'

His voice trailed off and he looked old, Alice thought.

'Father, I wonder if you and I might have a chat?' Alice asked. 'I'm afraid I have some disturbing news.'

The Rector's shoulders slumped.

'Very well,' he said, and set off across the hall – more of a shuffle than a walk. He opened a panelled door in the wainscoting that Alice had not noticed on her previous visits, and led the way down a staircase. Alice followed, into a kitchen in the basement, where weak light filtered through barred windows. On the table, someone had been making a big bouquet with fresh-cut flowers: roses, irises, sunflowers and hollyhocks.

'This is Brother Harkin's domain, so to speak,' said the Rector as he filled a yellow kettle. 'He looks after the flowers for our chapel.'

'Very artistic,' Alice said, as the Rector prepared a brew of Barry's Gold Blend in a flowery china pot and dispensed it into china cups.

'Indeed he is,' the Rector said. 'Did you know that he is also a very gifted picture restorer?'

'Brother Harkin?'

'Oh yes. A very considerable connoisseur of European art – although he has never aspired to more than the humble status of lay brother. I used to have the greatest admiration for Brother Harkin.'

Curiouser and curiouser, thought Alice as she sipped her tea. 'Father Rector, I'm afraid I've got some news that may upset you.'

His handsome features drooped so miserably that her heart went out to him; yet she made herself continue: 'We have been forced to the con-clusion that Jeremy Meadowfield, who stole our Caravaggio, drove here, to this house, with the painting, on the night of the theft.'

'What?' The Rector's eyes were enlarged and he struggled to find his breath. 'You mean . . .'

'We don't yet know why, but all the indications now are that he and Brother Harkin were involved in this together. We also think that the painting may still be here in Aylesmere,' Alice said.

'Harkin!' the Rector gasped. 'I knew it!'

'You knew it?' Alice asked.

The Rector sat down heavily on a kitchen chair. 'He never stops talk-ing about Caravaggio,' he said in a whisper. 'Did you know that Harkin has a criminal record?'

'Brother Harkin?'

'Oh yes,' said the Rector gloomily. 'Years ago, before he entered the religious life, he had convictions for stealing cars. We forgive, you see. Oh yes, we forgive.'

'So Harkin is a thief,' Alice said.

'There's a lot more to Brother Harkin than meets the eye,' the Rector said. 'Come, let me show you.'

Drawing aside a red velvet curtain, the suddenly animated Rector started down a dark passageway.

'Brother Harkin?' he called. 'Are you here?'

Alice, with mounting apprehension, followed. The Rector opened the door at the end of the passage and ushered her in, flicking light switches as he entered the room. Spotlights, floodlights, lamps, up-lighters sprang into life.

'This is where he spends all his time,' said the Rector.

Alice took in the whitewashed walls of the windowless room where portraits in oils, printed maps, medieval scenes of the Annunciation and lush blue landscape paintings hung side by side. The Rector flicked another switch and there, spotlit in an alcove, stood Brother Harkin.

'Oh!'

Alice drew in her breath.

'Never fails to get that response,' said the Rector. 'Uncanny, isn't it?'

Rendered in dark oils on uneven wooden boards, Brother Harkin was whelmed in a black cloak, the hood drawn down onto his oddly sinewy shoulders. One large white hand was fastened around a dark crucifix. His white hair and pale skin seemed to shimmer out of the darkness, while his colourless eyes on either side of his slightly bulbous nose fixed the viewer with chilling intensity.

'Pedro Velázquez de Cuellar, one of the first followers of St Ignatius Loyola, slain by a traitor in 1546 from within the Society's own ranks,' the Rector explained. 'Found here in an attic, almost ruined beyond redemption. Harkin has an amazing ability to transform even the most mundane objects.'

'It does look remarkably like him,' Alice murmured, as her eyes were drawn down to a corner of the alcove where, from behind a drape, metal glinted.

The Rector had moved along from the alcove to two large canvases hung in gold frames, each depicting a large, naked woman in a wood-land scene, surrounded by flowering bushes. Alice hung back. 'For a celibate lay brother, Harkin has a particular appreciation of the female form,' the Rector was saying. 'Here is Saint Susanna, for example. And a very lovely Mary Magdalene, showing all the temptations of created beauty.'

Alice wasn't listening. Stretching back her foot into the alcove, she nudged aside the hanging drape. A pair of ten-kilo cast-iron dumbbells winked at her from their hiding place. Her mind was working at high speed. Those heavy front doors, pulled back by the seemingly bent-over, wraith-like Brother Harkin; the six-inch-plus heels worn by Meadowfield's tall, mystery assailant, captured on CCTV in Liffey Valley.

They climbed back up the stairs. Alice was glad to have left the cellar; at any moment, she expected Brother Harkin to appear.

The Rector stood in the hall, his hands joined before him.

'What do you think I should do, Sister?' he asked. 'What you have suggested is a vista almost too appalling to contemplate. But if evil has taken place here, it must be expunged.'

'I want you to do nothing for the moment, Father,' she said. 'You are a good man, and I apologise for having upset you today. What I suggest is that you don't mention any of this to Brother Harkin, just let the gardaí deal with the case from now on.'

'I will say nothing to him,' the Rector said. He shivered. 'Do you think he's dangerous?'

'He could be, Father,' Alice said. 'I'll see to it that he's taken in for questioning this evening.'

They had reached the hall door.

'Do you think I should resign?' asked Father Rynne. 'I mean, I am ultimately responsible.'

'No way. Your help and conduct has been exemplary. I will testify to that,' Alice said.

'Thank you, Sister Alice,' he said as he reached for the long door. His voice fell away to a low tone. 'Would you like me to hear your confession?'

For a split-second, Alice was tempted to accept. To unburden herself of Bruno Scanlon Junior. But no. This was neither the place nor the time. Her modest, downcast eyes lingered. Then, suddenly, she was looking squarely at him.

'Thank you, but I must go,' she said.

The Rector was struggling to pull back the door; Alice heaved it with him.

Dublin Outskirts
18 June, 7.15 PM

As Alice drove towards Doonlish, the sky was darkening rapidly. She had just received a phone call from Sebastian: Sister Mercy Superior was vehemently denying that she had killed anyone. Sebastian was keeping the head nun and the novice mistress in the garda station overnight. Although he could have arrested them for theft and for misleading the gardaí, his superior had warned him to do nothing until it had been cleared with higher authorities.

'We can't be seen to be persecuting nuns,' Sebastian had said.

'That's a good decision,' Alice told him, 'because I've now got information that will make your hair stand on end.'

'Tell me,' Sebastian said.

But Alice's phone was showing red on the battery. 'I'll meet you in Naas Hospital,' she said, and explained what had happened to Maggie.

As she drove south, Alice's mind was awash with images – so many that they threatened to blot out her ability to see the road ahead. *Get a grip!* she swore, as she yanked the wheel and overtook a truck. The old Alice would have cut and sorted the images, her mind like cheese-wire.

'Damn!' she swore.

She pulled over on to the hard shoulder and sat back in the seat of the Berlingo, eyes closed, pinching the bridge of her nose and breathing deeply. Fifty seconds later she sat upright, as if a bolt of electricity had passed through her.

'Oh! My! God!' she cried out.

Sebastian answered on the first ring. 'Sebastian, listen carefully: this phone is almost out of juice, and I don't have a charger with me. But you've got the Liffey Valley CCTV images on your phone, right? The ones showing the murderer at the hotel?'

'Yes I do,' Sebastian replied, sounding puzzled. 'What has this got to . . . ?'

'Just forward them to me. Now.'

'Yes ma'am.' Sebastian sounded miffed by her curt tone.

She ended the call and sat there, waiting, going through all the facts with clinical precision. Two minutes later, her iPhone squeaked. She opened the file, scrolled down, found the detail she was looking for, enlarged it and zoomed in until she could be absolutely sure.

There was no doubt.

She called Sebastian back. 'Hi. Listen, I'm sorry I was so short with you just now, OK? But I've finally worked it . . .'

The iPhone died.

Alice found a turning place and in a sudden rain started out on the road back to Dublin as fast as the little van could go. The noise of the rain all but drowned out her thoughts. She was just going to take the next step, and then the step after that, and then keep going until she had settled the whole thing. No deviation. No hesitation. Back on the beat. She got on to the motorway and drove in the wake of big lorries that threw up bow waves like ships at sea. The lights of a filling station loomed through the downpour. She pulled in and, under the bright lights, removed the toolkit that she had earlier taken from her Renault 4. She found what she wanted, wrapped in an oil cloth, then drove on.

There was no time to lose, she now knew – not if she was to save the Caravaggio.

Dublin Southside
18 June, 8.30 PM

As she neared Aylesmere, Alice realised that her hands were balled into fists, locked onto the steering wheel in a white-knuckle grip. Relax, she told herself. Lighten up. In retrospect, all crimes seem so simple. Why had she not seen it before?

The rain cleared for a moment, and in the moonlight she could make out the shape of the Jesuit house. It looked almost derelict now. No lights were showing. She parked beside the steps leading up to the front door. Had Brother Harkin returned, she wondered? A flash of lightning lit the paintwork of the van. The grounds were dark, apart from a dim light in a distant glasshouse on the far side of the rolling front lawn. That must have been where the sunflowers and hollyhocks had come from.

She decided to go around the back, walking on the balls of her feet. Another door at the top of steps – in this case a narrower door than the one to which Brother Harkin normally attended. Alice climbed the steps and pushed. The door fell open before her.

She waited for a moment, then ventured into the hallway. There were no carpets, and the floor seemed to be missing several boards. After a moment, her eyes got used to the darkness, and she could make out a skylight towards the back of the house, and a stairway leading up to it.

'Brother Harkin?' she called. 'Are you here?'

Step by step, feeling her way, she began to climb, following the curve of the staircase and climbing a second flight until she was on the landing of the upper floor. Another sudden flash of lightning gave her a momentary vision of a large empty room, devoid of carpets and furniture. There was a crash of thunder. Then all was plunged into darkness once more. And silence.

The scent of candles, drifting through the darkness, led her forward. At the side of the landing was a small door, standing ajar. As she approached, she sensed the flickering glow, and then made out the profile of a man with a large nose, kneeling on a *prie-dieu* amid two banks of small candles. In his right hand he held a cutthroat razor. Before him was an easel, on which stood Judas Iscariot as painted by Michelangelo Merisi da Caravaggio.

'Good evening, Father Rector,' Alice said.

Slowly, he turned to face her, rising to his feet. 'Sister Alice. I was not expecting you back so soon.'

'Nor was I. But then I realised that it was you.'

By the light of the candles, she could see now that he had changed his clothing. Instead of the casual attire he had worn during her earlier visit, he was clad in full canonicals: a cope embroidered in cloth of gold, a purple stole, a white alb over a black cassock, shiny black patent leather shoes; only the purple socks remained unchanged.

'Ah,' he said with sudden interest. 'How?'

'Your socks,' she said. 'I saw them earlier, just as I was leaving. They're also visible above your ankle boots in the CCTV coverage in Liffey Valley.'

He was moving around the room in a wide arc.

'So I am guilty, Alice. A sinner, in need of grace. *Vanitas vanitatum, omnia vanitas.* I purchased them three years ago, in Rome, in

Barbiconi's, the ecclesiastical outfitters behind the Pantheon. As a senti-mental gesture, I have taken to wearing them in private. Today was to have been a private day,' he concluded reproachfully.

Alice felt that in different circumstances there might have been something pathetic, even endearing, about a priest being too embar-rassed to wear purple socks in public.

'Father Rector Rynne,' Alice said evenly, 'I am arresting you for the murder of Jeremy Meadowfield, and for handling stolen property, con-trary to the provisions of the Criminal Justice Act 2001. There may also be other charges.'

'You people never learn,' the Rector said sadly. 'That picture tells us everything about the need for betrayal, the need for crime and sin and loss. Without Judas, the story of the Crucifixion could never have occurred, and mankind would have remained unsaved. That is the power of art, the power of Judas, the power of Caravaggio. That is why Meadowfield had to die. I was only a poor foot-soldier carrying out my part in the universal scheme.'

'Drop the razor, Father Rector. Now.'

'You see, after your earlier visit,' he went on, ignoring her, 'I con-cluded that your pretty little nose had more than likely winkled out my secret. Therefore, the only sure way to avoid further complications is to destroy this sublime painting. It will melt into nothing by the flame of these holy candles, just as you will melt into nothingness very shortly, my dear.'

'Why are you telling me this?' Alice asked.

'Because nobody should go to her death without understanding,' the Rector said. 'We are human beings, not beasts.'

'What about the others you killed?'

'I always tried to explain first,' said the Rector indignantly. 'I always did my duty. Even your former boyfriend would have understood why he had to die, if his ridiculous girlfriend had not intervened.'

'I think I understand,' Alice said, as the Rector cast off the heavy cope and moved towards her.

He had slipped on a pair of black gloves and was swinging the blade of his cutthroat razor in the general direction of her neck with long, painterly strokes.

'Why the letter "M"?' Alice asked. 'What does it stand for?'

He sucked in his breath, as if she had struck him. 'Mama . . .' he began.

'The "M" you carved on Brice's back is for Mama?' Alice said, watching him circle her.

The Rector let out a cry of anguish. 'She shouldn't have called me that!' he cried. 'She made me what I am.'

He wiped his eyes and took a step towards her, his knife probing.

'Called you what?' Alice asked. 'What did your Mama call you, Jonathan?'

The big man was blubbering, his teeth grinding.

'This may be your last chance to tell,' Alice said.

He made a feint and Alice skipped to one side.

'She . . .' He was fighting for his breath. 'She . . . called me *monster!*' he screamed, and plunged for her heart.

Alice turned and ran. She stumbled down the great staircase, illuminated by lightning flashes, and twisted the handle of the door. It would not move. The Rector was swishing along behind her. She ran across the hallway in the darkness, and tripped and fell and tumbled down a flight of narrower wooden stairs.

Down here, strangely, the electricity was working. A series of dim bulbs set in the wall guided her as she ran along a curving tunnel for what seemed like fifty or a hundred yards. She imagined the Rector closing on her with every stride, but he had vanished.

She stopped, and listened. Silence. She walked on and found herself at the foot of a short flight of stairs, and went up, and through a door, and into a garden pavilion, with glass walls and shrubbery all around. She appeared to be somewhere between the main Jesuit house and the glasshouse she had seen earlier.

In the pavilion were comfortable chairs, low coffee tables of an oriental design, seemingly made of teak, Turkish rugs, bookshelves with paperback novels, a large glass-fronted drinks cabinet. She reached for the glass-panelled door of the pavilion, found it locked, looked for the key, and recoiled as the Rector himself came towards her across the well-mown grass. He was now outside the house and approaching her from the gardens, moving faster and with sharper movements than she remembered. He unlocked the door and stepped inside. Big drops of rain discoloured the shoulders of his alb. He was advancing with solemn deliberation, as though he was about to embrace her, or ask her to dance, then at the last moment he made a lasso of his purple stole and tried to sling it over Alice's head. As she evaded his move, he closed in again, this time with gloved hands grappling for her throat. Alice dropped to the floor, rolled on to her back, braced on her elbows and kicked upwards as the Rector turned to crash his weight on top of her. Again she was too quick for him, catching him in the stomach with her up-kick as he started to fall. As he collapsed forward, she wedged her other foot firmly under his chest and swung him back over her head and into the glass cabinet. Sherry bottles, Madeira decanters, glassware of all sorts, together with a great array of Waterford crystal drinking glasses, crashed out. Alice had a confused sense of these shattered, glittering items as the Rector picked himself off the floor, wiped blood from his face and throat, and seized the ice pick which lay beside an ice bucket on the highly polished wooden floor.

He advanced again, a glint of respect in his eyes, mingled with cold hatred and an energy she had not seen before. He swung the pick at Alice's head, and when she raised her left elbow to block his blow, he countered with a high kick. Alice's reactions were not as fast as they should have been; the sole of his polished black shoe grazed her ribs. She took a half-step backward, caught the shoe on its way down, grasped his well-turned ankle and gave it a sharp jerk. The Rector fell back sharply, striking his head off a broken vodka bottle. He was on his feet again, and bleeding heavily from his forehead. He sprang into a judo pose, and started to circle her with slow deliberation. The blood seeping down his face added an extra element of horror to his mask of hatred.

'Come, my dear,' he whispered. 'Come to mother.'

When it came, his attack was furious. A flurry of chopping fists, and she was thrown against a bookcase. He lunged at her with bleeding hands outstretched, grabbed at her throat but caught her mouth instead. She bit into a finger, which seemed to break, or perhaps she had only dislocated it.

He clasped Alice's throat in his good hand. He was laughing now as he dripped blood over her blouse. He tightened his grip on her throat. She was losing consciousness. For a split-second she thought this might be the end. He was going to have his way with her.

And still she hoped to take him alive.

Desperately, she jabbed her right knee into his groin. The Rector gave a shriek, followed by a howl. As he raised his left fist to club her again, she realised that this man would never give up. She dodged his blow, which went through the glass of the pavilion window. He pulled back, spurting blood, and looked in dismay at his bloody fist. Then he reached into the folds of his cassock and extracted a long stiletto, the handle fine-wrought gold.

'This is the end then,' he remarked conversationally, 'the Toledo dagger, made of the very finest steel, you know.' He kissed the hilt of his weapon as he waded towards her across Turkish rugs, holding the long knife on the heel of his fist. When he raised it high above his shoulder to strike down into her chest, Alice shot him once, a clean shot through the fabric of her denim jeans.

The Rector stood still, swayed, looked down, spread his fingers across the wound in his chest. Puzzled, he opened his mouth to speak, but eloquence deserted him and he sank to the floor like a soufflé exposed to sudden cold.

Alice looked into his face, but all she could see was the ghost of Bruno Scanlon Junior, peaceful, all done, falling asleep at last.

Epilogue

As autumn began, and the nights came in ever earlier, Sister Alice often lay half-awake, half-dreaming. The centuries sighed from the turrets and the elaborate finials that surmounted Doon Abbey's Gothic windows. Moonbeams bathed the moss-covered buttresses and conjured intricate shapes from the ancient escarpments. Sister Alice knew that later she would hear the passage of mice in the corridor going about their nocturnal business, as they had done for generations, safe from the attention of Panda, the convent's muscular tomcat, who slept with Sister Mary Magdalene Superior two cells to the east.

It had been a good summer season, in the end, Alice reflected dreamily. The return of the Caravaggio to Doonlish, and its reinstallation in the convent chapel, had been reported on national television, and the resulting response from tourists had been phenomenal. The nuns had put up the viewing fee to fifteen euro a head and the resulting revenues had already had an impact in reducing the convent's loan with the bank. Sister Mercy Superior had spent far too much on renovating the cottage in County Kerry and on the purchase of a car for Sister Winifred. But now, at last, financial equilibrium was in sight.

A special Mass was said in the convent chapel to celebrate God's goodness in overseeing the return of the painting to its owners. The celebrant was the recently ordained Father Rector Harkin. Even Sister Columba and Sister Mercy put aside their misgivings and sang in choir as if their lives depended on it alongside Alice, Maggie and Sister Diana. Incense curled heavenwards from the thurible as it gently swung from the strong hands of young Joe Foley, Sister Diana's nephew, who still milked the cows on the farm. In the front row of the congregation pews, beside the Misses Hogans, little baby Aurelia Rainbow gurgled happily on her mother Winnie's lap. A tear came to Alice's eye as she saw how proud Davy Rainbow was with his family. No drink for three months, and a new job as a crime reporter with the *Leinster Leader*. What could be better? And Winnie had been promised a position as an auxiliary teacher in the local primary school, when she was finished breast-feeding.

Alice's gaze drifted to the window of her cell, and to the vivid stars in the night sky. When it was all over, Maggie and she had kept their promise and gone back to the Shelbourne for a drink. Sitting on stools at the Horseshoe Bar, a bottle of Pinot Grigio in an ice bucket between them, they raised their glasses.

'We did it,' Alice said.

'*You* did it,' Maggie replied. 'I just tagged along.'

A couple of men with big smiles on their faces were approaching.

'Ladies . . .' the first one began.

'Get lost,' Alice said.

'Vamoose,' Maggie snapped, as one of them tried to draw in a stool near her.

As the men withdrew, the two nuns could scarcely stop giggling.

'It's over, isn't it?' Maggie said. 'I mean, it was awful, but it was also kind of fantastic. There were times, I have to admit, when I wondered if my vocation was slipping away. But then I tried to imagine myself as Mrs Sebastian Hayes, and all I could think of was the Crucifixion.'

Alice laughed. 'He's nice,' she said. 'He needs a good woman to straighten him out.'

'But not this woman,' Maggie said. 'How about you?'

Alice drank some wine and speared a stuffed olive with a little stick.

'I think Ned's found his comfort zone,' she said. 'He wants a conventional woman, someone who doesn't question . . . a mother for his children. I'm too much of a maverick for Ned. Too much of a rebel.'

'You mean, a bit like Caravaggio,' Maggie said.

'You and I would have got on with him, I think,' Alice said. 'We would have understood Caravaggio.'

'I'll drink to that,' Maggie said.

★

What had annoyed Alice more than anything was the absence of a single prosecution. It was the Irish way, she knew, but still: so many corpses, and not a single arrest warrant issued. Sebastian had driven to the convent to explain.

'The word has come down from on high,' he said. He added, 'I mean from *our* on-high as opposed to *your* on-high.'

'I understand,' Alice said.

'To make a fuss of this would offend so many separate interest groups that the powers-that-be have as good as stood down any further action. They could withstand pressure from the religiously minded population, or the transvestite community, or the feminist community, or the Society of Jesus, or organisations supporting nuns, or people who hate Caravaggio, or people who love Caravaggio – but not from all of them.'

Nonetheless, Alice's promise to Bruno Scanlon had been kept by the gardaí. Bruno and Natalie were living in an undisclosed location until such a time as his evidence could be used.

Alice even felt sorry for poor Cyril O'Meara, the farmer who had tried to warn them, but had gone about it the wrong way. His widow revealed that Cyril had had a dream in which he saw Alice being burned at the stake as a witch. He felt that if anything happened to her, he would be blamed. When he learned that she had left the convent to find the Caravaggio, he had set out in pursuit, God rest his soul.

The only person left to prosecute over the Caravaggio affair was Kazakhstan-born Mafia boss Matthias Taboroski, aka Metro, who lived in County Kildare. But Bruno had never had direct contact with him, so no criminal case could be taken against Metro, who, it was thought, was spending less time in Ireland. Sebastian did tell Alice, however, that since the summer, Bruno Scanlon had lost three stone in weight and had become a daily communicant.

★

The Rector, it seemed, was not expecting Jeremy Meadowfield to materialise in Aylesmere that night. But Meadowfield *did* materialise, and what he brought in with him was an exquisite small canvas, beautifully painted. His car had broken down, he explained. He told the Rector to hide the painting on his behalf, until such time as the heat died down, or he would expose Sister Winifred's pregnancy to the world.

The Rector hid the painting, as instructed, as he sent Brother Harkin to repair Meadowfield's car. But the stolen Caravaggio was not the only thing that Father Rector Jonathan Rynne was hiding. A thorough search of Aylesmere in the aftermath of the Caravaggio affair revealed a fascinating series of furnished wardrobes and cosmetics. No way was Dark Heart ever going to part with a painting that meant so much to her. She had to eliminate Meadowfield. The rest was history – or, at least, was on CCTV.

★

Alice sighed. She had hoped never again to use the gun with which she had shot Bruno Junior. And yet some old instinct of self-protection had made her report it to her superiors as stolen and then hide it in the tool-box of her car before she had enrolled in Doon Abbey.

She got up and began to dress in the grey, pre-dawn light. The convent was a far happier place now that Maggie was in charge, even if the

Aurelian tradition of silence was still observed. Three more applications for novitiates had been received, thanks to the publicity around the return of the Caravaggio. The future for Doon Abbey had never been brighter.

Alice made her way down the marble staircase. Fifteen minutes still remained until the bell rang for lauds. She liked to walk alone around the cloister in the slowly growing light, in personal contemplation. Tucking each hand into the opposite sleeve of her habit, she stepped outside.

Almost immediately, she saw Maggie standing alone outside the door to the chapel. Maggie had made herself personally responsible for locking and opening the chapel, each evening and morning. Now she stood there, looking at Alice, her eyes round. Alice frowned. Maggie was pointing. Alice saw that the chapel door was open. Maggie brandished the key.

Oh no, not again, Alice thought as she rushed into the cool space. She stumbled up the nave. The Caravaggio . . . was there. Thank God, Alice thought. So what was Maggie on about? Alice turned around. Maggie's sign language indicated that when she had come down there five minutes before, the door to the chapel was open.

What? Alice mouthed.

Maggie mimed that she had walked in there, checked the picture was still in place, then proceeded towards the altar.

OK, Alice signalled.

Maggie opened the altar rail and acted out what she had done: climbed the steps to the altar, looked around.

'And then?' Alice asked with eyebrows and hands.

Last night the altar was bare, Maggie indicated, with clean sweeps of her palms.

But when I came in here five minutes ago, I found this.

Alice stared.

Maggie opened her fist.

A Claddagh ring lay there, two hands in gold enclosing a frail human heart.